SIDEWALK SAINT

A selection of titles by Phillip DePoy

The Foggy Moscowitz series

COLD FLORIDA *
THREE SHOT BURST *
ICEPICK *
SIDEWALK SAINT *

The Fever Devilin series

THE DEVIL'S HEARTH
THE WITCH'S GRAVE
A MINISTER'S GHOST
A WIDOW'S CURSE
THE DRIFTER'S WHEEL
A CORPSE'S NIGHTMARE
DECEMBER'S THORN

* *available from Severn House*

SIDEWALK SAINT

Phillip DePoy

**SEVERN
HOUSE**

First world edition published 2019
in Great Britain and the USA by
SEVERN HOUSE PUBLISHERS LTD of
Eardley House, 4 Uxbridge Street, London W8 7SY.
Trade paperback edition first published
in Great Britain and the USA 2021 by
Severn House, an imprint of Canongate Books Ltd,
14 High Street, Edinburgh EH1 1TE.

British Library Cataloguing in Publication Data
A CIP catalogue record for this title is available from the British Library.

ISBN-13: 978-0-7278-8957-7 (cased)
ISBN-13: 978-1-78029-636-4 (trade paper)
ISBN-13: 978-1-4483-0335-9 (e-book)

Typeset by Palimpsest Book Production Ltd.,
Falkirk, Stirlingshire, Scotland.

ONE

Middle of the night, Florida, June 1976

It doesn't take long to wake up when there's a gun in your face. You feel something cold on your cheek, you open your eyes, and just like that: Good morning, Mr Moscowitz.

The shadow on my bed, the one holding the pistol, was well dressed. I could tell that. Nice fedora, sharp Windsor in the tie, smelled like witch hazel.

'You're Foggy Moscowitz,' he whispered.

'Who?' I mumbled. 'No.'

'Show me your hands,' he said politely.

'You think I sleep with a gun under the sheets?' I asked him.

He didn't move a muscle. I showed him my hands.

'Now.' He sighed. 'How much to find my kid?'

I blinked. I glanced at the clock on the bedside table. It was four in the morning.

'I'm sitting up now,' I told him, 'and I'm going to rub my eyes. Then I'm going to explain to you what Child Protective Services means. So, take the gun out of my face and get off my bed, or shoot me so I can go back to sleep. Your choice.'

He hesitated, but he stood up. The gun didn't disappear, but he lowered it.

As foretold, I sat up and rubbed my eyes. 'I am,' I began, 'through no fault of my own, the one and only guy in this part of Florida who is employed by the state under Public Law 93–247, the Child Abuse Prevention and Treatment Act. This means I *could* help find your kid, gratis. But I won't.'

'You won't?' The gun came up again.

'Because you woke me up out of a very nice dream about my Aunt Shayna's brisket, which I miss very much, and because you did it while you were pointing a gun at my face. I realize that my face is not that much to look at, but it's the only one I've got. I'd like to keep it intact.'

He nodded. 'You object to my manners.'

'I do,' I told him. 'Now I'm going to turn on my lamp to see who's in my bedroom.'

I reached for the lamp, but I did it slowly, so he'd know there wasn't any funny business afoot. The light popped on, the room was buttery, the guy was thin as a skeleton. His skin was grey, and his eyes were the saddest song you ever heard, times ten. It was a melody I'd only listened to, thank God. Never sang it myself. But I had sympathy.

'Tell me about the kid.' I sighed.

'She's eleven,' he said, but it sounded like a sob.

'Your daughter?'

He nodded but couldn't seem to muster a voice.

'How long has she been missing?'

'I'm not sure.'

I tried not to react in a negative manner, because a person who breaks into your house in the middle of the night, with a gun, is not someone you want to aggravate. But 'not sure' wasn't much of an answer from an anxious father.

I rubbed my eyes again. 'You'll excuse my asking, but how is it you're uncertain how long she's been gone?'

'Oh, I been in the joint.' That's what started the tears. Not a flood, but still: silver in the corner of the eyes. 'Her ma passed away, and the State took the kid. I tracked her all over Florida. All the way to this little town, whatever it is.'

'It's Fry's Bay, Florida,' I told him.

'Not your home town,' he said. 'You got a Brooklyn accent.'

'Right the first time,' I agreed. 'Park Slope – in the old days.'

He gave another very heavy sigh. 'I'm glad you're not one of these redneck types I been running into with Florida law enforcement.'

'First you point a gun,' I said. 'Now you insult me. I'm not a cop – of any sort. I have to tell you, you don't exactly make it easy to be on *your* side.'

I got out of bed, slipped on some pants and stifled a yawn. 'Kitchen,' I suggested. 'Coffee.'

He nodded and away we went. I started a kettle for the French press and then sat down at the kitchen table. It was new. The old one had blood on it.

'OK,' I said to him. 'Start at the beginning. What's the kid's name?'

He stared. 'Usually they ask me what *my* name is.'

I said, 'Take this the right way: I don't care about you. I *might* care about the kid, if you tell me a little more about her.'

He closed his eyes. 'Her name is Etta. After Etta James. She looks like a Raphael cherub. Blonde. Maybe a little on the chubby side, but you know: baby fat. And smart as a whip. Skipped two grades. Gets the brains from her mother, but she's tough like me.'

'First,' I began, 'it's impressive that you know Renaissance paintings. But second, I was hoping for something a little less romantic. Like a photo. Or where you saw her last. Or a last name to go with Etta.'

He sniffed and opened his eyes. 'Right. Etta Roan. Age eleven. About four foot five. Blonde hair, brown eyes, maybe seventy pounds. She was with her ma until fall of '75. That's when the wife died. Had the cancer. Etta was put into the system in Lake City, but I couldn't get very far with that office. Ex-cons and child welfare don't mix, it turns out.'

'Especially if you approach them the same way you did me,' I said.

'Are you going to help me or not?'

'Still not sure.' I leaned forward. 'What brought you to me?'

'Saw your name in the papers,' he said. 'You broke up some kind of human traffic ring; got a mother back to her kids. Local hero type of story. Also, you don't miss a name like *Foggy Moscowitz*. I asked around. You got a rep.'

'And you couldn't just come to my office in the morning?'

'I been patient,' he told me. 'I'm not patient any more.'

I studied the guy's face. He'd been through the ringer. Crazy hair, dark circles under the eyes, suit like a bartender's rag. And he still had the gun in his hand.

The kettle went off and I got up. Filled the French press and stood there watching it.

See, the trick for a guy with a gun is to keep quiet. Especially if he's a guy at the end of his rope like this one was. You let him stew in his thoughts. Eventually he'll start talking. Or he'll shoot you. But usually it's the talking.

I waited five minutes. I pushed the plunger down on the press. It sounded very loud in the silence of the kitchen. I got out two mugs and poured.

'Sugar?' I asked.

He shook his head. I brought him a mug and sat down. He sipped.

'Good coffee,' he said softly.

'Are you going to tell me what's really going on?' I asked. 'Because you broke into my apartment in the middle of the night and your story doesn't quite ring true.'

He set down his mug and sat back. 'All right,' he said after a minute. 'Maybe I'm in a little trouble.'

'You're on the run.'

He nodded. 'I've got to find Etta. I'm her father. She needs me.'

Sounded more like *he* needed *her*.

But there was something in his eyes. I couldn't look away. And I couldn't say no.

'Take a couple of hours on the sofa,' I told him, 'while I finish my dream about my aunt's cooking. And in the morning, bright and early, we'll go into my office and I'll make some calls. We'll find out who has Etta.'

'It's not going to be that simple,' he protested. 'You don't think I tried to find out who has her?'

'Maybe,' I said. 'But you're not a local hero. With a funny name.'

He didn't want to, but he cracked a smile. A little one.

'I could use a couple of Zs,' he admitted.

And the gun went away at last.

'OK,' I said, and finished my coffee.

'You're not going to rat me out, are you?' It was a tired question, not a worried question.

'I'm with Child Protective Services,' I told him. 'What do I know about escaped convicts?'

He smiled. 'More than you'd like to, that's my guess. But I'm too worn out. I'm going to trust you, which shows you how stupid I am.'

I got up. 'I'm letting a con with a gun sleep on my sofa.

Who's the one with questionable judgment? You want a blanket?'

'In Florida in the middle of September? I want an ice bag.'

I smiled. 'You'd be surprised how cold it can get here.'

'I think my internal thermostat broke down.' He yawned. 'I was always either too cold or too hot. Now I don't care. Now all I want to do is find Etta and go away someplace nice. Like Montreal.'

That was it. I went back to the bedroom and fell asleep in under five. I don't have any idea what Mr Roan did. Maybe he dreamed about Montreal. Maybe he stayed awake, staring at the ceiling, wondering where his Etta was.

All I know is that when I woke up at eight the next morning, he was gone.

TWO

I figured on an easy day. In the office by nine a.m., a little paperwork and then a long lunch starting at eleven. Check back in at the office by two, and then down to Mary's Shallow Grave by five, in time for happy hour.

The office was a second-floor cell. Peeling paint, moldy smell, letters missing from the sign. My chair squeaked like a train trying to stop, and you couldn't see the top of the desk from all the manila folders. I did my best to make order, but chaos was boss.

By 10:03 I'd decided that Mr Roan was a ghost or a dream or some otherwise negligible apparition. Then, for no apparent reason, at 10:37 I picked up the phone. I had to look up the number for Lake City Family Services. I got a gravel-throated civil servant on the phone.

'Child and Family Services, Bannon speaking,' she rumbled.

'Moscowitz over in Fry's Bay,' I told her. 'Looking for placement information on an Etta Roan, should be eleven years old, mother deceased, father incarcerated. You placed her in foster care, don't know when.'

'Not me,' Bannon said. 'I just got here. From Tampa.'

'Still,' I said.

'Yeah.' She lowered the phone from her face and hollered. 'Etta Roan. Who did her? It's that Jew from over at Fry's Bay, the famous one. He's looking.'

There was a long silence in which I reflected on the dubious nature of being a notorious Jew. Until a man's voice startled me.

'Mr Moscowitz,' he said in a very lush tone. 'May one inquire as to the nature of your interest in the aforementioned subject?'

'Certainly,' I assured him. 'A relative traced her to Fry's Bay and asked me about her. I have no record, so I've been calling around.'

It was *mostly* true.

'Ah,' he said.

There was a shuffling of papers, and then he began humming. At first, I didn't recognize the tune, but then it turned out to be a song from the radio called 'You Sexy Thing'. He was humming the part that talked about believing in miracles.

I took the phone away from my ear. I hated that song.

After a second, he stopped very abruptly.

'Oh,' he said. 'Oh, dear.'

'What is it?' I asked him.

'It's this one. I'd almost forgotten.'

I waited, but it turned out that he wasn't prepared to offer me anything more without a little prompting.

'Right,' I said. 'So, where is she?'

'I'm not really supposed to—' he began.

'Me neither,' I interrupted. 'But you wouldn't believe what my desk looks like, and I'd like to say goodbye to at least *one* folder today.'

'The reason it's difficult,' he went on, voice lowered, 'is that the child in question is not in foster care. She's been adopted. Our file is closed. And, um, you know how they are about adoptions right here in Lake City.'

I could hear him wink over the phone. So, she was still in Lake City.

'I know,' I told him. 'I can just imagine what the adoptive family would say if they found out you gave out their name.'

'Mr and Mrs Lambert? Oh, they'd be very unhappy.'

I smiled. 'OK, you have to tell me your name, now,' I said to the guy, 'because I think you're my new best friend.'

'It's Elvin, Mr Moscowitz. Elvin Bradley.' He sipped a fussy breath. 'Perhaps if you ever find yourself in Lake City, we might enjoy a cocktail or two.'

'We might, indeed. And it's Foggy, OK?'

'You *are* famous, you know. Like Mrs Bannon said. You've been in the papers a lot.'

'Fools names and fools faces, Elvin.'

'Nevertheless.' He paused. 'Even Etta Roan knows your name. I may have mentioned you to her.'

'What? Why?'

He whispered. 'There was something not right about that

adoption. I could tell that the child was in trouble. I didn't like it. So, I told her she should try to get in touch with you if she ever needed help.'

'Me?'

'Guess you don't realize how famous you are,' he whispered, 'for helping kids.'

And then I heard Mrs Bannon say something to him and he shut up.

'Next time I'm in Lake City, Elvin,' I promised, 'it's cocktails on me.'

He actually giggled, and I hung up.

So, that was easy. Etta Roan was in Lake City. Half an hour's worth of research told me that there were five Lamberts in Lake City; three were listed as *Mr and Mrs*, which wasn't a sure thing, by any means. But it *was* a place to start.

I reached for the phone, picked up the receiver, and set it down. Three times.

This wasn't a phone-call thing. It was an in-person thing. I just didn't want to spend two hours driving to Lake City, and another three knocking on doors and getting yelled at.

But I knew that's what I had to do.

So. Up from the desk, down to the street, and into my car, the world's saddest ride.

I know some people would try to tell you that a raven-black '57 Thunderbird is only one among a parade of fine automobiles. But for my money, it was the T-Bird. Not that I actually spent money on it. It was the last car I boosted in my previous incarnation as Brooklyn's finest Jewish car thief. Sure, that was a select club, but I was supreme. Right up until the moment I climbed into the driver's seat of a car with a crib in the back. A baby crib. I was halfway down the street when the nipper started squawking. And two seconds later, the mother came running after the car, screaming to high heaven.

Long story short: I got arrested; I escaped (in my T-Bird) all the way to Fry's Bay, Florida. Through no fault of my own, I ended up as the guy from Child Protective Services, a new crew in tangential law enforcement. I took care of kids.

Anybody could see the obvious Freudian motivations. I was

protecting children from people who might do them harm. People like me.

But I digress. There I was, in my Thunderbird, sailing out of town on a Tuesday morning, top down, aimed in the general direction of Lake City. For the first hour I got a college station that played jazz, so that was lucky. But after a while it was all that country crap. Both songs: the happy one, and the sad one. You know: the former involved a girl in a pickup truck, the latter dealt with drunken loss and mother. Over and over again.

I was in Lake City by lunchtime.

The first Mr and Mrs Lambert were in their eighties. She was in a wheelchair and he was very hard of hearing. They never got past the idea that I was trying to sell them something. I even showed them my badge, which was very official looking. Their response was that they couldn't afford tickets to the Policeman's Ball.

The second house was empty. No curtains, no furniture, no dust: neat and clean as a pin.

The last one on my list was a couple from Cuba. Loud, funny, kind. And they had filled up the house, a two-bedroom job, with plenty of kids of their own. They thought it was hilarious, the idea of adopting a little blonde cherub.

So, feeling ill-used by fate, I opted for a small diner I'd seen close to the second house, the vacant one. It had a lot of signs in the window. One told me that Elvis Presley was coming to the Colosseum in Jacksonville, but the one that caught my eye said 'Authentic Deli Sandwiches'.

I should have known better. The place inside was a vinyl and Formica number. Three people at the bar, another ten in various booths. Seashell pink and aquamarine blue – too bright; smelled like clams.

I ordered the chopped liver on rye. My expectations were low, but still a little generous for what came next. The rye was whole wheat, the livers were chicken, and there was mayonnaise involved. Plus, no pickle. I was still staring at it when the waitress came over to fill my water glass.

'It don't get no better,' she told me. 'No matter how long you say grace.'

'You think I'm praying over this sorry excuse for a lunch?'
I asked her.

'I take you for the religious type, yes.'

I looked up. She was in her late forties, greying hair,
sagging eyes; a waitress uniform that looked as tired as she
did. The pin on her apron said 'Madge'.

'Madge,' I began, 'I take you for a keen observer of life
around this neighborhood.'

She set the pitcher of water down on my table. 'I keep to
myself.' But that phrase ended with an upward inflection, the
kind that expected you to continue the conversation.

'There's a vacant house down the block, number 212,' I said.
'My friends the Lamberts used to live there, but they seem to
be gone now. Any idea where?'

'Lamberts?' She shook her head. 'Don't know no Lamberts.'

It was worth a shot.

'Maybe just the check, then,' I told her.

'No pie?' She was surprised. 'We don't get much call for
that sammich you ordered, but our pie has got enthusiastic
fans.'

'Enthusiasm for pie is a subjective thing.'

'Key lime,' she murmured enticingly. 'But hurry up. We
about to close.'

And I succumbed. Key lime pie was a delight unknown
to me before I came to Florida. It was tart, it was sweet, and
at this particular diner, it was vaguely green. It was also gone
in about thirty seconds.

'Told you,' said my friend as she slipped the check under
my plate.

Maybe it was the sugar rush, or maybe it was desperation
– I sometimes get those two confused. But whatever it was,
I had the idea to ask Madge an odd question.

'The people I'm looking for had a daughter,' I said, reaching
for my wallet so I could pay her. 'Looked like a little cherub,
blonde hair, about eleven years old.'

'Etta!' Madge said instantly. 'Sweetest kid in five states. You
didn't say it was her family you's looking for?'

'So, you know them?'

'Didn't know they was named Lambert. But you couldn't

miss Etta. Cutest thing you ever saw. Ain't been in for . . .
I'd say at least a week. Always get fried chicken sammich,
extra fries, co-cola, and that key lime pie. Big tippers, too.
Usually left a dollar. Whole dollar. Where'd they go to?'

'Yeah,' I said. 'That's what I need to find out.'

I glanced at the check and doubled it.

She raised her eyebrows. 'I get off at six,' she suggested.

'Let's not spoil what we have,' I told her.

She sighed, and that was that. I was out to the parking lot.

In my car I got an envelope out of the glove compartment,
wrote on it, and headed for the post office.

THREE

The local post office was a tidy affair. Nice square room, well swept, one employee behind the counter. No waiting at 2:45 in the afternoon.

'Hi,' I said, ambling toward the grey-haired postman. 'I wonder if you can help me.'

He smiled. 'Do what I can.'

'It's about the Lamberts, over on Bell,' I told him, arriving at the counter. 'Did they leave a forwarding address? This letter came to them at their old place, and it looks important.'

I held up the envelope from my glove compartment.

'Okey doke,' he said. 'Just let me have a look.'

He disappeared into the back room, stayed gone for longer than seemed necessary, and returned frowning.

'There *is* a forwarding address for the Lamberts' mail,' he said, shaking his head, 'but it doesn't make any sense.'

'How's that?' I asked.

He held up a spiral notebook. The forwarding address was written on it. I stared. It said: 'Office of Child Protective Services, Fry's Bay, Florida. C/O Moscowitz'.

'That's way south of here,' the postman said.

'Yeah,' I told him. 'I know.'

'And, plus, it ain't a residence,' he went on.

I nodded, still staring at the piece of paper.

The postman leaned forward and lowered his voice. 'You think they were arrested, maybe?' he asked. 'Something to do with a child?'

'From what I know about the Lamberts,' I assured him, 'that would be hard to say.'

I certainly hadn't gotten any of their mail in my office.

'And, plus, that ain't Daisy's handwriting,' he went on.

'Daisy?'

He grinned. 'We got a lady postman. Daisy Fuller. Got very

distinctive handwriting. Dots her I's with little hearts. So, she didn't write this note.'

'Right. So, could it be that Mr Lambert wrote this himself and brought it in?' I asked.

'Wouldn't be procedure. He's supposed to fill out the form.'

'But there's no form.'

'Right,' he said. 'Just this note. Looks like a child's handwriting, to me.'

I thanked the guy and beat it.

Now, it was true that some people in north central Florida might have known my name, being that it was kind of unusual for the region. But what would make a total stranger forward mail to my office?

So. Off to the local police precinct office for a little research, because I was beginning to suspect there was more to Etta's father than he'd let on when he had a gun in my face.

There's a funny smell in police stations. It's a combination of sweat, fear, and boredom. Not the worst thing in the world, but something that had very uncomfortable associations for me. They say the smells can bring back powerful memories. And who likes to remember?

The police station in Lake City was small. Double glass doors into a waiting room filled with empty wooden benches. A big window that hadn't been cleaned since World War Two, and a desk sergeant you could say the same thing about.

I flashed my badge and he was singularly unimpressed.

'Run along,' he growled. 'I ain't gonna buy your girl scout cookies.'

'Very amusing,' I told him, 'but I need to know about a felon at large, name of Roan. It's for a case over in Fry's Bay.'

It was worth a shot.

He gave me the once-over. I was wearing the grey seersucker with an unfashionably thin black tie. And two-tone Florsheims. He shook his head. 'What is the nature of your *case*?' He said it like he knew I was making it up. Maybe it was my haberdashery.

'Missing child,' I said. 'Etta Roan, possibly kidnapped by her father, the aforementioned felon. See?'

He snarled, but he got up out of his chair. Went to a nearby file cabinet. Took him forever to find the file he was looking for. I heard him singing the schooldays alphabet song three times under his breath.

Then, after about a century and a half, he ambled back my way with a couple of papers in his hand.

'Nelson Roan.' He sighed. 'Only served a couple months of a life sentence. He was up for a retrial, so that's odd. Says here he popped a guard and jacked a police motorcycle. Considered armed and dangerous. Don't say nothing about no missing child.'

'When was this?' I asked. 'When did he bust out?'

'Last week.'

'Where'd he escape from?'

'Had him in Cross City Correctional, for some reason,' he told me. 'Opened a couple of years ago on the grounds of that decommissioned Air Force station. Rinky-dink, if you ask me.'

I hadn't planned on asking him that, but I did have a few other questions.

'What was Roan in for?'

He held the pages at a distance, the way you do if your eyes are bad.

'Killed a guy in Lake City. A *doctor.*'

'Doctor. Name?'

'Adam Bainbridge. Cancer doctor.' He squinted. 'Wait. Says here that there was twenty malpractice actions against him, this Dr Bainbridge.'

He set the papers down and stared at me in a way that let me know he was done.

'Well.' I looked around the empty room. 'I'll let you get back to your busy schedule.'

He said a few words I didn't like the sound of, so I left.

And as I did, I had to ask myself some questions. Like, was it possible that Dr Bainbridge was Mrs Roan's doctor? And if he was, had he botched an operation or a diagnosis involving the very same Mrs Roan? And is that why Mr Roan ended up in stir, because he killed a rotten physician?

It didn't seem like much of a leap, and I had a very firm kind of intuition about it.

Still, it got me nowhere finding the kid. And that's all I really wanted to do, for some reason.

Maybe it was because Roan reminded me of my Brooklyn friends, or because I was a sucker for a lovelorn parent. Something had made me drive a long way from my home on a case that wasn't a case, not officially. But it seemed important.

And beyond that, it was what I was doing. I was always a big believer in *is*. Not *should be*, or *ought to*. *Is*. That's very powerful, because it's the only reality. Whatever it is you were doing, that was the only thing that truly existed. Everything else was a fantasy.

In other words, I was outside a crappy police station in Lake City. That's where I was. Everything else – like I was *supposed* to be back in my office, or I was going to get in *trouble* for pursuing an unofficial investigation – wasn't real.

In such a philosophical frame of mind as that, I felt lucky. So, I went back to the empty house near Madge's diner. Now that I knew it was the last place Etta lived, I thought I might commit a little breaking and entering, and meander around the homestead. You never could tell what someone might have left behind in the way of a clue.

I parked my car a block away and sauntered over to the side yard of the vacancy. Around back was just right: bushes on either side hid me from the neighbors and the backdoor handle was a Kwikset. I was very familiar with the knob in question. I was inside the house in seven seconds.

It was more than empty. It had been cleaned like a crime scene. Smelled like ammonia and obsession. Floors were polished, windows were spotless, kitchen looked new. It was well beyond any occupant's due diligence, or owner's responsibility. Maybe Mrs Roan was a neat freak. Or maybe a professional cleaning service had been paid to do the place twice.

Whatever it was, it didn't feel right. In my experience, *that* much cleanliness was next to hiding something.

But what was it hiding?

I decided to take off my shoes so as not to track anything in.

I set them by the back door and wandered around for a while in my stocking feet, feeling more than a little ridiculous.

The house was a single-story job, what they called a 'ranch', though I never understood that name. It was nothing like the ranches I'd seen on television. No bunkhouse, no horses, no cactus. It was a flat box with a bunch of smaller boxes inside: living room, dining room, kitchen, two bedrooms, and a bath. And about as much character as a Kleenex.

Just as I was about to give up and skate on back to the kitchen where the door was, I had another intuition. I remembered what I was like when I was a nipper. For instance, I had a couple of hiding places in the apartment, and one on the street, next to our stoop. I hid the usual things any kid might: stuff I'd pickpocketed, nudie magazines I'd shoplifted, a gun from my uncle once.

Anyway, I wondered if Etta was the kind of kid to have a hiding place or two. I started in the closet of the smaller bedroom. Maybe there was a loose floorboard or a hole in the drywall. But no luck.

Then I wondered if there might be something in the bathroom. It's the only place I ever got any genuine privacy.

Nothing behind the toilet bowl. Nothing behind the medicine cabinet over the sink. Then I thought about kid height, and I knelt down to get that perspective. When I did, I realized that I could get under the sink pretty easy. And under the cast-iron porcelain sink, in the folds way in back, there was a rolled-up scroll, tied with a thin white ribbon.

I dislodged it carefully and stood up. I slid it out of the ribbon, and unfurled two pieces of notebook paper. One of the pages was a poem.

Blueberries roll around my table
Like little ocean waves.
I love my blueberry ocean
More than the sea at the beach.
In my ocean, no one can drown.

Etta

The second page was a note.

> *Dad, I hope you find this. I'm hiding it where you told me to.*
>
> *Me and the Lamberts had to leave in a hurry. I think something is wrong.*
>
> *We're not taking Den. Go get him at the vet. There's something for you on his collar. I love you. Etta.*

And there we were: a couple of pretty good clues.

I slipped both pages into my inside coat pocket just as I heard a click at the front door. I shot out of the bathroom, into the kitchen, scooped up my shoes, and was in the back yard before I took a breath. I had time to slip on my Florsheims, but not to tie them, because I saw two people in the kitchen, like they were headed for the back door.

I rounded the house and ran like an idiot out into the street and across to the other sidewalk. Then I came to a very sudden standstill, dropped, and tied my shoes.

I looked around. Nobody out on the streets. No cars. Nobody following me from the back yard of the deserted house.

There was a blue Dodge Dart parked in front of the house. Not a cop car or a hood-mobile. Just regular citizens, I figured. Maybe the new renters, or real-estate types, or a landlord checking up on the place. Nothing to worry about.

Still, I beat it back to my car and got out of the neighborhood as fast as I could, all the while thinking where I might find the closest veterinarian. And hoping Den wasn't a German shepherd.

FOUR

t only occurred to me after I'd rounded the corner that it was odd for a kid and a con to share a hiding space under a bathroom sink, even if the con was the father. Why had Roan told his kid to hide stuff? And what kind of eleven-year-old thinks to leave something for her dad on a dog's collar? And if Roan knew where the kid was living, why bother me in the middle of the night?

Maybe there was something on the dog collar in the way of further explanation. I'd seen a phone booth on the same corner as Madge's diner. I was hoping there was only one vet in that part of Lake City.

I pulled up to the booth, looked around before I got out. Almost getting caught in an empty house had me a little off balance. Couldn't say exactly why.

No one around that I could see. I jumped out of the car and into the booth. The phone book was tattered, but it was there. There were three vets in the Yellow Pages inside the city limits. I didn't know the city well enough to know which one was closest. I thought about going back into the diner to see if Madge had any ideas, but the lunch crowd was long gone, and the place looked closed. No lights inside.

I stood there wondering what I was going to do about it, when a guy wearing a pink shirt with green palm trees on it came motoring my way with a little wiener dog on a leash in front of him. I stepped his way and smiled.

'Hi,' I said to him, smiling. 'I'm glad I ran into you. I got a sick beagle and I wonder if you could tell me where's the nearest vet?'

He stopped short and eyed me like I was the flu.

'I'm new to the area,' I went on. 'Just had some key lime pie from Madge.'

I nodded in the direction of the diner. That broke a little of the ice.

'It's good pie.' He pronounced it like *pah*, and out of the corner of his mouth.

'It is. So. My beagle.'

'They get sick all the time. Them beagles.' He shook his head.

'Right. So . . .' I began.

'Dr Carroll,' he interrupted. 'Two blocks down that way; one to the left. Can't miss it.'

'Oh. Great. Thanks.'

'Next time you go in there at the diner,' he advised me, 'you tell Madge that Morris says give you the pecan pie. She's always pushing the key lime on account of the locals won't eat it. We eat pecan.'

That was pronounced *pee-can*.

'It's good to have the inside track,' I told him.

He didn't comment on my philosophy. He just clicked at his dachshund and took off.

Five minutes later I was standing at Dr Carroll's front desk.

The person behind the desk was a well-dressed high school kid, with all the know-nothing enthusiasm that comes with it.

'I've come to get my dog, Den,' I told her.

'Ooh, what a great dog!' she told me. Then: 'Wait. That's not your dog. That's Etta's dog.'

'Right. Etta Roan. They moved, and she asked me to come pick it up. And pay the bill.'

The phrase 'pay the bill' usually got respect, but she treated me like bad news.

'What's going on?' she said slowly. 'Everybody wants Etta's dog.'

'They do?' I tried to sound innocent, but I had an idea what she was talking about. Someone else had come to collect the dog.

'First that rude man day before yesterday,' she sniffed, 'and now you.'

'He didn't offer to pay the tab, though,' I guessed.

'No.' She frowned. 'But, look, Den is *Etta's dog*.'

I reached in my coat pocket and produced Etta's poem about blueberries.

'She likes to give me these little poems,' I said, holding

it out. 'I like to keep them with me because I think they're great.'

The kid read the poem, sniffed, and then nodded. 'Gee. Isn't Etta, like, the best?'

'Yes,' I agreed. 'She probably is.'

'OK.' With that, the kid shuffled into the back room. There was a great noise of animals and metal doors. The kid spoke very lovingly to everyone and returned with a dog the color of caramels. The chewy kind.

Den was very happy to see me. I got the impression he was very happy to see anyone. His tail was going like a windshield wiper and he jumped up with his front feet all over my nice clean suit coat.

'*That's* a golden retriever,' the high school kid said, laughing.

I tried to smile. All I could see was Den's teeth.

I paid the tab and made my way out the door.

I may have neglected to mention that I'd always been afraid of dogs. German shepherds, mostly, but every dog was a devil dog, potentially. I'd had a bad experience when I was a kid; I didn't like to talk about it.

Luckily, Den did all the work. He was happy to see me, happy to get out of stir, and when he realized he was going for a ride in a Thunderbird, I thought he might explode.

I let him in the passenger seat and I got in my side. He sat down very sedately, I thought, and waited for his ride to begin.

'Look, Den,' I said to him. 'I want to have a gander at what's on your collar. OK?'

He didn't seem to care, so I patted his head and looked at his collar. Beside his dog tag, there was a locket-type item hanging there, about the size of a silver dollar. Den was very polite about it. He was still as a picture while I took it off.

I sat back in the driver's seat and opened the locket. Inside there was a small square of paper. I unfolded it.

'Fry's Bay. Yudda's Restaurant.'

Written very carefully in kid's printing. The same writing as the forwarding address I'd seen at the post office.

I was chasing rainbows all over Florida while something else was pointing toward my adopted home town. And apparently the kid was headed for my favorite eatery.

I looked at Den. He didn't seem to know much about the strange turn of events, but I could tell he was anxious to get on the road. So, I cranked up the T-Bird and pointed it back toward Fry's Bay. The sun was headed toward the western sea, and I was headed for dinner.

The ride was pleasant. The air was warm, and Den was a great travelling companion. He didn't bother me with a lot of gab, and he didn't mind when I turned on the jazz station. Gave me plenty of room to ruminate.

And here was my thinking: Yudda was the owner of the worst-looking fine-dining establishment in the eastern United States. Mostly sea food, whatever was fresh, but he was an experimenter. That meant that one day you'd be eating like the King of France, with John Dory in a caper sauce made for God, and the next day you'd ask for your money back over the cod and pickled peaches. Yudda had also become a friend. He was 230 pounds of irascible Cajun in a stained apron and flip-flops, but he was also the most reliable person I knew in Fry's Bay.

His story was that he left New Orleans to get away from an ex-wife, but I found out, over time, that he was actually escaping his criminal escapades, hiding out in Nowhere, Florida. Which made him something of a kindred spirit.

The sun was sinking low and I was nearing Fry's Bay, and I thought: what if Roan was somehow connected to Yudda's nefarious enterprises? I knew that Yudda had been involved in the weed trade. Probably still was. Benign, but it might sometimes put you next to some more serious criminals.

Or what if Roan was somehow hooked up with my old friends in Brooklyn? I had only been a car thief – and, not to brag, the best one in five boroughs – but it had acquainted me with some very serious offenders. In my past.

See, I always thought that you dragged your chains around behind you like Marley in that stupid Christmas movie. Or like the old Robert Johnson blues song: there were hellhounds on my trail.

And at that, I turned to Den. 'You're not a hellhound, are you?' I asked him.

He turned, looked at me like I'd lost my mind, and then put his face back into the wind.

So, at least that was settled.

The sun was almost down by the time I pulled into my parking spot. Den bounded out, peed in two places, and then headed for the sand at the side of my apartment building to take care of some more serious business.

I unlocked my front door and stood there waiting. I was afraid he might want to explore, run off down the beach. But after a minute or two of looking around, he loped back my way and came into my apartment like he owned the place. Straight into the kitchen.

'Oh.' I locked the door behind me and followed him. 'I thought we'd dine out.'

He stared up at me, and I suddenly thought he might be thirsty. I hauled out a big silver mixing bowl and filled it up from the tap. He drank it up, every drop.

'More?'

Den sniffed, so I filled the bowl again.

Most of that was gone in seconds. Thirsty dog.

'Look,' I said to him, 'I don't have any dog-style food here, and I don't know if I should take you with me or not. But I have to go to Yudda's. Do you have an opinion?'

Swear to God, the dog nodded once and went to the front door to wait for me.

I shrugged. On impulse, I went to the bedroom and got my Colt Defender, slipped it into the special pocket in the small of my back. You never could tell.

'All right,' I told Den. 'I hope you like seafood. Because Yudda's gumbo is way too spicy for a dog.'

I opened the door and Den was in the passenger seat before I could turn around.

FIVE

Yudda's place was nothing more than a tin shack with a rusted roof. The whole joint was the size of a dining car from the old days in the railroad game. But people in the know came from far and wide to get a crack at what he'd dreamed up. He was creative, unencumbered by the constraints of middle-class cuisine, and willing to fail spectacularly if it meant occasionally succeeding in the same way.

Or you could just order the soup and a burger, which was also great, and available for the less adventurous stomach.

The sky was darkening and there was a little haze from the nearby water. The windows of Yudda's place were orange, cheery. The place was packed. Which it usually was around the dinner hour. Which was why I always ate late. But I figured if, in fact, the Lamberts or little Etta might show up, it would be during the more popular times.

I opened the door and stood in the doorway. Den was calm, but clearly interested in everything he was smelling. I surveyed the customers. Mostly locals, people I'd seen before. No little kids. Four teenagers on a double date. One guy on his way to the bathroom in back. A normal night.

When Yudda finally looked over at me, he tilted his head at a very unusual angle. 'That's Etta's dog,' he said over the noise of the place.

So, there was an answer to something; I just wasn't sure what the right question was.

'It is,' I said, like I knew what I was doing. 'His name is Den.'

'I'm familiar.' Yudda wasn't smiling. 'No dogs allowed. Take him around back.'

'The thing is—' I began.

'Take him around back,' Yudda said again, only louder.

I nodded. Den and I made our way around the diner to the kitchen door. Yudda was there. He had a .44 in his hand. I stopped short. Yudda was a good friend, but I didn't care for the look on his face.

'Where's Etta?' he wanted to know.

'That seems to be the question,' I agreed.

'I mean, what are you doing with her dog?'

'Taking him out for a bite to eat,' I said. 'They say the food here is good.'

'Foggy,' Yudda snapped.

'The kid's father woke me up in the middle of last night,' I told him. 'He wanted me to find Etta. I did pretty good for a day's work. I found out the name of her adoptive parents, where they lived, and what kind of pie they liked. I got a hold of the dog, and just now I found out that my favorite local chef is involved. Somehow. Not bad for under twenty-four hours. And now it's time for dinner.'

'You were followed.'

I shook my head. 'I don't think so.'

He pointed his gun up the street and repeated himself. 'You were followed.'

I turned. A block away, in a darker part of the street that led up to Yudda's, there was a car parked. It was a sky-blue Dodge Dart.

'Huh,' I said, glaring at Den. 'You couldn't have told me there was a car behind us all the way from Lake City?'

Den lowered his head.

'Who's in the Dodge?' Yudda wanted to know.

'Yeah, that's my new favorite question.' I looked down at Den. 'You want to come with me over to the Dodge, or would you rather stay here close to the kitchen?'

The dog thought about it, then sauntered over to Yudda and sat beside him. Yudda couldn't help smiling.

'Looks like you're on your own,' he told me. 'You want to borrow my forty-four?'

'Not even a little bit,' I assured him. 'But if anything untoward happens, you can use it all you want.'

He nodded.

I headed for the car in question.

As I got closer, I could see that there were two people in it. A man and a woman. The woman was in the driver's seat.

When they realized I was headed their way, they scrambled. The woman started the car, lights off, and began to back up. Right into a low post, something that you used to tie your horse to in the old days. Cast iron sunk into concrete. Did more damage to the car than the post.

Momentarily confused, neither of them knew what to do. I'd picked up my pace considerably, and I was standing at the driver's door before they realized it. The window was open. I reached into the car, switched off the ignition, and pulled out the keys. All one move, nice as you please.

They were both talking at once, so I couldn't understand either of them. I pounded on the roof of the car to get their attention.

'You followed me all the way from Lake City,' I said, doing my best to sound mean and intimidating. 'Now you're going to tell me why!'

'You broke into our house!' the woman said, high-pitched. 'You took Etta's poems!'

'You stole our dog!' the man added, nearly as shrill.

I took a breath. 'First, not your house. You moved out. Second, not your poems. They belong to Etta – and her dad. Third, I'm trying to find Etta *for* her dad, see?'

That shut them up more than I expected.

'And you can have the dog,' I told them, more softly, 'if you tell me how the dog knows Yudda.'

'Who?' the woman asked.

I turned. 'You can kind of see him over there, the big guy in the light from the kitchen of his diner. He's got a gun in his hand and that's the dog sitting next to him.'

'We don't know any of your *hoodlum* friends!' the man ventured, bravely.

I nodded. 'Let's start over again.'

I reached for my wallet.

The woman screamed, and the man lunged my way. Neither action prevented me from showing them my badge.

'I work for Florida Child Protective Services,' I said calmly, sticking the badge in their faces. 'I'm concerned about the welfare of Etta Roan. You, I assume, are the Lamberts.'

They were both frozen for a moment. Then the man sat

back, and the woman put her hand up to her chest like she was fending off a heart attack.

'We thought . . . we thought . . .' Mr Lambert struggled.

'You look like those other men,' Mrs Lambert jumped in.

'What *other* men?' I asked as I handed Mr Lambert his keys.

Before he could answer, there were gunshots.

I looked over my shoulder, and Yudda was nowhere to be seen. The dog was lying very still by the back door of the diner. And two guys who were all business headed my way in a very big hurry.

'Stay put,' I said to the Lamberts.

I launched myself in the direction of two men with guns.

As I got closer, I could tell they were angry. That was to my advantage. They also weren't shooting at me, which I took as a good sign. So, you know what they say about the best defense.

'You guys haven't found Roan *yet*?' I shouted. 'I thought you'd have him with you by now!'

See, the beauty of such an accusation was that if I was right, and they were after Roan, they'd figure I was someone in the know. Which I was not, but that was my secret. And if I was wrong, and they were out for some other kind of nefarious mischief, they'd at least be momentarily confused.

Either way, it worked. Their ire turned to curiosity, and in the time it took for that to happen, I was all over them. I kicked the gun out of one guy's hand with a high sort of side swipe of the old Florsheim. Something I learned from a French guy in Owls Head. The other guy was easier because he couldn't believe what I did to the first guy. All I had to do was backhand the second guy's wrist, and his gun went sailing away down the street like a fat pigeon.

I shook my head. 'Now, if I can handle you guys that easy, it's no wonder Roan's still in the wind.'

I reached into the small of my back and got my Colt.

'Where'd you learn that fancy foot thing?' assailant number one asked me, rubbing his empty gun hand.

His accent was very Canadian, which was a puzzle. It was widely known in my previous circle that there was a war on between the Sicilian and the Calabrian factions in Canada at the time. There was plenty of trouble right there in Montreal if you were in any way connected. So, it was unusual that these guys would be so far south. Because it was obvious to me that they were Canadian hoods.

I was beginning to realize that Etta Roan was somehow mixed up in something much bigger than a family adoption matter.

'You guys are a long way from home.' I put my gun away as a sign of good faith. 'Let me give you some local advice: you just killed a very nice dog and pissed off the owner of the only really good place to eat within 500 miles. And I'm unhappy with you, which is your third strike. Choice one: fill me in on everything you've done since you came down here. Choice two: beat it back to Montreal.'

Guy One shook his head and said, 'It's too cold in Montreal right now.'

Guy Two agreed. 'Early snow, can you believe it?'

'My understanding,' I said, 'is that it's actually pretty hot in your city right now.'

'Oh.' Guy One glanced at Guy Two. 'In a manner of speaking.'

'Names, gents,' I insisted, 'or the Colt comes out again.'

'Scarlatti,' said Guy One.

'Mordecai,' the other one told me.

'Fine Canadian names,' I said. 'Now. What gives? Why shoot a dog? And what do you want with Etta Roan?'

'In the first place,' Scarlatti assured me, 'we did *not* shoot no *dog*.'

'And in the second,' Mordecai piped up, 'Etta Roan is the Holy Grail.'

Both statements caught me off guard.

'Yudda!' I hollered.

Yudda appeared at the kitchen door. 'What?' he wanted to know.

'How's the dog?'

Yudda said something to the limp body, and Den jumped up, wagging his tail. Yudda gave him a bite of something, and the dog seemed very happy.

'Fine,' Yudda told me. 'I taught him how to play dead in emergencies. It's come in handy more than once.'

'Very effective,' I shouted. 'You'll have to teach me sometime.'

'You're too old of a dog,' he informed me.

And then he went back in the diner. Den followed.

'OK,' I admitted. 'You didn't kill the dog. Now explain to me why Etta Roan is the Holy Grail.'

At that, the Lamberts' car started up and the engine raced. I barely got out of the way, and they clipped Mordecai pretty good. The tires squealed, and they almost hit the diner turning the sharp corner next to it. I could still hear the engine headed down the main street and out of town as I knelt over Mordecai. He wasn't breathing.

SIX

Turns out that Yudda had called the cops. At the first sign of the Canadian gents, he said. He sized them up right away when the shooting started. He told the dog to play dead, for some reason – just showing off, I figured. Then he retreated to his position behind the bar and traded his .44 for the shotgun. He referred to the entire enterprise as 'simple Cajun precautionary measures'. I didn't buy it. What self-respecting miscreant calls the cops as the first order of business? I had so many questions for Yudda I couldn't even remember them all. But they had to wait. There was a guy bleeding all over the street.

The constabulary in Fry's Bay had recently undergone a sort of shake-up, so the officers who showed up were new to me. One was young, maybe twenty. His suit was cheap, and he had Brylcreem in his hair. The other guy, around fifty, seemed to be the sort who'd had a tough beat, like in Miami, and was looking to ease out the last few years of public service in a nice little town like Fry's Bay. Someplace where he wouldn't have to deal with hoods from Canada run down by a strange couple from Lake City.

The ambulance arrived about the same time the cops did.

The older cop climbed out of the passenger side of his car, took one look around, and asked, 'Who shot him?'

Scarlatti was suddenly dumb, and I just shook my head.

The old guy looked around. 'The call said shots fired.'

'Yeah,' I said to Scarlatti, 'what about that? What were you guys shooting at if you didn't kill the dog?'

'Somebody killed a dog?' the younger cop asked, high-pitched.

I looked at the older cop. 'There's a lot to the story. I'm going to reach for my wallet now, to show you my badge. I'm telling you this because I haven't always had great luck with the police in a situation like this.'

He lifted his chin. 'Situation like *what*?'

'The shoot-first-and-ask-questions-later type,' I said, reaching behind me.

I showed him my badge, then flashed it in junior's direction. He was kneeling over Mordecai's body, fishing for a wallet or some sort of ID.

'Child Protective Services – where's the child?' Oldster wanted to know.

'This is what I'm telling you,' I said. 'It's a little complicated. It's not a short answer.'

The old guy heaved a sigh like I'd just told him his mother died.

'I was shooting at the guy in the diner,' Scarlatti whispered, a little late in his timing.

We all stared at him.

'The guy in the diner?' I asked before anyone else could.

'Came out of the bathroom, pistol in hand, ready for Freddie,' Scarlatti explained, still *sotto voce*.

'Yudda!' I hollered.

It only took a second for Yudda to appear in his back door again.

'Stop yelling at me!' he shouted.

'Was there a guy in your bathroom with a gun?'

'Uh, *yeah*,' he said, like I was an idiot. 'Why do you think I called the police?'

'OK, but, where is he now?'

'Who?'

'The guy in the bathroom with the gun,' I said, like *he* was the idiot.

'Oh.' He shrugged. 'He's gone. Anything else? I got fishcakes I don't want to burn, OK?'

'The ones with the fennel seed?' I asked him.

'Naturally.'

'By all means,' I encouraged.

He vanished.

The ambulance guys were picking up Mordecai, and Scarlatti was doing his best to be invisible.

The old cop headed my way, but I was way ahead of him.

'Look,' I said, 'we have a ton of stuff to discuss, but these

fishcakes that Yudda's making? You don't want to miss. So, let's
go back down the street and wait for them to be done and then
eat, like, a whole lot of them. Meantime, I'll clue you in, right?'

The old guy only thought about it for a second, then looked
Scarlatti up and down.

'Who's this?' the cop asked.

'Never saw him before,' I told him honestly.

'Smith,' Scarlatti said. 'Benny Smith. Me and my pal, there
on the stretcher, we come here for a little deep-sea fishing and
some peace and quiet. What kind of a town are you running
here, where a decent citizen gets run down in the middle of
the street at dinner time? Geez!'

I had to smile. I hoped the cops didn't notice.

Old Guy sighed again. 'Show me some ID.'

Like he was flipping out a switchblade for some kind
of rumble, Scarlatti flashed a perfect Illinois driver's license.
Name of Benny Smith.

'Look, Mr Smith,' I said to the guy, 'if you want an apology,
there's nothing better than these fishcakes.'

'I should probably go with my friend, Mr Jones,' Scarlatti
said, heading for the ambulance.

'Of course,' I said sympathetically.

Old Guy just shook his head. 'Listen, Moscowitz: I'm wise
to you.'

'In what way?' I asked him.

'I've heard of you. You're supposed to be some kind of
local hero,' he said. 'But I peg you for a wise guy.'

It was impossible to tell if he meant 'wise guy' in the New
York way or the Woody Woodpecker way.

I stepped toward him quick enough to make him flinch.
'Look, Officer Whatever-Your-Name-Is,' I lashed out, 'this is
my town, Fry's Bay. I have friends here. I do good work. I
save a lot of kids. That doesn't make me a local hero, it just
makes me somebody who does his job reasonably well. If I
find out that you're *not* that sort of person, I'll have you out
of town faster than Officer Brady.'

Brady was the name of the previous cop in town, a bad
guy from the ground up, and everybody knew it. So, in a very
complicated way, I'd gotten rid of him.

The officer squinted so hard I thought his eyes were closed. 'I was thirty years in Miami, Hialeah neighborhood,' he said steadily. 'Where the rats run the streets. Then the wife died of cancer, about a year ago. I have recently come to Fry's Bay as a kind of early retirement, see? So, don't get up *my* nose!'

There was a moment of silence, the kind where they say an angel passes overhead.

'Um, boss?' the younger cop said. 'It's skid marks right here, and over there it looks like a car maybe ran into that iron post thing. This all looks legit. I mean, like they say.'

Old Guy took a moment to think, or maybe just to calm down. 'It's Haley, my name,' he said. 'Like the comet. The partner's Banquer. Straight from Louisiana.'

I stuck out my hand. 'Happy to meet you, Officer Haley. Now. About these fishcakes.'

An hour later I was sitting back in a booth at Yudda's holding my belly like it might burst.

Haley put his hand over his mouth and belched as politely as I ever heard.

Banquer was at the bar talking to Yudda in some kind of odd French.

The place had emptied out for the most part, and I was a little sleepy. Den had taken up residence in the booth beside me. Yudda had given him the biggest steak he could find, and the dog looked sleepier than me.

I'd explained to Haley, as best I could between bites, about Roan, and his kid, and my odyssey to Lake City. I only left out the part about the Canadian hoods, partly because I still wasn't sure about Haley, partly because I didn't understand who they were or what they were doing in my town.

Haley had listened, nodding and eating, without saying much at all.

'Just so you know,' he told me at length, 'there's a general bulletin about Roan. Busted out of Raiford, just outside Lake City.'

'You know Roan got busted because *his* wife died of cancer too,' I said, 'and he popped some doctor in charge of her case.'

'That was the story.' He looked unimpressed.

'You got kids?' I asked.

'None of your business,' he said affably, 'but I got a son who went to Vietnam. When he came back, he wasn't my son any more. Don't know where he is now.'

'I see. What did you think of the fishcakes?'

He glanced down at the clean plate. 'I don't know what those were, but they weren't fishcakes. *Jesus* don't eat that well. This guy, Yudda. He cooks like this all the time?'

'All the time,' I confirmed. 'He misses about one in twenty. But the rest of the time it's nirvana.'

'Hey!' Yudda yelled out. 'This guy knows my cousin!'

'Yeah,' I said to Yudda, reluctantly. 'I'm sorry to ask about all this now, but I think you have to tell me what the hell is going on.'

Yudda nodded. 'You mean about the dog.'

'And all things attendant,' I added.

He closed his eyes. 'You mean Roan.'

Then Yudda told us all a story.

In 1966, Yudda was in New Orleans, cooking for a 'private club', dealing a little weed on the side and fighting with his ex-wife in his spare time. Roan was a guest at the club and Yudda happened to overhear the part where Roan was going to Manhattan on the next flight from Moisant Field. A couple of friendly drinks later, Roan had a heavy carry-on bag: coffee with chicory from Café Du Monde. Inside each bag of coffee was half a cup of grounds and a couple of dime bags of premium weed. All Roan had to do was leave the bag on a bench at JFK.

It all worked out. Roan got 500 bucks for nothing, Yudda became the exclusive supplier to a certain Manhattan family with an interest in New Orleans music. A nice little side business was born.

Roan's goal had been to marry the girl of his dreams, which the extra money allowed him to do. They had a kid right away. Then Roan's bosses sent him to Miami. When the wife got sick all the money went to her treatments. But there was something hinky about the doctor; Yudda was uncertain or unwilling with details. Roan killed doc, wife died anyway, kid got 'adopted'.

'But all that illegal activity is in my past, Officer Haley,' Yudda swore.

He fell silent for a couple of minutes before I realized he was done.

'What about the dog?' I asked.

'Oh.' Yudda smiled at the sleeping mutt beside me. 'Etta got Den as a present, like, at Christmas two years ago. I taught the dog a few tricks. The usual. Roll over, play dead, growl when you see a cop.'

We both looked at Haley.

'Which is how I know you ain't a real cop,' Yudda went on. Only this time he had his sawed-off shotgun in his hand.

Haley was calm. His younger buddy, Banquer, not so much.

Banquer stumbled backward off his stool, flapping around. He made the mistake of pulling his gun.

I glanced at Haley. 'We should get under the table.'

I patted Den. Haley slid down. Then the three of us did a duck and cover.

And Yudda's shotgun went off. It was unusual. I'd seen Yudda threaten people with it plenty of times, I'd just never seen him shoot it. Something had put him on edge. Of course, the kicker was that a guy pretending to be a policeman had pulled a gun on him. I guess anybody would have fired a shotgun under similar circumstances.

The thing about a sawed-off shotgun is that it's an equal-opportunity weapon. It sprays shot everywhere, regardless of affiliation. So, while Banquer got the worst of it, there was also damage to the bar, several booths, and the wall behind me.

Banquer went down. Haley had his gun out, and my Colt appeared. In no seconds flat, Den had Haley's gun hand in some very vicious teeth and Banquer was shouting in French.

'Hold it!' I shouted. 'Hold on!'

I took Haley's gun away and my head popped up over the table. 'Let's sort this out before we all go shooting each other,' I went on. Then: 'Good dog.'

Haley sat up. 'Shut up, Banquer.'

Banquer stopped yelling.

Haley shrugged. 'He's wearing a vest. Me too.'

A quick examination revealed that Banquer had a bit of

shot in one arm, but the main blast had been largely stopped by the vest. Banquer was just scared, mostly. Although buckshot really stings, they tell me.

'We really are the new cops in town,' Haley told me wearily. 'And I really did work in Miami. Thing is we're *also* a little employed by the family Yudda mentioned. From Manhattan. They got fingers in one or two police departments around the country. Chicago, New Orleans, Miami. We got sent to this little berg, like, a month ago because they found out about Roan and Yudda. I tell you all of this because you mostly know it already or would figure it out soon enough. And I don't want to get shot. And I think we might be after the same thing. Namely: Etta Roan.'

I held my Colt in plain sight of everyone. 'Yeah, one of the guys in the street said something about Etta Roan being the Holy Grail. What does *that* mean?'

Yudda chimed in. He was still holding his shotgun. Still had one loaded barrel.

'You don't know about Etta's talent,' he said to me.

'She's not a bad poet,' I ventured.

'Got some kind of brain disease,' Haley told me. 'She can remember every second of her life like it was right now.'

He let that sink in.

'Poor kid,' he went on. 'It's a real problem.'

I assumed that what he meant was that Etta had been hanging around when illegal business had transpired. Certain things that certain people would prefer no one remembered. Certain things that certain *other* people would pay a lot of money to know about.

What it meant was that Etta Roan was going to get bought, or sold, or dead.

If I didn't do something about it.

SEVEN

'So, the two Canadians are from one of the warring factions in Montreal, I guess,' I volunteered. I knew people in Manhattan. I'd never even *been* to Canada. I knew where my loyalties were. Or at least that's what I wanted Haley to think. You really want a guy who's both a hood *and* a cop to be on your side.

He nodded. 'The Sicilians.'

'Scarlatti, maybe,' I allowed. 'But the other guy's named Mordecai. That's their real names, the Canadians.'

The younger cop, Banquer, who had been lying on the floor breathing to calm himself, suddenly sat up.

'Mordecai?' he moaned. 'Jesus, Haley, you didn't tell me this was a *suicide* mission!'

Haley turned my way. 'Some would tell you that a guy named Mordecai is the finest hitman in the western hemisphere.'

'I don't know,' I said. 'Ever hear of Sammy "Icepick" Franks?'

Haley nodded. 'He's good, but he's not subtle. Whereas with Mordecai, he will very often *scare* a person to death. Like, he'll take a guy, lock him in a trunk or maybe a room in a creepy house, and just mess with the guy until the guy has a heart attack or something, see, all on his own. Without Mordecai *actually* killing him, in the traditional sense. Icepick is just a person who lives up to his nickname.'

'But if Mordecai doesn't like you,' Banquer whispered, 'he might just start whittling you down. Like, cutting off fingers and toes and other stuff I don't even want to think about. Until you'd *prefer* not to be alive. What there is left of you.'

Sounded to me like a hoodlum ghost story. Something to tell around a gangster campfire. I was beginning to get the idea, though. Montreal and Manhattan both wanted Etta.

'Yudda,' I began. 'You know Roan well enough to teach his little girl's dog some tricks? I'd like to know more about that.'

He lowered his shotgun at last. 'If you knew Etta,' he told me, 'you'd understand.'

I wasn't sure what that meant, and I certainly didn't understand it. But I did wonder if maybe I understood something else all of a sudden.

So, I asked. 'And what were those gunshots from in here, in the diner, when I was out on the street playing with the Lamberts? It wasn't you, because the shots came from the front door and you were there in the kitchen. There was somebody here in the diner that shot at them, and they shot back, and you told the dog to hit the deck. And I have an idea who shot first.'

Yudda licked his lips. That meant he was trying to think of what to say. In other words, he was searching for a good lie.

'Don't bother,' I said to him. 'It was Roan. That's why you told the dog to take a dive, so he wouldn't come into the diner, see Roan, and act all happy to see him and maybe get shot.'

He hesitated, but he nodded.

'And I didn't see Roan when I came in because he saw me first and headed for the bathroom. He was waiting in there and saw the Canadians come in. He started the fracas.'

Yudda sighed. 'Sometimes I forget how good you are at this stuff.'

'And you told the Canadians – what, exactly?'

'That Etta's new parents were in a Dodge Dart out in back,' he said.

'Then the adoptive parents, the Lamberts, panicked,' I explained to Haley. 'They clipped Mordecai with the Dart on their way out of town.'

Banquer got to his feet. His arm was wet. You couldn't see that it was blood on account of his dark suit coat.

'We should go over to the hospital right now and ice Mordecai, while he's in a weakened condition,' he said. His voice was shaky.

Haley rolled his head. 'In the first place, kid, we are *policemen* in Fry's Bay, Florida. We do *not* ice people. Not without a warrant. But in the second place, and more importantly, Mordecai would smell you coming and have your mother killed before you got within a half-mile of him. Then he'd pay for the funeral and bury you alive in the same casket as your mother's corpse.'

The kid nodded slowly. 'That sounds like something he'd do.'

Haley turned back to me. 'You, Mr Moscowitz, should do your job. You should protect the child. You have the full support of the Fry's Bay Police Department.'

I had a pretty good idea that what he *really* meant was that he wanted me to find the kid and turn her over to him. That way he could, in turn, hand her over to his bosses. Which was not something I was particularly interested in seeing happen. Because it was not really protecting the child at all.

I turned to Yudda. 'Roan was here because he figured to meet Etta,' I said. 'Or the Lamberts. The Lamberts were scared because somebody took Etta. And Roan was stupid to be here in the first place. I figure the Canadians have been on him for a while, hoping he'd lead them to Etta. Anyway, there was supposed to be some sort of meeting here in your place.'

Yudda just nodded.

'So.' I sat back and looked around. 'Just what is it that Etta knows that everybody wants so bad?'

No one was willing to share. For a minute, Yudda's place was quiet as a morgue.

And who should walk into the joint at that exact moment but the one and only John Horse.

Now, as everyone knew, John Horse was not so much a *person* as he was an *idea*. The rumor had it that he was hundreds of years old, and maybe couldn't die. The truth: he was a wanted criminal and the tribal boss of the local Seminoles. He was also my best friend in Fry's Bay, if you could call a walking chunk of mythology a *friend*.

No matter what, he always knew how to make an entrance.

The front door to Yudda's slammed open and he stood in the doorway, backlit by streetlamps, and surveyed the place.

'Foggy?' he mumbled after a moment. 'Is that a dog you got there?'

Den raised his head, sniffed, stared, and then his tail started going a million miles an hour.

'Seems to be,' I answered. 'What's new?'

'I think I'm going to vote in the presidential election,' he said, not moving.

'I thought you couldn't vote because of your outstanding warrants,' I said.

'I'm still registered to vote.' He took a step inside the diner. 'The only way they can stop me from voting is to catch me here at the polling station. Which they won't do because the new cops in town are even stupider than the last ones we had.'

He slammed the door shut behind him; you could see his face. He was grinning like he'd just told a hilarious joke.

Haley wasn't laughing. He turned to look at John Horse. 'Who's this?' Haley asked no one in particular.

After another one of those uncomfortable silences, John Horse took a couple steps toward Haley, holding out his hand.

'My name is John Horse,' he said, still smiling. 'I used to be called Young John Horse so that I wouldn't be confused with another Seminole, but since he died in 1882, I think we're safe.'

Haley stood up and took John Horse's hand. That's the effect John Horse could have. Impossible to explain.

'He's the leader or grandfather or something-important for the Seminoles in this part of Florida,' I finally managed to say. 'And the only reason he's here now is because he knows something.'

John Horse nodded.

The dog got up and went to John Horse, who knelt and scratched the dog's chest. 'This dog has knowledge,' he told me, looking up.

I agreed. 'He speaks English, as far as I can tell. Don't know how much Seminole he knows.'

John Horse leaned forward and whispered something in the dog's ear. The dog sat back and, swear to God, shook his head.

'He speaks Seminole, too,' John Horse said, getting to his feet. 'I asked him if he trusted these two policemen. One of them is bleeding and the other one has a pistol in his hand under your table, there.'

I nodded. 'They're crooked. But they admit it, so that makes them easier to deal with.'

Haley put his gun on the table top. He was still holding it.

'You wanted to see me?' I went on.

'Couldn't I just be here for a nice dinner?' he asked.

Yudda and I both said 'No' at the same time.

John Horse nodded. 'All right. I have some friends in Lake City that are trying to open a smoke shop. They can sell tribal tobacco tax free. Legally, they can do it because of the so-called Indian Self-Determination and Education Assistance Act that just got passed last year.'

'But the local merchants in Lake City don't like it,' I surmised, 'because everyone will buy cigarettes from your guys cheaper.'

'Better tobacco too,' John Horse said.

'You know they give you cancer, them things,' Haley chimed in.

John Horse looked down. 'If white people don't know how to smoke tobacco, or how much tobacco to smoke, that's not our fault.'

The thing was that John Horse was still at war. The Seminole tribe was the only one that had never signed a peace treaty with the American Government. He wasn't suggesting that tobacco was a tribal conspiracy to wipe out white people. But his folks had been treated so badly for so long, it was hard for him to feel sorry for white people who couldn't keep themselves from smoking too much.

'Your point is,' I assumed, 'that you somehow know I just got back from Lake City, and you see some kind of connection.'

'I do,' he said.

I sat back. 'I'm only interested in finding Etta, the dog's owner.'

John Horse smiled. 'That's what the dog wants.'

None of my companions there in Yudda's knew about the note on the dog's collar. They didn't realize that all I had to do was sit at Yudda's and wait for Etta to come to me. Because despite what the Lamberts thought, Etta wasn't taken by anyone. She ran away. There may have been people *wanting* to take her, but my thinking was that she outsmarted them.

The reason Roan had been waiting in a booth at Yudda's was that he knew Etta was planning to show up. He'd gone to the vet's office in Lake City; he'd been the guy who'd visited Den before me. He'd seen the note, left the dog, and come to my apartment. Why he'd done that was unclear; why he'd disappeared from my place was also hard to figure. Maybe he wanted me to know what was going on so that his business would be, in some way, legal. Or maybe he wanted me to chase myself up to Lake City to get me out of the way, for some reason.

Didn't matter. He knew more than he'd told me when he was sitting on my bed. And one of the things he knew was that Etta was coming to Yudda's. But for the moment, the Canadians and the Lamberts had scared her off.

All that was guesswork, of course. But I always trusted my intuition. And if I was right, it probably meant there was an eleven-year-old kid hanging out in Fry's Bay, somewhere, trying to be invisible.

EIGHT

I helped Haley decide he ought to take his bleeding partner to the hospital. The bleeding partner, Banquer, disagreed.

'You want me to go to the same hospital as Mordecai?' he stammered. 'I don't *think* so.'

In the end Yudda prevailed upon the walking wounded, in the same baffling Cajun French as before. Something to the effect that bleeding to death wasn't his best choice. So off they went, the town's new crooked cops.

John Horse took a seat in the booth across from me. The dog joined him. 'Good,' he said. 'Now they're gone I can tell you why I'm really here.'

I nodded and waited.

'You're looking for a little girl,' he said.

I'd given up trying to figure out how John Horse knew what he knew. But he was always right.

'You have information about her,' I said.

It wasn't a question, because he wouldn't have been there otherwise.

'She might be in trouble because of me.' He closed his eyes.

His story was short and clear. It was true that a few Lake City Seminoles wanted to open smoke shops owing to the new law. And that was irritating the local merchants. But that wasn't the real problem. The Seminoles had opened a tax-free gaming casino in Lake City. That's what had New York and Montreal upset, I figured. They wouldn't like someone trying to muscle in on their Florida gambling income.

'Seminoles don't care about these games,' John Horse concluded, 'but white people gamble on everything. They gamble with their lives when they drive a car too fast or fly in an airplane. They wager their health on the terrible food that they eat. And they don't even know which drugs are good for them to take.'

He shook his head.

'It was your idea to set up the casino,' I surmised.

'Yes. And I'm not certain what it is, but something bad is going to happen there.'

'The Lamberts have something to do with it.' It was a guess. But the Lamberts were crooked, I was sure of that.

'Mr Lambert works for the Florida DBPR,' he said. 'Department of Business and Professional Regulation.'

'That's the department that would hand out the license for the casino,' I said. 'Lambert works for the Division of Pari-Mutuel Wagering, that's my guess.'

'I forget how good you are at this kind of thing,' he said.

'I told him that,' Yudda chimed in.

'It's my only advantage,' I told them both. 'People underestimate me.'

'It's because your name is *Foggy*,' Yudda mumbled.

'The point is,' John Horse said, 'that Lambert is crooked.'

That's why the guy at the Child Services place in Lake City, Elvin, was suspicious of Etta's adoption. I wondered if maybe the Lamberts knew Roan or knew about his nefarious activities. Maybe even knew about Etta's talent. Why any of that would matter wasn't clear yet.

'Lambert is being paid by someone, probably in New York,' I said, 'so when this casino business came up to him, he alerted his connections.'

The old man sighed. 'Is there an honest person left in this sorry world?'

'No,' Yudda and I both said at the same time.

'I just want to find Etta,' I went on. 'You understand that her father's in town. He was here in Yudda's just before you came in. And I think Etta's somewhere around here too. Yudda could be more help than he's being, because he knows these people, and that's Etta's dog you've got beside you there. To sum up: this ought to be easier than it's been so far. And why did I drive all the way to Lake City when everything I need to know is in Fry's Bay? And why is everything in Fry's Bay?'

Yudda leaned forward. 'Are you done?'

'I think that covers it for the moment,' I answered.

'Good,' he continued, 'because now that there's not cops around, I can tell you where I think Roan is.'

But before he could say anything else, there was a lot of car noise outside on the street, and a lot of horn honking.

Yudda's shotgun was out. But John Horse didn't move, and the dog didn't bark.

'That's probably my friends,' John Horse said calmly. 'I'm being followed. Whoever's following me just got too close, I guess.'

I wanted to see for myself, so I headed for the door. Sure enough, two Seminoles, a guy I knew named Philip and a stranger, were honking the horn of their Jeep at a big black Cadillac Deville. It looked like John Horse was being followed by the FBI or a Manhattan mob boss. And while the difference between the two was often difficult to discern, I was more worried about the FBI. The criminals I could deal with. I'd dealt with them my whole life, they were like family. What can you do with the government – except run?

Nobody in the Caddy was honking back at Philip and his cohort, or doing anything, really. But the sinister car didn't move.

I nudged the door open a little more. 'Hi, Philip.'

He turned. 'Oh, hey, Foggy. Sorry for the noise.'

'Who's in the limo?' I asked.

'I don't know their names. White guys in suits.'

'You met them?'

'Sure. They were here in town, asking people for directions to the village.'

He meant a rocky place in the middle of the swamp that John Horse and his partially illegal group of friends and family called home. It was a difficult aggregation of cinderblock houses, log sheds, and chicken bones.

'But no one would tell them,' I assumed.

'So, they started following John Horse around. You know how he attracts attention.'

'He does,' I agreed.

'They ended up here.' Philip turned his head toward the Caddy. 'That's why I started honking, to let John Horse know.'

'I can see that.'

I looked back to the booth where I'd been sitting, and it

was empty. John Horse and the dog had split out the back. And Yudda was nowhere to be seen.

I knew better than to follow John Horse. It was easy for him to be invisible. I'd never find him if he didn't want to be found. And if Den was under his protection, I wasn't worried about the dog either.

I was worried about me. Canada, Manhattan, crooked cops, and now maybe the FBI were all looking for the same little kid. Not to mention the Lamberts and the kid's own father. My best move was to back away. Go sit in the sand somewhere and watch the sun go up and down for a couple of weeks. Everybody said Key West was nice.

But what did I do?

I went to the donut shop.

See, the donut shop in Fry's Bay was something of a gathering place. It's not just the taste of the donuts, although they are superior. The thing was, you could smell the shop from blocks away. It got into your brain before you realized it. You started thinking, I could use a donut! Then you realized it was just because the smell got into your nose. But by then it was too late.

The shop was a left and two rights up from Yudda's place. Once you got outside the diner, all you could smell was the bay. But once you turned toward town, you could smell hot donuts.

My thinking was that if the kid had been anywhere near Yudda's and got spooked, like by the Lamberts car or the sound of gunshots, the hot donuts would be a magnet.

I was there in no time. The red neon said *Hot! Donuts! Now!* But it didn't need to. The air was filled with that information. The place was crowded. It usually was.

Bibi was at the counter, a little harried. She'd had the job for a year, but she wasn't really built for it. The previous long-time server, Cass, had gone away under strange circumstances, unlikely to return. But Bibi made the best of her situation, and always with a smile.

'Foggy!' she called out when I came in.

'Hey, kid.' I looked around. 'Man, you're slammed.'

She offered a weary shrug. 'Every time the sign comes on.'

'Cruller and coffee?' I asked.

She nodded and was gone.

I spotted the only empty stool at the counter. Second to the end. Sitting in the last stool there was a small person in a black sweater and a big, floppy disco hat. Face covered, head down. I had the intuition it was Etta, but I wasn't usually *that* lucky.

When I got closer to the situation, I could see the reason no one was sitting next to the Disco Kid. The empty stool was taken up by a small blue backpack that said ZOOM. All caps.

I stood there for a second, but the kid didn't move or look my way.

'Can I move your backpack?' I asked.

'No.'

She was trying to make her voice sound low and tough.

'Thing is,' I said, 'I'm getting a donut and the backpack hasn't ordered anything.'

'Maybe it's trying to decide,' she said.

'It's taking a long time,' I told her, 'for something that's got a *Zoom* on its back.'

'Miss!' the kid sang out in Bibi's direction. 'This old man is messing with me.'

Bibi didn't even look our way.

'Let him sit there or take off, kid. Can't you see how packed we are?' Bibi sighed.

I lifted the backpack off the stool and said, 'Excuse me, *Zoom.*'

The kid's head lifted slightly.

'It's not named *Zoom*,' she corrected. 'I got it from a television show.'

'*Zoom* on PBS?' I set the pack on the counter next to the kid. 'I love that show. Karen's my favorite.'

Because I'd had the gig with Child Protective Services for a couple of years at that point, I had occasion to talk to kids about their interests. Also, I watched *Zoom* all on my own, because it was good.

'I liked Bernadette Yao from the original cast,' the kid told me.

'She's the one with the arm thing, right?'

The kid finally looked up. And while she still had the *punim* of a cherub, she looked tired. Tired and scared.

I sat down. Bibi slid my cruller and Joe across the counter in my general direction. I tore the cruller in two, ate my half, and shoved the rest of it to the kid. She stared at it.

After a second I said, 'You don't want it?' and made as if to take it back.

She grabbed it off the plate and stuffed the whole thing in her mouth.

I let her finish, and then I reached into my pocket and took out the locket I'd found around Den's neck. Set it down on the counter beside the empty place.

The kid froze.

I fished out the poem about blueberries and unfolded it.

'I'm a fan of your work,' I told her.

She still didn't move. I understood. She seemed like a pretty smart kid. She wasn't about to trust a stranger in a donut shop. So, I just kept talking.

'I think the Lamberts are no good. I think Den is a great dog. I think your father really wants to see you. A lot of people are after you, and you're not exactly certain why that is. Also, I really do like your poem about blueberries and *Zoom* doesn't sell merchandise. You made this backpack yourself from iron-on letters. And a person your age should not be using an iron.'

'A person my age should not be talking to old men in donut shops.'

'You have to stop calling me an old man,' I told her in no uncertain terms. 'I'm younger than your father.'

'Miss!' she sang out again. 'This man is still bothering me! Could you please call the police?'

Bibi made a sort of growling sound and shot over to the kid.

'Listen, little girl,' she snarled. 'He's probably trying to help you but you're too stupid to know it. And I'm too busy to care. So, that's it for you. Out!'

'You're throwing me out?' The kid blinked.

'Vacate the stool!' Bibi said, louder.

'Now you've done it,' I told the kid. 'Once you get thrown out of a donut shop, your life takes a downward spiral and you end up homeless in the gutter and addicted to drugs.'

Somebody from the other end of the bar complained about Bibi's inattention to his lack of coffee, and Bibi explained to the customer where she was going to put his next cup.

I stood up. 'I'm uncomfortable with this level of discourse. Let's beat it.'

I put my hand on the backpack, but the kid grabbed it, body-blocked me like Mean Joe Greene, and shot out the door. A couple of the customers laughed. I probably would have too, if the shoe had been on the other foot. I was a ridiculous sight.

I got my balance, if not my dignity, and hustled out the door.

That time of year the sun went down around 7:45, so the streets were more shadow than light. The sky was a sinister kind of purple. Meant rain later on. And there was no sign of the kid.

I stood there in front of the donut shop for a minute or two, feeling foolish and incompetent. Then I remembered about how the Lamberts had left my office as their forwarding address. Except that it wasn't the Lamberts who'd left that. It had been a kid's handwriting.

Which made me think that the kid was smarter than people thought she was, and she'd somehow orchestrated a lot of action, including leaving the forwarding address.

In which case she might be trying to find my office.

NINE

I hadn't *moseyed* in a long time, so I thought I'd give it a try. Give the kid time to find my office, if that's what was happening. It was a fine, warm evening. The humidity was going down and the moon was coming up. I went back to Yudda's, but the lights were off and the place was locked up. Unusual. I watched the fishing boats bob up and down at the docks on the bay for a while. Hypnotic. Then I got bored. Under any other circumstance it would have been happy hour. Unfortunately, I was still working, so I wasn't all that happy.

I headed toward my crummy office. The building was what you'd call nondescript. Squat, brick, fifties-era office shell. If you were there at night, you could hear the cockroaches everywhere. In the daytime it was only depressing and soulless. The reason I didn't mind it was that I wasn't there very much. The job was mostly legwork. And if I wanted to, I could always do the paperwork at home.

I fished for keys in my pocket at the same time I leaned into the glass front door of the building. Someone had turned the hall lights on. I decided to whistle. It was hard to be scary to a kid if you were whistling. The tune I chose was 'Swinging on a Star'. It was happy.

I got nearer to my office door and I saw her. She was sitting on the floor, knees to her chin, floppy hat over her face. She could tell I was getting closer, but there was nowhere for her to go. By the time I was about five feet away she looked up. Saw it was me. Panicked.

'Look, mister,' she roared, getting to her feet, 'I got an appointment with the man who works here. He's a government official and he's probably right outside.'

I ignored her, got to my door, unlocked it, and swung it wide.

'He's probably here, actually,' I said.

Her eyes widened.

I held out my hand. 'I'm Foggy Moscowitz. I work for Child Protective Services. I've been looking for you.'

'ID,' she demanded, shivering a little.

I hauled out my wallet and she examined my badge and my driver's license like it was counterfeit money.

'I would have gotten to introductions in the donut shop,' I said, putting away the wallet. 'But you split.'

She still wasn't certain about me and kept eyeing the hallway like she might take off any second.

'Your dad paid me a visit last night,' I went on. 'He really wants to see you.'

'Where did you get my poems?'

'At your house in Lake City. I also had pie with Madge. Key lime, same as you.'

Her demeanor shifted, but only a little.

'Where's Den?' she asked me.

'He's with a mutual friend,' I assured her. 'Very safe. He wants to see you too. Come on in, OK?'

'You got all my clues,' she said.

'I did.'

'And you don't work for the Lamberts?'

'I work for the State of Florida,' I said, 'and for my own peace of mind.'

'I don't know what that means,' she admitted, 'but if you really do work in this office, I have to talk to you.'

I stepped aside. 'Then, like I said: come on in.'

She clutched her backpack in front of her and slid past me into the office. I flipped on the light. It was hard to say whether the place looked better with the lights on or off. Either way, it was dismal. The kid took a chair in front of the desk. I took the other one. I decided to let her be in charge.

'OK,' I said, 'you came to my office. How may I be of service?'

'A nice man named Elvin Bradley told me to find you,' she said softly.

'I am only recently acquainted with him,' I said, 'but he does seem to be a very nice man.'

'He didn't like the Lamberts.'

'My first impression of them? They're cartoons.'

Her face lit up. 'They *are* cartoons.'

I decided she was smart enough, so I skipped ahead.

'How long did it take you to figure out that they adopted you for the wrong reasons?' I asked her calmly.

She exhaled and settled back into her chair. The backpack slipped to her lap.

'You have no idea what a relief it is,' she told me, 'to talk to someone that doesn't treat me like a child.'

'Well,' I began, 'in all fairness, you *are*, technically, a child.'

'Yeah, but.'

'Good point.' I settled in too. 'So, how long?'

'About the Lamberts?' She shook her head. 'In the car on the way home from the foster family. They're morons.'

'You don't mind my saying you're a pretty tough cookie, do you?'

'Is it a compliment?'

'It is. Your dad's incarcerated, your mom's dead, and you're in a whole lot of trouble.' I shook my head. 'And look at you: cool as a cucumber.'

'I ask about the cookie thing,' she went on, 'because I prefer my cookies bendy.'

'But we digress,' I said. 'Could we get back to the Lamberts?'

'They work for the Delany family.'

I'd heard people say that their blood ran cold, but I'd never experienced it until that very moment. The Delanys were an Irish organization in New York built on supernatural violence and impenetrable rage. Even my former associates in Brooklyn were afraid of them, because there was no talking to those lunatics.

'It's hard to imagine those two little rabbits working for the Delany family,' I told the kid.

'They're idiots,' she agreed. 'And they're afraid of everything.'

'Well, to be fair: *everybody's* afraid of the Delanys.'

'Yeah, they're scary. They needed innocent dupes with clean records. They picked the Lamberts.'

'How long have you been with them?' I asked her.

'Mom died about six months ago,' she said, hard as steel, 'and I was in foster care for a few months, so I think it's been about eighty days.'

'They treat you OK?'

She nodded. 'No idea how to take care of a kid. I was fed. I got clothes. They didn't let me go to school, though.'

'Why not?'

She just shrugged.

'OK.' I leaned forward. 'So, here's the deal: my job is to protect children. And, as it turns out, I'm really good at it. From now on, you're safe. The Lamberts and the Delanys and the mob from Montreal, even the FBI – they can't touch you.'

She glared at me. 'Are you drunk?' That was her first question.

'No.'

'You can't promise something like that to a child. Children are trusting and impressionable. You say that kind of stuff to most children, they're liable to believe you. And *then* where are you?'

'You're a doubter.'

'I'm a realist.'

'You know you're too smart for your own good, right?' I suggested.

'Oh, yes,' she said. 'That's my main problem.'

'OK, well, the proof is in the pudding, as they say,' I told her. 'Although I have no idea where that saying comes from. You just stick with me and *see* if you're not completely aces.'

She blinked. 'It's an English proverb from the fourteenth century.'

'What?' I stared.

'The original saying is, "The proof of the pudding is in the eating".'

'Oh! Well, that's exactly my point. You have to take me for a test drive to see if I'm legit.'

She sighed. 'Right.'

'Where did you get that? How do you know that stuff?'

'I read it once and I have a good memory.' She stood up. 'Are we going to stay here in this crappy office, or are you going to take me to Yudda's to get something good to eat?'

I shook my head. 'Yudda's is closed. And I think you know why. But I can make you an omelet at my place.'

'I don't want an omelet; I want a crepe.'

'I'll make you a crepe.'

'What do you know about making crepes?'

I stood up. 'Didn't we just decide about the pudding thing?'

'I guess,' she grumbled.

'So, off to my apartment.'

TEN

Etta sat at my kitchen table eating a crepe. It was filled with smooth peanut butter and blueberry preserves. The secret to a good crepe has always been a thin batter. The secret to making a kid love it will always be peanut butter and jelly.

She was in the middle of her third bite when she said, apropos of nothing, 'He's not incarcerated.'

I was standing at the stove tending to the construction of my own crepe: spinach and mushroom.

'What?' I mumbled.

'My dad,' she said. 'You said he was incarcerated. He's not.'

'Yeah, I know,' I told her. 'He visited me last night. Jesus, last night. This has been kind of a long day for me. I drove to Lake City and got a dog. And that's just for starters.'

'I want to see Den,' she said, staring down at her crepe. 'This is good, by the way.'

I struggled for a moment, trying not to be Mr I-told-you-so.

'Den's safe,' I assured her. 'Do you have any idea why all these guys are after you?'

That put a real dent in the conversation. Etta stopped eating, closed her eyes, and put down her fork.

'Pari-mutuel betting was first authorized by the Florida Legislature in 1931,' she intoned. 'Pari-mutuel is a gambling system where all bets are placed together in a pool, taxes and the vig are excluded, and the pay-off odds are calculated by sharing the pool among all winning bets.'

I blinked. 'Yeah, I know what – and by the way, how would you know *anything* about the vigorish?'

She opened her eyes. 'The juice, the cut, the take,' she told me impatiently. 'The amount charged by the bookie, for taking the bet in the first place.'

'You'll excuse my saying that you are one spooky kid,' I said softly.

'I told you: I read, and I remember.' She shook her head. 'I think all these guys are after me because I know some stuff about gambling in Florida, and the Indians.'

I nodded. But I thought it was only part of the story. One little kid knowing that you were trying to keep the Seminole tribes from making a little green didn't seem to be reason enough for the gaggle of suits chasing after her. There was something much more. And it was something that the kid wouldn't notice. Like the Purloined Letter.

My sort-of-uncle Red had told me the story. I don't know where he got it, but it was all about this stolen letter that was really important. It was hidden in some room. Everybody and his brother looked for it. Turned the room inside out. Only the thing was, it was right there on top of the desk in the room the whole time. Hidden in plain sight, Red called it. Something so obvious that you *couldn't* see it.

Anyway, that's what I *thought* Etta's brain was up to: couldn't see the obvious, the real reason for all the brouhaha.

But what I *said* to her was, 'The thing is, they're not Indians because they're not from India. That's just a bone-headed Caucasian mistake. Don't use that word, OK?'

She looked up at me. 'OK. What should I call them?'

'In this case, the people in question are Seminoles,' I said. 'And my friend John Horse is kind of their leader, although he would tell you that he's not. And he's the person taking care of Den.'

She thought about it for a second, then went back to her crepe.

I tried to gather my thoughts. I didn't want to press too hard about the kid's father. He was obviously in Fry's Bay. He obviously knew where his kid had been, since I figured he'd beat me to the veterinarian where Den had been staying. So why the nighttime visit with the gun in my face? The Lamberts were easy to figure: stooges caught in the middle. But what exactly were the Canadians and the Delany mob up to?

The kid had something in her brain that was worth a lot of trouble. Which made me, once again, consider walking away.

All I had to do was fill out a few forms at the office, maybe call up my new best friend, Elvin, in Lake City, and get the kid into a real home. Done and done.

But I made the mistake of looking down at her in that stupid floppy hat. She was going at her crepe like she hadn't eaten in a week. She'd gotten a series of tough breaks. And trying to place her with a so-called good family would only be a temporary fix. Because Montreal and Manhattan would keep looking. And in a week or two she'd be right back where she was: on the lam in a bad hat.

I folded my arms and let out a breath. 'Look,' I began. 'I've never gone wrong treating a kid like an adult. Which is why I'm going to tell you some things and you're going to have to take it like someone twice your age. At least. Stop me now if you don't want it.'

She swallowed the last bite of crepe, put down her fork, wiped her mouth with the back of her hand, and nodded.

'Go,' she said.

'The reason you're in this situation,' I said squarely, 'is that you've got something in your head that everyone wants, and it's not about Seminole gambling rights. Your dad busted out of prison to find you. A very scary man came all the way from Canada to find you. The cops, maybe the FBI, *and* the Delany family want to get a hold of you. And you're way too smart for your own good.'

She took her hat off. 'You're trying to scare me.'

'A little. But mostly I'm trying to apprise you of the situation in order that we may discover what everyone is *really* after.'

She thinned her lips. 'And how do we do that, Mr Know-It-All?'

I picked up her plate and put it in the sink.

'For starters?' I began, buttoning my coat. 'Let's go visit your dog.'

ELEVEN

knew where the dog was. He was with John Horse. I knew where John Horse was. He'd gone back to his house. The house was in the swamp. The swamp was a perfect place to hide. I'd been to the camp enough times to know a few shortcuts. And I knew most of the guards. You'd never see them, but I had a pretty good idea where they hid themselves. I was positive I could get in. Mostly because I was sure that's what John Horse wanted: me and the kid in his house, with the dog.

So, the moon was up, close to full, and when the road turned to dirt and the swamp got noisy with frogs and night birds, I stopped the car. We'd been driving a little more than half an hour.

When I turned off the engine, Etta clutched the door handle. 'I'm not getting out here,' she told me firmly.

'It's a short walk to camp,' I said. 'There's a pretty good moon; I have a flashlight. And even though you can't see them, there are, like, twenty Seminole warriors all around us. You're safer here than in church.'

'I don't go to church,' she said.

'Well, neither do I, but I hear it's safe. Get out of the car.'

She shook her head.

'We're going to see your dog,' I said.

She squinted in my direction. 'No.'

'Yes,' I insisted. 'Den is with John Horse. And, incidentally, John Horse probably knows where your father is.'

'Everybody knows that,' she sneered. 'He's somewhere in Fry's Bay.'

'I mean in particular.' I opened my door.

Some bird or other sang out. It was pretty. It seemed to make the kid more disposed to a little walk in the swamp. She opened her door and slid out.

The first time I was in the swamp at night, it was a nightmare.

I'd been in back alleys with guys who wanted to pull my teeth out with pliers. Wasn't half as scary as my first five minutes in the swamp. I knew how to handle hoods. What's the possibility of reasoning with a gator? Or convincing a snake not to bite you? Nature's got no give. You eat it, or it eats you. Those are the choices.

In short, I had a pretty good idea how the kid felt.

So, I went over to her, patted her on the shoulder, and tested my luck. Thought I'd see if I could guess who was hiding in the shadows.

'Philip?' I called out.

A lot of the frog and bird noise stopped. There was a heartbeat of silence. Then: 'Swear to God, Foggy,' Philip answered in the dark, 'you haven't learned anything about being in the swamp after all the times you've been here?'

'What?' I said, probably louder than I needed to. 'I got a kid here. She's nervous.'

Philip emerged from the underbrush and switched on the lantern flashlight in his hand.

'You don't just shout out like that,' he went on. 'Especially not with the kid, when everybody in the world is after her. What if it wasn't me out here? What if it was the bad guys? They got *guns*, Foggy! Jesus.'

Etta tugged on my coat. 'How did you know who was out there?'

'Philip and I have always had a kind of simpatico. Remind me to tell you about how he was lost in another swamp one time and we scared off some bears.'

Etta shifted closer to me. 'There are bears here?'

'Not any more,' Philip answered, disgusted. 'Foggy Fog Horn here scared them all away. And how *did* you know it was me out here?'

'I smelled your patchouli,' I said.

'It's not *patchouli*,' he complained. 'I told you, like, a hundred times it's lavender and rosemary.'

'It still smells,' I told him.

'It's very soothing,' he went on. 'I got anger issues.'

I looked down at Etta. 'He does. The other kids used to bully him when he was younger.'

Etta's eyes widened, staring at Philip. He was twice the size of a normal human being, built more like a Viking god than a Seminole warrior.

'Who would bully someone like that?' Etta whispered.

'They used to make fun of his name,' I began.

'*Philip.*' She nodded. 'Derived from the Greek; means *lover of horses.*'

'Right,' I said. 'Some of the mean boys in his camp suggested a lewd interpretation of that meaning.'

Etta looked back up at me. 'I don't understand.'

'She's *eleven*, Foggy. Geez,' Philip admonished. 'She doesn't know what you're talking about.'

'Oh.' I thought about it for a second. 'Right.'

Philip sighed like I was the biggest idiot in the state. 'Come on,' he said, shaking his head. 'John Horse is waiting for you.'

Etta whispered, 'I think he smells nice.'

I shook my head, she shut up, and we followed Philip into the swamp.

Now, when you first got to John Horse's house, you wondered if maybe it was an abandoned shack. Concrete blocks, tin roof, no heat. And he wasn't much for decor. A couple of ratty items of furniture that a junkyard wouldn't take, a hot plate, and some weird stuff on shelves that I was always afraid to ask him about.

Still, when you walked in the front door, there was an eerie sense of well-being. Like the room was filled up with *calm*. As a bonus that particular night: child and dog were reunited.

'Den!' Etta screamed when she saw the pooch at John Horse's feet.

The dog scrambled to his feet and shot over to Etta like an arrow. He knocked her to the dirt floor and the two of them rolled around laughing and yelping for what must have been five minutes. John Horse watched and smiled. I was less patient.

I sidled up to the man and said, 'Are you going to tell me what the hell is going on, or not?'

His eyes were still on dog and kid. 'You're not delighted by this?'

'Why is the entire world after this little girl?' I demanded.

His eyes darted my way. 'Well, that's an exaggeration, don't you think? Can't be more than a couple hundred people after Etta.'

I shook my head. 'Stop trying to be funny.'

He turned to me, suddenly very concerned. 'I may be wrong about the reason they're after her. I thought it was about the gambling. It might not be. I've been having a conversation with the dog, and he's been trying to explain it to me. I'm just not as good at speaking *dog* as I used to be. I don't understand him. Yet.'

You could never tell with John Horse if he was pulling your leg with that kind of talk. 'Indian Schtick' he called it. Something for the rubes.

But in this case, I knew what he meant.

'You understand – that's why I brought Etta here,' I said softly. 'I want you to watch out for her while I go back into the belly of the beast and find out what's really going on.'

He nodded, returning his attention to the dog-and-child show.

I went over to Etta. She sat up and the dog gave me his full attention.

'Would you mind staying here for a while,' I asked her, 'while I go back into town and find your father?'

She looked around the smudgy room. 'Seriously?'

Den barked twice.

'See?' John Horse said. 'The dog wants to stay.'

'And Philip's mother is a really good cook,' I added.

Etta stood up. 'You misunderstand. I meant, like, "Seriously, I *get* to stay in an Ind— in a Seminole village? Unbelievably cool.'

I turned to John Horse. 'She says she's eleven, but I don't believe it.'

'Yes,' he told me, 'her spirit is *much* older than that.'

So, it was settled. I bid a brief farewell and made it back to my car. Only got lost twice, a personal record. But as I put the T-Bird in reverse and started to ease a turn-around, a Seminole woman appeared on the road. Someone I'd never seen before. Dressed in jeans and a black T-shirt. She was holding a deer antler in one hand and a bone knife in the other. She was scraping the knife on the antler and making a cricket sound. I stopped the car and stared at her. She smiled back. Just as I was about to say something to her, I heard Philip's voice.

'Foggy! Wait!'

I turned and there was Philip loping out of the undergrowth with a mason jar in his hand.

'You almost left without taking some of my mother's turtle soup,' he scolded me, arriving at the driver's-side window.

He held the jar out.

I took it. 'Man, I can't believe I almost missed this. You know it's the best soup I ever tasted.'

'I know.' He smiled. 'My mother made it just for you.'

I gave up a long time ago trying to figure out how his mother knew I was going to be in the camp. But she always did. And always with the soup, which was, in fact, the greatest soup in the world.

I set the jar on the seat beside me. 'Look, who's that woman?' I asked him.

He tilted his head. 'What woman?'

I turned to see her. 'The one with the . . .'

She wasn't there. She wasn't anywhere.

'There was a woman in the road,' I began. 'Doing a weird antler thing.'

Philip interrupted. 'Was she scraping a knife on an antler?'

'Yeah, that's the one. Made a kind of cricket sound.'

'Get out of the car!' he shouted. 'Get out of the car *right* now; back to the camp!'

And then he disappeared.

I sat there for a second with the motor running. I'd never seen Philip panic. But that was panic.

I switched off the engine and climbed out of the car.

TWELVE

The camp was chaos. I heard the gunshots when I was still in the underbrush. I got out my Colt, and like an idiot I just went running into the open. I saw three guys in suits with M3 submachine guns, what they called 'grease guns'. Easy to use and impossible to dodge.

Running low, I ducked behind the nearest cinderblock house. I got sight of one of the guys and managed to pop him in the leg with the Colt. He looked around like someone had tapped him on the shoulder, then just kept firing. Someone was throwing rocks at him. One of the rocks connected and hit him square in the forehead. That had more effect. He lowered his gun and rubbed his head. It was all red there too.

I used that moment to get closer to him. Ran around the house, up behind the guy. I stuck the muzzle of my pistol in his ear, hard.

'You won't be so able to shake it off if I put a bullet through your brain,' I said.

He agreed and dropped his gun.

'Which gang are you from?' I asked him.

There was a short pause. Then: 'Foggy?'

I kept the gun in his ear, but I moved around to the side a little. It was Tony Tedeschi, from my old neighborhood in Brooklyn.

'Tony? What the hell?'

He grinned. 'You look good,' he said. 'Florida must agree with you.'

'We have our arguments,' I said. 'What are you doing here, shooting up a peaceful Seminole housing project?'

'Oh. That.' He nodded. 'I got a gig with the Delanys.'

He was clearly embarrassed.

'Can you get your other guys to stop shooting for a minute?' I asked him. 'I can help. You're looking for the little girl, right?'

'Hey!' he shouted immediately. 'Stop shooting! Come over here, see who I got talking to me with a gun to my head!'

The shooting stopped. The two other guys wandered over. I didn't recognize them.

'It's Foggy Moscowitz!' Tony said affably.

The two guys stared.

'You're looking for Etta Roan, am I right?' I asked everyone.

'Yes,' Tony said. 'Could you move your gun, it's making my ear itch.'

'Oh, Jesus, sorry, Tony.' I put my gun away. 'But why in the world you want to come in here shooting things up? You didn't ask anybody about the kid first?'

'Ask?' one of the strangers exploded.

He had the look of a Delany. And his face certainly displayed a certain disposition to the violence-before-reason creed of that family. He was dressed in a suit he bought on sale at Woolworth's and his eyes were redder than Tony's forehead. Heavy drinker.

'The kid's not here,' I said. 'That's what you would have found out if you'd asked.'

Tony looked at his shoes. 'We followed you here, Foggy. We saw you bring the kid. I mean, I wasn't sure it was you. We kept our distance. But we got pictures of the kid. She's here all right.'

'Sure,' I said. 'I brought her here, but this guy, John Horse, already took her into the swamp.'

I didn't know that for a fact, but it was something John Horse would do. My hope was that Den and Etta and John Horse had all vanished into the weirder part of the swamp.

'I'll show you,' I said.

It was a bold move, but I guessed that keeping these guys occupied would give Philip and his cohorts a chance to organize.

I led the out-of-towners to John Horse's house, opened the door, peeked in, and sighed a little when I saw it was empty.

'This is where I brought the girl,' I told Tony. 'See? All gone.'

He peered in.

'What a dump,' he mumbled.

'Yeah,' I said. 'You should have someone look at your leg. You're bleeding.'

He looked down. His pants were red.

Before he could look up again, we were surrounded by twenty Seminole men and women. They all had guns. And all the guns were pointed at us.

'All they have to do,' I explained slowly, 'is put about fifty slugs in each of you guys, and then drag your bodies to the edge of the water over there. Gators would have you in five minutes.'

'And they don't just eat your body,' Philip said solemnly. 'They eat your memory.'

'It's true,' I said, playing along. 'Once they're done, no one on earth will remember you ever existed.'

'Your spirit is just . . . *gone*,' Philip said softly.

It was hard to keep from smiling, because we both knew it was schtick, but the boys from New York City didn't know that. It sounded really spooky under the circumstances.

Tony whispered, 'So, what's the move here, Foggy?'

'My advice?' I said. 'Drop the guns, apologize, and back away. I mean all the way to downtown Manhattan.'

'*Apologize?*' the loudmouth screamed.

His gun arm twitched about a quarter of an inch before a younger woman in the crowd shot him in that very arm. Three times. He dropped his gun then. And he might have been trying to apologize. It was hard to tell with all the whimpering.

Tony and the other guy let go of their guns so fast that the guns bounced on the hard dirt in front of John Horse's house.

The woman who'd shot Loudmouth handed her pellet gun to someone, took a kerchief from around her neck, and started dabbing the blood on Loudmouth's arm. He just stared at her.

'He should go to a hospital,' she said to no one in particular.

'That's what I was just saying to Tony,' I said. 'Before I was so rudely interrupted by you guys, I was on my way back to town. You come with me, the other guys can follow. I'll take you to the hospital. Although you should probably know that Mordecai is there.'

I said it just to see what the reaction would be. It was worth it. Loudmouth went completely silent and his face turned even whiter than it was naturally. The other guy swallowed and couldn't stop blinking.

Tony had a more practical approach. 'I quit,' he said to his cohorts.

I looked at Philip. 'Can we leave?'

'After I make sure no one in the village was hurt,' he said quietly.

'They broke my window,' said the girl tending Loudmouth's arm.

'Twenty bucks,' Philip said.

Tony had a Franklin in his hand before anyone else moved. He held it out in Philip's direction.

'For the inconvenience,' he said.

Philip looked at me. 'I like this one.'

I nodded.

'Should we just feed these other two to the gators?' he went on.

I shrugged. 'OK by me.'

'I'm good with that,' Tony agreed.

'Gee,' I said to the goons from Manhattan. 'Gators in the swamp or Mordecai in the hospital?'

They both thought about it for a minute.

Loudmouth drew in a breath and looked at the girl tending to his arm.

'Nobody ever did nothing nice to me before,' he said to her, almost whispering. 'I'd like to stay here.'

'I need to get the pellets out of your arm,' she said. 'They didn't do too much harm, but they have to come out.'

'I can do that myself,' he told her. 'I done it plenty of times. You got tweezers somewhere?'

She looked at Philip. 'Can I take him to your mother's house? She's got tweezers.'

'John Horse told me a story about a lion with a thorn in his paw,' Philip said.

Without another word, the girl took Loudmouth by his good hand and led him away.

The other goon said, 'This means I ain't gotta go to where Mordecai is, right?'

I nodded.

'Then I think I'm gonna go to Hialeah,' he said. 'Make a little vacation out of it. I got a pal there that bets on the dogs.'

And without further comment, he turned and headed for his car somewhere in the swamp. He left his grease gun on the ground.

I turned to Tony. 'And now you're coming back to town with me.'

'Not to see Mordecai, I'm not.'

'No, I mean – I gotta find a guy. If you're truly quit from the Delany clan, you could help. But we've got to get your leg looked at.'

'It zipped me,' he said. 'Hurts a little, but the bullet did more damage to my pants than my leg. I'll put something on it. When we get back to town.'

I looked at Philip. 'OK?'

Philip waved the hundred-dollar bill in the air.

We both took that as a yes, Tony and me.

But just as we turned to leave, I thought to ask, 'So, who exactly was the woman with the antler, Philip? Some kind of early-warning system you guys got here? She alerted you to trouble in the camp?'

He nodded. 'She did. She's my grandmother.'

'Oh.' I looked around. 'I don't think I ever met her.'

'Probably not,' he said. 'She's been dead for ten years.'

THIRTEEN

The ride back to Fry's Bay was quiet. No idea what Tony was thinking about. I was thinking about the woman with the antler.

A lot of times, John Horse or someone in the Seminole Jokers Union would try to pull my leg about one thing or another. That's because they thought it was amusing to mess with my non-Seminole perceptions of their world. Like how John Horse would pretend to read minds, or astral travel, or know the future.

The problem was he was always right when he read my mind or told me what was going to happen. Of course, the astral travelling thing was harder to set in stone.

About halfway back to town I gave up trying to suss the woman and turned my attention to the very confusing details of the previous thirty-six hours or so.

First, Etta was with John Horse, so she was safe as Fort Knox.

Second, this Mordecai character, who was supposed to be the most wicked hitman in the country, was neatly stuck in the hospital.

Third, the Delany boys were dissipated and out of the picture, at least for the moment, so that was reassuring.

But thereafter, in no particular order: crooked cops, Canadian Scarlatti, the Lamberts, and Etta's missing father.

And behind everything was the King of Questions: why was everybody in the world after Etta Roan?

When we got back to town, I headed to my apartment.

'You mind if I stop off at my place,' I asked Tony, 'before I take you to the hospital?'

'I'm in no hurry to go to a hospital where Mordecai is,' he said. 'Just get me some hydrogen peroxide and a rag, I'll be fine.'

'OK, but you gotta wait in the car. I don't want you getting blood all over my living room.'

I always changed my shoes after I'd been in the swamp because you could never tell what you'd stepped in. I also had to get the hydrogen peroxide and a rag for Tony's leg. But mainly I got a little extra ammo for the Colt. Just for my peace of mind.

When I got back to him, I handed Tony the rag and the peroxide. He dabbed, hissed, and sat back.

'That ought to do it,' he said. 'But I'm eventually gonna have to change these pants.'

And off we went.

I was hoping that even after Roan had seen everything that went down at Yudda's, he'd still be close by because he wanted to see Etta. The siren scent of hot donuts was mighty, and he might be in the place. It worked with Etta. It was worth a shot with her father.

I parked around the corner, in front of what used to be the Kress store, a five and dime. Been closed for years. The downtown development group kept saying it was going to be a Macy's one day. They'd been saying that since 1958.

We got out of the car and into the shop; Tony disappeared into the gents' room. I sat at the counter. Bibi wasn't around, which either meant she was on a smoke break, or at her tap class. She thought if she got good enough, she could beat it down to Orlando and get into some show at the new Disney franchise there.

Warren was the guy in the kitchen. Made the donuts, kept to himself, had a slow eye. He saw me, nodded, and a couple of seconds later he appeared with a coffee pot in his hand.

'Cruller?' He sniffed.

'Yes, and my friend will have two cream-filled.'

He poured two cups and went back to the kitchen.

The place wasn't nearly as crowded as it had been earlier. Getting near closing time. Maybe Bibi had just taken off early.

Tony joined me at the counter, sipped his coffee, and was content to wait for me to start the conversation.

'Working for the Delanys,' I said, eyes straight forward, shaking my head.

He set his cup down. 'You got no idea how times are in Manhattan. You Brooklyn guys, you got it easy.'

'I'm a Florida guy,' I reminded him.

'Yeah,' he growled. 'Your body's in Florida. But your legend's in New York.'

Warren brought our donuts and left as silently as he had arrived.

Tony stared down at the plate in front of him. 'What's this?'

'They're kind of like an éclair, like something you'd get at Ferrara Bakery on Grand in Little Italy.'

'I know where Ferrara's is,' he said, staring at the donuts. 'This don't look like nothing you'd get there.'

'Taste it.'

He obliged. He grinned.

'See?' I said when he'd finished the second one.

'I do. I see.' He wiped his mouth with the back of his hand. 'Now, so, what are we doing here? Because it ain't just for these delicious donuts.'

'Hoping to see the kid's father. Nelson Roan.'

Tony looked around. 'And you think he's hiding in a donut shop?'

'He's in Fry's Bay,' I answered. 'This is one of the few places open now. And you get the smell; it's hard to resist.'

He nodded. 'Yeah, well don't look now, but I think the only people who can't resist it at the moment are the Feds.'

I turned to the side a little, like I was about to make a point with Tony. Out of the corner of my eye I saw what he meant: the big Cadillac Deville was parking in front of the shop.

'Is there a back way out of here?' he asked me.

'Through the kitchen,' I told him. 'But it won't be necessary. I'm on *their* side of the law at the moment, remember?'

'Right. I keep forgetting that. What a weird world this is.'

The car parked. Two guys got out. Government suits, all right. No self-respecting criminal would be caught dead in white socks, for instance.

They came in, looked around, then flanked us. One sat by me, the other by Tony.

Without a word I reached very slowly into my suit coat and produced my ID and badge from Child Protective Services, then slid it toward the guy on my side. Tony sat still as a statue.

The guy by me nodded once. 'I heard of you.'

I took my wallet back.

'Now let's see yours,' I said.

He hesitated. Then he hauled out his FBI credentials. Agent Dover.

I nodded. 'You're looking for Etta Roan.'

'Yes.'

'Why?'

The question was met with silence.

'Well,' I said after a minute, 'I'm looking for her *father*.'

He hesitated. 'Yeah. We're looking for him, too.'

Seemed odd.

'We know you have the kid,' he went on.

'*Had* the kid,' I corrected. 'She's in the swamp now.'

Warren appeared with half-a-dozen glazed. Dover fished in his suit for a smoke, but he couldn't find any matches.

I could tell that Tony was getting itchy sitting so close to FBI agents, so I decided to give him a job; keep him busy.

'Got a light?' I asked, knowing that he didn't. Tony was anti-smoking. Even weed.

Tony glared at me.

'I got a lighter in the glove compartment of my car,' I went on. 'Do you mind?'

Tony got wise right away. 'Oh. Sure. No problem.' He slid off his stool and was out the door before the stool stopped spinning.

'Who's that?' Dover asked me, gulping water.

'Friend of mine from the city,' I said. 'Never been deep-sea fishing. Thought I'd take him out tomorrow.'

'Seems nervous,' Dover said, looking over his shoulder to where Tony had gone.

'Well, he's a small-time hood from New York,' I said. 'The FBI makes him uncomfortable.'

I always heard that the best lies were the ones that were true.

The other agent finished a donut and belched.

'When I said I heard of you,' Dover began, 'I meant that I know about your former criminal affiliations. There's supposed to be an outstanding warrant on you but nobody can seem to find it.'

Technically speaking, I'd skipped out of an arrest. I'd popped out of the back seat of a squad car and absconded. I absconded all the way to Florida. The reason there wasn't a warrant on me was that the two cops who'd had me in custody were embarrassed to admit that I'd slipped away. So, no paperwork, no follow-up.

Then there was the matter of my rep, which was ridiculous, but palpable nonetheless. I was supposed to be the hood with a heart. All I did was send money to a certain child in New York. Every week. For the past couple of years.

See, I was responsible for making the kid an orphan, so I figured it was my responsibility to take care of him. My own personal Yom Kippur. It wasn't much money, and it was anonymous. But word got around, as word will do. All of a sudden, I was supposed to be some kind of sidewalk saint. Which not only was I *not*, but it was also very confusing to me on the religious front, because as far as I knew there weren't any Jewish saints. But apparently, even a non-religious Jew has got scruples. And when I say *scruples*, I mean, of course, *guilt* that could crush Samson. Mainly I was the guy who was off fighting alligators and saving children. No cop in New York wanted to mess with that, and every hood wanted to *be* that.

Of course, the whole thing was a legend. But I wasn't above using the legend.

'There isn't a warrant,' I told Dover. 'Don't you know I'm a *saint*?'

'Yeah,' he muttered, 'I thought that was more of a Catholic thing: *saints*.'

What happened next was very unfortunate.

Dover produced a set of good old-fashioned handcuffs, and his partner hauled out a pistol. Just as I was about to protest, Warren came out of the kitchen with a cast-iron frying pan and whomped the gun out of the partner's hand. Fast as lightning. The gun went skittering across the Formica countertop, and rattled on to the floor. Everyone else at the counter stood up and backed away. All I had to do was grab the handcuffs away from Dover.

'Warren doesn't mean anything,' I explained to Dover. 'See, he saw you threaten me, and locals protect locals. That's all.'

'I am an FBI agent in pursuit of my duty!' Dover steamed.

'Yeah?' Warren sneered. 'The last time we had FBI in town, they was crooked as your grandpa's dick!'

'And twice as useless,' someone else in the crowd volunteered.

There was a general mutter of agreement in the joint.

'You're outnumbered.' I shrugged.

Tony burst in then with a gun in his hand and put it right against the back of Dover's skull.

The other FBI agent was breathing hard. I thought maybe Warren broke his hand with the frying pan.

'If you really are FBI,' I said, 'then I apologize for all this, but you played your hand wrong. If, however, you're actually more nefarious characters bumming up my town, I'll just let my friend shoot you in the head and we'll take your bodies into the swamp. Never to be seen again.'

Another mutter of general agreement thanks to the hoi polloi.

I turned to Warren. 'Would you mind calling those new cops?' I asked. 'They might want to talk to these guys.'

Warren nodded, then set the cast-iron pan down in the order window between the kitchen and the counter area. A second later he was on the phone.

'This isn't going to go well for you,' Dover hissed.

'What's Etta's middle name?' I shot back.

Dover was confused. He blinked. Which was all it took for me to know that he was not, in fact, FBI.

'Lee Harvey Oswald,' I said.

Again, he blinked.

'Before he shot Kennedy, even most of his close friends didn't know Oswald's middle name. They just called him Lee. It's a law enforcement thing, using the middle name to identify people, to make sure you get the right one. That's how we know John Booth had the ridiculous middle name of *Wilkes*. You think his friends called him that? *If* you were FBI and you were looking for Etta Roan, you'd know her middle name.'

'They're on their way,' Warren sang out.

I smiled at Dover. 'I think maybe it's not going to go well for *you*. The great thing about our new cops is that they're crooked. Which means you're in a lot more trouble than you would be if they were straight.'

I reached over and snapped the cuffs on Dover. Warren picked up his frying pan again and leveled a genuinely evil look at the partner.

'This has been fun,' I told them both, 'but I have to go to work now.'

'I'll keep them here until the cops show up,' Warren promised.

And with that, Tony and I strolled out of the diner and into the soft evening air.

FOURTEEN

While I was a little let down that I didn't find Etta's dad in the donut shop, I was feeling pretty good about out-foxing the fake Feds. Tony, on the other hand, was not doing so well. His leg was hurting, his breath was labored, and he was clearly exhausted. Time for a little honesty.

As we got into my car, I said, 'What kind of a shot do you think I am?'

He stared. 'How do you mean?'

'Do you think I'm a pretty good shot or what?'

He settled into the passenger seat. 'You *meant* to nick my leg,' he realized. 'You weren't aiming to really hurt me.'

I nodded.

'For old times' sake,' he said.

'Not really.' I started the car. 'I don't know you that well.'

'Yeah, I kind of wondered why you were willing to take me back to town and buy me a nice donut.'

'I zipped your leg,' I told him, 'so I could get you into the hospital. I need somebody inside to keep an eye on Mordecai.'

Even though the car was moving at that point, he reached for the door handle and started to get out.

I slammed on the brakes; he shot forward and conked his forehead smack on the windshield.

He squeezed his eyes shut. 'That was uncalled for.'

'He's not going to know you're there,' I said. 'I have a friend at the hospital who's going to put you into a room close to him under a fake name, like you're a local. Shot in a hunting accident.'

'Hunting accident?' he whined.

I shrugged. 'People around here, they hunt.'

Five minutes later we were at the hospital.

Maggie Redhawk was head of nursing at the local hospital. It was a good one because it served the entire county. It was in Fry's Bay as a leftover from the town's glory days before the Depression.

Maggie was smart and large, two qualities she used every day. A Seminole woman in that kind of position needed to. It didn't hurt that her brother was one of the richest men in Florida. Which was another anomaly: a wealthy Seminole. But they came from parents who were serious about their children. Sent Maggie to UNC Chapel Hill when she was seventeen. Named her brother Mister. Seriously, so anyone talking to him would have to call him *Mister.*

Maggie and I had been friends from the start, and her brother and I were on good terms. I knew she'd help me, especially when I told her that Etta, my current charge, was hiding out with John Horse in the swamp.

She was standing at the nurses' station with a chart in her hand when she saw me.

'It's about time,' she mumbled.

'Sorry?' I asked.

She sighed. 'A guy who looks more like a hoodlum than *you* do, even, checks in, I expect to see you the next minute. Who's your friend?'

I glanced at Tony. 'My *acquaintance* is another hood. He's from New York. The other guy's from Canada.'

'Tomato/to*mah*to,' she intoned.

'Yeah, but the guy from Canada is someone to watch out for, they tell me,' I said. 'Did he give his name as Mordecai?'

She took a second to consult some paperwork, then shook her head.

'Henry Jones,' she told me. 'Victim of a hit-and-run.'

'How's he doing?'

'Still unconscious,' Maggie said.

'What about his friend?' I asked. 'The guy he came in with.'

'Mr Smith? Last time I saw him he was asleep in the chair beside Mr Jones's bed.'

I filled Maggie in on just who Mordecai was, and why it was important to keep him under sedation. With very little further talk, we got Tony checked into a room down the hall. Under the name of Johnson. The idea was that he'd keep an eye on Mordecai, but I knew Maggie would tell her brother about the whole mess.

Tony limped down the hall and I peeked in on *Smith* and *Jones*.

Scarlatti was sound asleep, sunk down in an uncomfortable hospital chair. Mordecai was hooked up to a couple of machines that went *beep*. I thought about waking Scarlatti until I remembered how you were supposed to treat a sleeping dog.

Which, in turn, encouraged me to think about the weird relationship between Yudda and Den, Etta's dog. He wasn't that old a dog. And Yudda had taught him the play-dead trick. Which meant that Yudda maybe knew even more about the Roan family than I thought. Like, not just an old connection from the New Orleans drug days, but a more recent relationship with the wife and dog. Which also meant that maybe Roan was with Yudda now.

I'd never been inside Yudda's home, but I knew where it was. It was a rusty bucket parked on the bay, a houseboat he claimed he'd sailed from New Orleans. He once told me that a houseboat was a perfect getaway. I'd seen it from a distance. It didn't look like it could travel faster than the speed of smell; certainly couldn't outrun a cop's boat.

One of its advantages, though, was that it was situated in a part of the bay that was hard to sneak up on. Entirely bounded by a craggy inlet on one side, deep salt water on the other. How Yudda navigated his bulk over the rocks, in flip-flops no less, was a mystery all its own.

I approached the tub with a fair degree of caution, because my estimation of Yudda had shifted a little. He had guns, he used to be in the drug trade, maybe still was, and he was mixed up in this business of Etta a little too much. In other words, I had no idea what he'd do if he saw me sneaking up on his house. In my experience, your hoodlum friends were always on your side right up until they weren't.

There was no one around that I could see. The sky was gun-metal grey. There were seagulls floating on the sulfur-smelling water. The rocks were slippery.

When I got close enough to the boat so that I was an easy target, I hollered.

'Yudda! It's Foggy! Could I speak with you for a moment?'

No answer.

Could have meant that Yudda wasn't home.

But it didn't.

A second later, there were gunshots. Little bits of rock exploded all over my left shoe. I scrambled. Ducked low, trying to look like another rock.

Two more shots, both close. Either Yudda was a bad shot, or he was just trying to scare me away. And if that was the case, it was working. I was very interested in getting as far away from his boat as possible. Like Pennsylvania, maybe.

I stumbled backward, fell on the rocks. My left shoulder blade stung. I was staring up at the grey clouds. Then the back of my head felt wet. I figured I'd fallen into a little tide pool, but when I touched it, the water was warm. And when I looked at it, the water was red.

My vision was blurry, and my balance was off. I couldn't decide if I should haul out my gun or play dead. Felt more like a dead day, with the clouds and all.

Then there was another gunshot and it was very motivational. I scrambled up and shoved off, stumbling over the rocks and wheezing like a broken accordion. By the time I got past the rocks and around a bend of palmetto grass, my head was pounding. But more than that, my brain was working overtime trying to figure why Yudda would shoot at me that way.

I managed to get around the smelly water and up on to the path that ran back to the main docks. And just as I stepped up to it, I saw Yudda coming my way. From the docks.

'What the hell, Foggy?' he yelled. 'Was that you shooting at my house?'

I shook my head. 'Your house was shooting at me.'

I held out my bloody fingertips as some sort of proof as he came closer.

'You hit?' he asked. He sounded concerned.

'I fell on the rocks,' I told him. Showed him the back of my head.

'That ain't so bad,' he said. 'Hard as your head is.'

'Uh-huh,' I said. 'Who's in your house that doesn't want to talk to me so bad he'd rather shoot me?'

Yudda squinted. 'Place was empty when I left.'

'Not really an answer,' I told him. 'I think it's Roan, hiding out there. Why he'd shoot at me is the question.'

'Maybe he saw you talking with the Canadians, or the cops, or that Delany crew from Manhattan.' Yudda looked down at his exposed toes. 'Maybe he don't trust you or he don't like your associations.'

'Yeah,' I said. 'There's a bit of that going around.'

'Where's the little girl, Foggy? Where's Etta?'

'She and her dog are with John Horse, somewhere in the swamp,' I said steadily. 'They left the camp when the Delany bunch showed up, guns blazing, as they say.'

'I see.'

He was clearly skeptical. I figured he was that way because he thought he'd seen something, or heard something, so I wanted to nip it in the bud.

'An acquaintance of mine, Tony Tedeschi, from the old neighborhood in Brooklyn, *was* working with the Delanys, but he quit when I shot him. He's in the hospital now. Ask Maggie Redhawk.'

Yudda stared. 'You got him in there keeping an eye on that crazy bastard Mordecai?'

'Yes.'

'And you took Etta to the Seminole camp so that John Horse could make her disappear?'

'Yes.'

'And you ain't working any angles,' he concluded. 'You just want to help Etta?'

I shrugged. 'That's the job.'

He let go a sigh that would have broken a lesser man's heart. 'I don't know what to do, Foggy,' he moaned. 'I'm in trouble.'

He wasn't going to cry, but he was close.

'I used to think I'd know what that meant in your case,' I told him carefully. 'Now I don't know how to respond, exactly. Just what kind of trouble are you in?'

'Same as you,' he said hoarsely. 'All these gangland types wandering around in my little corner of paradise.'

I waited. That was something Red Levine taught me. Have your say and then shut up. Just wait. Let the other guy get uncomfortable with the silence and maybe say something he shouldn't.

'I know you talked with Etta,' he said at length, his voice much softer. 'Did she tell you what she knows?'

'My opinion is that she doesn't *know* what she knows,' I said.

He could hear the truth of that in my voice.

'Maybe not,' he went on. 'But that ain't what everybody else thinks. Everybody else thinks that she's got the key to the kingdom and knows where the door is.'

'*What* kingdom?'

He nodded. 'Yeah. That's a little unclear to me.'

'But the general thought is that she was in a room sometime or other when somebody said something that's worth all this bustle? And she knows how to use the information?'

He nodded.

'See,' I explained, 'kids don't think like adults. This is a key mistake that adults make. I remember when I was a kid about Etta's age, a friend of my father came to the apartment. There was some talk about a little gun hidden in a big box of chocolates. What was my thinking on the subject at the time? "How do I get my hands on a chocolate?" Not: "What's the deal with the gun?"'

He nodded again. 'I see how that could be true. But these hoods, they don't have the benefit of your experience, both as a child and as a grown man whose job is helping children. See? They think like adults and that's as far as it goes.'

'Still don't quite understand what kind of trouble you think you're in,' I said to Yudda.

He closed his eyes. 'On account of I'm old buddies with Roan, and close enough to Etta that I taught her dog some tricks, these gangland characters think *I* know something. I don't. I was hoping to get it out of Etta. See?'

The good news was that Etta's *life* wasn't in danger. Nobody would ice her if they thought she had this important information locked in her head. The bad news was everything else, but mostly what they'd do to her if they got her. Guys like the Delanys had a limited number of ways to extract information from a person. Most of them involved dental instruments, and all of them were bad.

So. How to convince the various factions that Etta didn't really know anything? How to hook the kid up with her father *after* that so maybe the both of them could scram? Also, how to do all that without getting myself shot up – or worse, if this Mordecai character woke up and got out of the hospital?

My thinking at that moment, standing there banged up and a little wet, trying to decide how I felt about Yudda, was fairly simple. I thought I should find out what Etta knew, her key to whatever kingdom, and just give it to the bad guys. What the hell did she care, or did I care, for that matter? Like they say, there's a time to keep secrets and a time to give secrets away. It's Ecclesiastes. A time for every purpose under heaven. That way the secret's not a secret any more, and everybody leaves the kid alone so that she can grow up and have a nice life.

Feeling pretty good about my conclusion, I told Yudda what I thought he should know.

'You should see who's in your house shooting at people.' I glanced back in the direction of his boat. 'I think I'm going to my office to see if I can't figure how to get the kid out of her legal status with the Lamberts.'

'The *who?*' he asked me.

'The couple who *adopted* Etta. So-called. I need to get her away from them, legit.'

'Oh, right,' he said. 'Good idea.'

He was already headed toward his home. He'd bought my story.

Which left me feeling comfortable about heading back to the swamp to find John Horse and the kid, get the secret out of her head, and, in general, save the day.

FIFTEEN

The Seminole camp was empty when I got there. I'd seen it quiet, I'd seen it sparse, but I'd never seen it deserted. It was spooky.

The place was abandoned because the people there had been hassled more than usual in the previous couple of days: phony FBI, Delanys, me. But a bunch that had been screwed with as much as these particular Seminoles, they were running toward something, not away from something.

The camp was really only a couple dozen cinderblock houses and some storage sheds. A few people lived on the outskirts. Philip had a house that was built in a cluster of trees. No kidding: using the trees as the basic support beams, he'd built a house. It was an architectural marvel as far as I was concerned. And one that the rest of the world was unlikely ever to see.

But I had the suspicion that his house was empty too.

The camp seemed to have a life of its own. It wasn't just the leftover smells, cook fires, swamp herbs and tobacco. It was like an eerie echo was still reverberating around the concrete walls. Like old conversations were still hanging in the air. Like ghosts were wandering free.

And just when that thought occurred to me, of course, I saw the old woman again, the one with the antler and bone knife. Philip's grandmother. The one who'd been dead for ten years.

Clear as day, at the edge of the camp, she was making a racket with the bones and mouthing something to me. Didn't seem like the same thing as before. Before it was alarming. This time it was more instructive, like she was trying to explain something to me.

Then, closer to me, a white ibis landed on John Horse's roof. Biggest one I ever saw. Size of a pterodactyl, swear to God.

And when I looked back, the woman was gone. Or maybe I'd just imagined her.

Still, I looked up at the bird.

'Thanks,' I said to it. 'I was just about to get a telegram from the spirit world. Then *you* had to show up.'

The ibis made a little creaky noise, opened up its wings, and looked south. Then, very slowly, it lifted off from the roof and headed in that direction.

I actually thought, believe it or not, that the bird might be the telegram. That I was supposed to follow the bird. Which I did. I know it sounds crazy, but in the first place you get kind of loopy in a deserted camp in the middle of a swamp, and in the second place you had to follow the signs – even if they weren't signs – because John Horse was involved.

It wasn't hard. The bird was flying lazily and there was a pretty wide path going south. And it didn't take long. Ten minutes into it, I heard distant voices. Another five minutes and there was singing, closer to hand. The swamp all around me was humid and green, all plants and clear water, the occasional small bird or red lizard. The sky was clear, and the day was bright. No idea what time it was.

And just as I rounded a turn in the path, there they were: just about everybody from the camp. They were gathered in a huge flat circle of land, a couple acres of it, surrounded by tall standing stones. In the middle of the swamp. Like some big industrial company had come in, cleared the land, tamped down a foundation, and then gone away. And the standing stones weren't anything like rocks you'd find in the swamp, or anywhere in Florida as far as I knew.

John Horse was sitting on a blanket singing, with a cup of something in his hand. When he saw me, he started laughing, and several others turned around to look at me. I'm pretty sure I looked like an idiot: sharp suit, good shoes, baffled expression.

John Horse got up and ambled my way. Conversation and singing continued. I couldn't make out the song at first, but it wasn't Seminole or remotely ceremonial.

'I'm glad you got my message,' he called out over the other sounds.

It was the kind of thing he'd say ordinarily just to get my brain thinking that a sound in the swamp or a gleam of sunlight had been his message. Only in this case it was a ghost and a giant bird. Harder to dismiss.

'The big white bird was a nice touch,' I said, mostly to see how he'd react.

He didn't.

'That little girl, Etta, is not normal,' he told me.

I came closer to him. 'How do you mean?'

'There's an extra spirit in her brain.'

'An extra spirit,' I repeated. 'No idea what that means.'

'She's a child of eleven *and* an ancient woman. Both.'

'OK,' I said. 'Where is she?'

John Horse turned around to face the group, scanned, then pointed.

'Over there beside the well.'

Sure enough, the kid was sitting on a pile of stones, dog by her side, staring out into space.

'What is this place?' I asked him, looking around.

'I'm not sure,' John Horse said, joining me in my survey of the place. 'The story is that it's thousands of years old. But it's possible that Humble Oil was going to build something here when they thought he might get the oil rights to our land.'

I stared at his profile. 'You're talking about what happened with the Bear Island Field.'

He nodded once.

Oil had been discovered in Bear Island in 1972, and production started a year later. And even though it had become a part of the Big Cypress National Preserve almost immediately after that, in 1974, Humble was still taking oil out of it.

Still, it was some kind of mind trick he was trying to pull off, saying the place might be more than a thousand years old or less than a thousand days. Maybe he meant to distract me, but I wasn't interested.

'OK,' I told him. 'I'm going to talk to the kid now.'

He shrugged, and I was off.

Etta saw me coming and smiled. Den was more enthusiastic. He barked, he wagged, and then he met me halfway, walked me to the well.

'Hi,' I said.

'I've been thinking,' she told me right away.

I sat beside her on the stones. 'About what it is that's in your brain that everyone wants a look at?'

'Right.' She was staring into the well.

The well was very clear, and probably fresh. It was maybe ten feet wide and looked deep. No gunk or growth on the well stones.

'And?' I asked.

She looked up at me. 'I want to see my dad.'

Her face clouded up and her eyes got a little red. She wasn't the tough kid in a disco hat any more. She was a little girl who wanted her father and probably missed her mother.

And that, after all, was what I'd promised to do: find her and put her next to her dad.

'Yeah,' I told her. 'The thing is, I want to keep you safe, so you've really got to stay here for now.'

'Safe.' She nodded. 'But you could bring my dad *here*, right?'

I wasn't really in the mood to tell her that her dad had taken shots at me very recently. Because what if I was wrong and it hadn't been her dad in Yudda's house? Although, who else would have been staying there? Roan and Yudda were friends from way back. Which was also messing with me.

Suddenly I was kind of mixed up. What was I doing? Who could I trust? And why the *hell* were there so many people out to get Etta Roan?

Next thing I knew, John Horse was sitting next to Etta on the stones and patting Den on the head. That's all. He just sat there.

Then, over his shoulder, I saw an ibis standing in the water outside the circle of stones. It was just standing there.

For a second, everything around me was still, not moving, not making a sound. I felt like I was in the perfect center of everything. Everything.

It didn't last. Den started wagging his tail; someone sniffed; the ibis went for a fish in the water at its feet. The world turned.

'I saw that,' John Horse said after a moment.

I tilted my head in his direction.

He went on. 'I saw something happen. Don't know what, and you probably don't know either. But whatever it was, it was the answer.'

I shook my head. 'I know you're always trying to get me to buy into your "wise man" hooey, and sometimes it actually works on me. But all that happened just now was that I was tired, and I had a blank moment. Used to happen to me a lot in Brooklyn. I'd be sitting on a stoop or standing in the street, and it was like I blacked out for a second, only it wasn't *black* – it was *blank*. When I told my ma about it, she took me to see a doctor. He said it might be a touch of epilepsy. What they call a *petit mal* seizure. He told my mother that I had lost awareness of my surroundings for a couple of seconds. But I knew that wasn't right. I didn't lose awareness: I was *hyper* aware. Personally, I like when it happens. It's a little moment of calm in the storm.'

'What storm?'

'You know.' I glanced at Etta.

He nodded.

'You said it happened a lot in Brooklyn,' he went on. 'Not so much here in Florida?'

'Not so much.' I glanced down at Etta. 'By the way, the FBI guys who were following you around town in that black Caddy? Fake. Not sure who they are, but they're not Feds.'

'Huh.' John Horse stuck out his lower lip. 'You have epilepsy and I guessed wrong. This is certainly a strange day for something.'

'I don't have epilepsy,' I began.

'I like it here,' Etta interrupted. 'I like John Horse, and so does Den. But I gotta get to my dad. He needs me.'

'He does?' I asked her.

'Yes. He's been very sad since Mom died.'

'And you haven't?' I went on.

'Sure. But I'm a kid. We get over things faster. Adults take too long to do everything. Plus, my dad was in jail, so that's not a good environment for getting over somebody dying.'

'Have to agree with you there,' I said.

'Come on then,' she nagged. 'Take me to my dad. Please?'

John Horse stared me down. 'You really shouldn't do

that. She's safe here. She won't be if you take her into Fry's Bay.'

'I don't *want* to be safe,' Etta complained. 'I want to be with my dad! And he wants to be with me!'

I had to agree. 'Well, that *is* why he paid me a visit in the middle of the night.'

'Yes,' she snapped. 'Exactly. So, which way is your car?'

John Horse closed his eyes. 'OK. But I'm coming with you.'

'Why?' she asked him.

He looked down at her little face. 'Because you have an important spirit. And because I want to know what your secret is.'

'My secret?'

'The thing you know that everyone is so interested in finding out,' he told her. 'I'm curious.'

'Yeah, but I don't *know* what my secret is,' she said.

He smiled. 'That's why it's such a great secret.'

I knew it was wrong to take the kid back into Fry's Bay. I knew she was safe where she was, and she wouldn't be safe back in town. It was against every instinct I had, but you could actually feel the longing, like a strange heat, coming off the kid. She *had* to be with her father. It was too much for me. Not to mention that seeing her father might help her figure out what her secret was. *And* I also knew that I had a better chance of finding out her secret if John Horse worked on it with me.

All in all, it added up to taking the kid back to Fry's Bay, over to Yudda's houseboat.

'I think I do know where your father is,' I said. 'And my car is that way.'

I glanced down the path, the dog stood up, and off we went: the strangest quartet in all of Florida. If I'd known what was about to happen, I probably would have just jumped in the well instead.

SIXTEEN

Back in town, I stood on the docks watching the boats bob up and down on the bay. John Horse was sitting down with his eyes closed. Etta was throwing stones into the water. The dog was considering chasing seagulls.

And Yudda was closing up his restaurant. Not sure what time it was. I always hated watches. But it was too early for him to close up, and he wasn't happy with me. The sun was low, I could see that. But in Florida that never told me anything. In Brooklyn you knew what time it was, more or less, when the sun went down behind the buildings. In Florida there was all that ocean to deal with.

Yudda waddled my way at last, cursing under his breath in his dirty apron and his flip-flops.

'There was nobody in the joint when we showed up,' I said, just as he was about to tell me what he thought of my plan.

'I live by the walk-in trade,' he told me.

'You *live* by the weed trade,' I reminded him. 'You enjoy a little walk-in business, every once in a while, to your fine dining establishment.'

He started to protest, but then he shrugged. 'Yeah, all right.'

'So, that's Roan in your house, right?' I asked him.

'Yeah.'

We'd already determined that it was Roan who'd been shooting at me from Yudda's houseboat. Roan was, Yudda told me, near-sighted. He had no idea it was me in the rocks. He thought I was some crook or cop, one of the many after him.

All this had been determined while Etta sat in the back booth sipping what Yudda called a 'cherry smash', which was just Coca-Cola with mushed maraschinos in it. I didn't want the kid to get all excited about seeing her father if anything went south.

To prevent further gunplay, I'd convinced Yudda to lead the way, just in case. But he wasn't happy about it. And there was a strange attitude in the air. For instance, I couldn't figure out why John Horse was so silent.

'Come on,' I said to everyone, 'let's go to Yudda's house.'

Etta looked my way. 'I'm not stupid, you know. If that's where my father is, why don't you just tell me that?'

I smiled. 'I don't think you're stupid, I just don't want you getting your hopes up in case something is wrong.'

'Such as?' she asked.

No point avoiding the issue, because Etta was right: she wasn't stupid.

'All those people after you are after him too,' I said. 'What if your dad had to leave in a hurry because of all that?'

'But he was there,' she said, with a kind of heartbreaking hope in her voice.

'He was,' Yudda confirmed.

Etta dropped all the pebbles in her hands and marched toward me. 'Then let's go.'

And off we went, across the docks, around the path, over the tricky rocks toward the inlet where Yudda had parked his houseboat. It was low tide, and there were all manner of smelly dead things near the water's edge. Seagulls were arguing. The sky was growing dark, and there were clouds blowing in from the east.

Yudda suddenly called out in the direction of his houseboat. 'It's me. I got people with me!'

Etta was moving faster than the rest of us, except for Den, who bounded along beside her. Yudda had a well-practiced path; John Horse was gliding serenely but slowly over the stones. I was the bum, stumbling and slipping all the way.

As we approached the makeshift plank that rose up from the stones to the boat, I called out.

'Etta! Just wait a second!'

I did it partly to let me catch up with her, but mostly to call out loud so that Roan, if he was there, would hear her name.

She turned around to face me. 'Well, come on then!'

I picked up my graceless pace and landed beside her in no time. I took her hand and called out. 'Roan?'

No answer.

I turned around to glare at Yudda. 'Is he there or not?'

Yudda didn't say anything. He didn't look at me. He was concentrating on walking over sharp, slippery rocks, trying to keep his flip-flops under control.

Etta wouldn't wait. She shot forward. Den was ahead of her.

'Dad?' she hollered.

The dog started barking.

A voice from the houseboat coughed a very painful: 'Etta?'

Etta raced up the plank toward the front door of the houseboat, but she couldn't get it open. Too excited.

The dog was going wild, spinning, barking, growling.

I made it to the boat, up the plank, and grabbed the door handle.

It was locked.

'Hey!' I shouted. 'Open the damn door!'

'Dad!' Etta was crying, pounding on the door.

At last it swung open, and there he was: the guy who'd sat on my bed in the middle of the night. He had his gun pointed right at my heart.

Etta froze. Den snarled. I blinked.

'That's not my dad,' Etta croaked.

'Sorry, Foggy,' Yudda said, coming up the plank. 'You got to understand. They had my guts in a vise. And that maniac Mordecai is here!'

Etta looked up at me. 'That's not my dad, Foggy.'

I looked over my shoulder at Yudda. His face was made out of ashes. And behind him, the rocks were empty. John Horse was nowhere to be seen.

SEVENTEEN

Before I could recover, the guy with the gun had a hold of Etta's arm. Den snapped and lunged, but the guy kicked the dog. Den rolled across the deck but was up in a flash.

'Sit!' Yudda shouted.

Den wasn't having it. He snapped again and ran. But Yudda grabbed the dog's collar and held on tight.

'Sit, Den,' he said more gently. 'It's for your own good.'

Den strained at the leash, but Yudda held firm.

'You came to the Lamberts' house,' Etta said to the man with the gun.

'Came to my house too,' I added. 'And you lied to me.'

'Shut up,' he said calmly. 'Both of you.'

I stared him in the eye, but I spoke to the owner of the houseboat.

'Yudda, I think this might be the end of a beautiful friendship.'

'Foggy . . .' Yudda began.

'Yeah,' Gun Guy snapped. 'You shut up too, fat boy. Keep the dog outside. Moscowitz? In.'

With that he dragged the kid inside and waved his gun at me. I moved toward the gun; Yudda pulled the dog outside.

'Now, I been looking all over for this little brat,' he told me. 'If you got any idea about screwing with me, I'll just pop her one or two in the bean, and that's that. My job is to find the kid. If I find her dead, I still get paid. Got me?'

His voice sounded like the Italian tough guys in my old neighborhood, but it had a definite whiff of brogue.

'You're here with Scarlatti,' I said. A guess.

He squinted. It made him look even stupider.

'How you know Scarlatti?'

'We worked together when I was in Brooklyn,' I lied. 'You never knew him when he was doing business with Red Levine?'

'You knew *Red*?'

'He was, like, my God-Uncle or something,' I said. That was true. 'I learned a lot about life from the guy.'

'This is all very touching,' Etta said to the guy, 'but you're hurting my arm.'

'Let her go,' I said gently.

He stared down at her. She smiled. Then she kicked her leg high, like Bruce Lee, right up into the guy's groin.

His eyes went wide. His gun went off. I grabbed his forearm and twisted. The gun dropped to the floor. Etta grabbed it and backed away. I popped the guy in the nose, hard. I felt it break. There was blood all over his face.

I shoved the guy backward, and he stumbled over a stuffed chair, then tumbled to the floor.

'Ever fire a gun?' I asked Etta.

'No, but there's a first time for everything.'

'Better give it to me. I've done it lots of times.' I held out my hand; she gave me the gun.

Yudda was in the doorway, still holding Den's collar.

'What the hell?' he demanded.

'I think I'm going to shoot this guy,' I told Yudda, 'and then I'm thinking about doing the same to you.'

'Go!' Etta yelled.

Den broke free from Yudda and was all over the guy with the busted nose. It was pretty frightening. The guy was screaming; the dog was snarling.

Yudda stared for about three seconds and then he turned around and took off. It was a foolish endeavor. He'd never outrun a bullet in those flip-flops.

But I let him go and concentrated my attention on the dog. 'Call him off,' I told Etta. 'That guy's had enough.'

'You won't let me shoot him, you won't let my dog eat him,' she complained. 'What *can* I do?'

'How about we get a little information out of him?' I suggested.

That settled, the dog was called off, the guy was given a wad of paper towels for his nose, zero sympathy for his groin, and we all sat down.

'You gotta understand,' he whimpered. 'Working with

Mordecai around, it's like a nightmare. You never know from one second to the next what he's gonna do. He ate a guy's kneecap off once.'

'*Ate* it off?' I said. 'You saw this?'

'No, but everybody knows he did it. The victim was in the hospital for a month getting a new plastic kneecap.'

I glanced at Etta. She was glaring at the man with the broken nose and there was something more than curiosity on her face.

'What's your name?' she asked him.

'Bobby.' He sighed.

'You came to the Lamberts' house,' she went on. 'You were there with another man.'

'You *are* with the Delany crew, right?' I asked.

He nodded. 'She's talking about a business meeting. See, the Lamberts work for the Delany family. I was there to make them an offer.'

'You and Mordecai?'

'No,' he said. 'I don't know where he was. He's been away on some other job for a long time. Like almost a year. I was there with Scarlatti.'

'What was the offer?' I asked.

'We were supposed to take the little girl,' he said, 'since they couldn't get anything out of her.'

Etta looked my way. 'I was hiding in the kitchen. I heard. That's when I split. Left a message for my dad, took Den to the vet, and came here, to this crummy town.'

'When the Lamberts couldn't find the kid,' Bobby went on, 'they cleared out fast. They knew what the Delanys would do to them, because they lost the prize.'

'Yeah, about that,' I said. 'Why is Etta such a prize? What does she know that's worth all this?'

Bobby looked at Etta. 'What color were my socks that day, the day we came to the Lamberts' house?' he asked her.

'Sky blue,' she said without a second's hesitation.

Then Bobby looked at me.

'And what color are my socks right now, Moscowitz?' he asked.

I had to look. They were black. But I saw his point.

'She sees or hears or reads something once,' Bobby said,

'and it's stuck in her bean forever. That's what everybody says. All I could figure was that she saw or heard something important that somebody wants to find out, or somebody wants to hide. No idea what that *something* is, but it's big, obviously. To be worth all this, like you said.'

'And you're sure you don't know what it is?' I asked Etta.

She stared and tapped the side of her head with her index finger. 'Here's what it's like: everything in my head is three-dimensional, and it won't ever go away. Right now, if I don't keep my head on straight, I can see the dried-up green bean in the dark corner of John Horse's house. Multiply that by, like, a billion, and you've got the problem. I remember *everything*. All I can do is focus on what's in front of me and hope for the best. Focus *really* hard. Plus, I sing a certain song in my head that my mom taught me. Before she died. Helps me.'

I couldn't even pretend to understand. So instead of prying, I asked the obvious. 'What's the song?'

She smiled. 'It's called "Quicksilver Girl". My mom loved it. Whenever I got lost in my memory forest, she'd sing it.'

I'd never heard of it, but Bobby had.

'I love that song,' he said softly. 'Stevie Miller's first record. Right?'

'The point is,' Etta told me, ignoring Bobby, 'that because I try so hard to keep the images from taking over my whole brain, I can't afford to spend any time looking for one single memory. I'd get lost. Like in a forest. And I might not find my way back out. See? So, I don't know what it is they want. I don't *want* to know. That's what these assholes don't seem to understand: whatever it is they want, it's safely buried somewhere in the forest.'

'OK, but don't say *assholes*,' I admonished. 'You're too young for that kind of language.'

'Bite me,' she said, but she said it sweetly.

'I think you broke my nose,' Bobby whined. 'Can I go get it looked at?'

Etta and I both said *no* at the same time.

He shrugged. 'Worth a shot.'

'Why *did* you come to my apartment in the middle of the

night pretending to be Roan?' I asked him. 'Just because you thought I could find Etta better than you could?'

'What's your connection with Roan?' he asked me right back.

'None.'

'Then why did he leave your business address for me to find?' he wanted to know.

Etta laughed. 'You're a moron,' she told Bobby. 'I'm the one who left Foggy's address, and I only did it because Elvin mentioned it.'

He stared. 'Who's Elvin?'

I sat back. Still kept the gun on Bobby, but he really wasn't in any condition to make a move. I looked around Yudda's place for the first time. It wasn't what I expected.

The room we were sitting in was small, half the size of my apartment living room. But twice the flair. Persian rug on the floor, sleek art-deco furniture all around, original art on the walls. The light was low, mostly from a standing lamp, but there were also deco wall sconces. No idea what the rest of the small place looked like, but that particular room would have made Louise Brooks very comfortable.

But that's as far as I got in my thinking, because John Horse appeared in the doorway.

'You're all just sitting around?' he asked, glaring.

'Where'd you go when the trouble started?' I asked him right back.

'I didn't go anywhere,' he snapped. 'I just turned invisible.'

I lowered my eyes. 'I see.'

'That man isn't Etta's father,' he went on. 'And you shouldn't have dragged her out of the safety of our hiding place. I'm taking her back there with me right now.'

'No,' Etta began.

'And *you*,' John Horse said to the dog. 'You did a terrible job of protecting her. I thought we discussed that.'

The dog looked down and whined a little.

'Come on, both of you,' he commanded.

'Hang on,' I protested, standing. 'You're not going to wander through Fry's Bay all by yourself with gangsters and miscreants on the loose all over the place?'

He shook his head. 'I'm not all by myself.'

He stepped aside, and I could see, out on the rocky shore, maybe a dozen Seminole warriors, men and women. Grim and silent. Where they'd come from, God knows. But they had a fierce presence that *nobody* would mess with.

I stood and took a couple of steps in Etta's direction. 'You know he's right.'

'I'm not *asking*,' John Horse insisted.

A heavy sigh from the kid, then she stood up. 'OK.'

Den hopped along toward John Horse, wagging his tail.

'I'm going to find your dad,' I promised Etta. 'And I'm going to figure out what the rest of these goons want from you.'

'*Sure* you are,' she snapped without looking at me.

John Horse caught her eye. 'He can do it. I know Foggy. If he says he'll do something, it gets done.'

I appreciated the support from John Horse. I only wished I was as confident as he was.

EIGHTEEN

After John Horse and his formidable entourage took off with the kid, I offered Bobby the option of going to jail. But he'd already decided he would limp off into the sunset. Back to New York, he said. I kept his gun. He protested, but there really wasn't much he could do. I left him on Yudda's sofa and headed to my office.

I had to find Etta's real father. He wanted to see her, I knew that. People who busted out of prison generally fell into three categories.

1: You were a guy who was wrongly accused.

2: You were a guy who was getting a raw deal on the inside.

3: You were a guy who had something important on the outside that couldn't wait.

Etta seemed worth the risk to me. And the fact that John Horse thought there was something more to the kid than met the eye only doubled my opinion.

So, back to my crummy little office. I found it remarkable that after a couple of years in the place, I still wasn't used to the smell – a spicy combination of wet cardboard and roach powder.

And my desk was a perfect little island of chaos in a larger ocean of boredom. Still, there were people I needed to call in my official capacity, and that was best done from the office. For one thing, all the official phone numbers were in my desk. For another thing, the atmosphere in the office made my voice sound different than it sounded when I was in my apartment.

So, first call: Lake City police station. Guy that answered sounded like the one I'd met before.

'What?' was all he said.

'It's Moscowitz from over in Fry's Bay,' I said. 'I spoke with you about—'

'The Jew with the two-tone Florsheim shoes,' he said. 'I remember.'

How he was so sure I was a Jew puzzled me, but I went on. 'You told me that they had Nelson Roan in some new correctional facility,' I said.

'Cross City,' he reminded me. 'Old airforce base.'

'And he was in for killing a doctor.'

'Adam Bainbridge.' He sighed. 'Cancer doctor. Geez, you got a memory like a sieve.'

The *fact* was that I remembered everything. The *trick* was to let the officer feel superior. It worked almost every time. Let a guy think he's smarter than you, and he'll either end up telling you things he really shouldn't or helping in ways he really didn't want to. For instance, I only flashed my badge at him for a second, and I never gave him my name. He didn't seem the observant type, so how is it that he knew my name, remembered my shoes, and was aware of my ethnic heritage?

But all I said was, 'Right. Adam Bainbridge. Let me write that down. Now. Where exactly is this Cross City place?'

'It's in Cross City.'

'Uh-huh, but . . .'

'Northeast 255th Street,' he snapped.

'Anywhere near the Cross City airport?'

'Look,' he said, 'what are you doing?'

'Well, you know I'm looking for Nelson Roan's daughter, Etta.'

He was quiet for a second. I let the silence hang.

'I thought you already found her.'

And there it was: he was working with somebody. How else would he know that I'd found her?

'Found her and lost her again,' I said. 'No idea where she is now.'

'Oh.'

He was beginning to realize what he'd done, the dawning realization of his idiocy.

'And what was your name, again?' I asked him. 'I have to put it in my report, you know.'

He hung up.

So, the first call was fruitful in its own way. The second call was to my friend Maggie Redhawk at the hospital.

'Nurses' station, Redhawk.'

'Maggie, it's Foggy.'

'Everything's fine,' she began.

'I'm calling about a doctor named Bainbridge,' I interrupted. 'Know who he is?'

'Adam Bainbridge?'

'That's the guy.'

'Monster,' she told me. 'Peddled all these fake cancer treatments, crap that he concocted himself, instead of treating his patients with radiation and chemotherapy like he should have. Made a lot of money, and all his patients died. He was essentially a mass murderer.'

'But it caught up with him,' I said.

'Yeah. Somebody killed him. Whoever did it should have gotten a medal, in my opinion.'

'Right.' My brain was starting to tingle. 'Thanks, Maggie. And be careful. There are a lot more goons in town than usual.'

'I've noticed,' she said.

We hung up and my brain really began to itch. Roan killed Bainbridge, but with a good lawyer he wouldn't have gotten life, not if the truth about Bainbridge had come out. He might even have gotten off, because homicide is 'justified when it prevents greater harm to innocents'. That was a concept I'd memorized from the legal statutes, since occasionally I'd run into a situation where killing some guy was the best possible thing you could do for a kid. Also, Roan had been up for a retrial. That's what Officer Idiot in Lake City had told me when I'd visited the station. Why would he bust out if he had a chance to get free in a retrial?

Something was wrong with Roan's situation. Maybe the story that Bobby had made up when he was pretending to be Roan was a little accurate. Maybe when Roan learned that the Lamberts had his kid, he also learned that they were working with the Delany family. Retrial or not, he had to get out. He had to find Etta. But the Lamberts heard that Roan busted out and panicked, was that it? Was *that* why they moved out of their house so fast?

I stood up from my desk, got Bobby's gun out of my suit coat and put it in a drawer. Then I checked my own Colt Defender, a nervous habit.

It was ironic, really, that I had a gun at all. Never owned one when I was a crook in Brooklyn. And in Brooklyn my father, a guy who died when I was a baby, was a well-respected member of The Combination before his untimely death as a result of payback-ignition problems. His car blew up. Twice in three seconds. They wanted him to be *really* dead. My point is that I was quite familiar with the activities of certain families in certain businesses. All that nefarious influence and not one pistol in New York State. I had to go straight and work for children before firearms became a necessary thing.

That's what I mean about irony.

My next stop had to be Yudda's, and I didn't like it. Before that day, I'd come to think of Yudda as a friend. I didn't care for the idea that he'd ratted me out. And put Etta in danger. It was obvious that I had to find out what he was doing. Yudda knew the *real* father, and almost certainly knew more about the whole business than he'd let on. I figured he'd get me to Roan, or at least point me in the right direction. With the right inducement. So, all I had to do was come up with something that would convince Yudda to be honest with me, for a change.

If I hauled out my gun, he'd get one of his and things would get messy. If I threatened him with anything legal, he'd just laugh. What would get him on my side, so he'd *want* to tell me what I had to know?

NINETEEN

Twenty minutes later I was sitting at the bar in Yudda's. The stool was uncomfortable, the place smelled funny, and Yudda was nervous. Maybe that was because I let my suit coat fall open so that he could see I had my Colt in a shoulder holster.

'I got nothing ready yet,' he muttered, 'if you're here for a bite to eat. If you're here to shoot me, go ahead. It couldn't make me feel any worse than I do now.'

I leaned forward and got eye contact. 'About five pounds of ground fish,' I began, 'and two medium onions, peeled and ground.'

He stared. 'What are you doing?'

'I'm giving you a secret more closely guarded than the nuclear codes,' I said. 'It's my Aunt Shayna's recipe for gefilte fish.'

He blinked. There may even have been a tear in his eye. 'How long I been asking you about that gefilte fish?'

'As long as you've known me.'

'So, after all this bullshit, why you give it to me now?'

'Because I want something from you in return,' I said.

'I probably don't have as much money as you think I do,' he told me.

'Yeah, I want to know about Roan.' I sat up. 'I want to know what could possibly make you rat me out. Me? I think I saved your life, like, three times already.'

'You ain't believe me when I told you I was under maybe three warrants in New Orleans?'

'I thought you were being colorful.'

'I got some ex-wife trouble,' he said. 'I got a drug conviction that I jumped bail. And it might be a murder rap I'm in on.'

'And?' I knew that wasn't everything.

'*And*,' he sighed, 'there's some guys who want me to give

a whole lot of their product back, which I ain't got because I sold it to get here. To Fry's Bay.'

'Cops, courts, and cons.' I nodded. 'All three after you.'

'These goons come into town and say to me, like, "We knock you on the head, ship you back to New Orleans in a fish crate, let the vultures pick at the bones." And *plus* which: Mordecai!'

'Yeah, there's a lot of talk about him. But he's in the hospital, bad off. The Lamberts hit him with their car. Have you seen him?'

'No! I never saw him, and I hope to God I never do.' Yudda started to sweat. 'You know anything about the guy?'

I shook my head because I wanted him to keep talking.

'He peeled a guy's skin off in front of the guy's whole family. Slow! They say the guy lived for, like, two days. He used the skin to make a waste basket and a couple of seat covers, for God's sake!'

I nodded. What I didn't say was that at least part of his story was actually about Ed Gein, a serial killer from Wisconsin. Famous case. Basis for Alfred Hitchcock's movie *Psycho*.

But Yudda was genuinely scared. He was in real trouble.

All I said was, 'Don't care. Tell me about Roan.'

'What do you want to know? He's a nice guy with a swell kid who got a wrong deal.'

'No,' I interrupted. 'I want to know where he is now.'

Yudda squinted. 'In prison. I thought you'd know that.'

He seemed genuine. Bobby, the guy who had pretended to be Roan, hadn't told Yudda anything.

'I'm serious, Foggy,' Yudda went on. 'These guys, they threatened to shoot me, to send me back to New Orleans in a box – all kinds of crap. You know I'm on your side.'

I knew the only side Yudda was truly on was Yudda's. But his eyes were sad, and his voice was shaky, so I let him off the hook.

'Two tablespoons of kosher salt,' I told him, 'five eggs, three tablespoons of water, and at least a cup of sugar.'

He nodded. I knew he was writing it down in his brain.

'What about the stock?' he asked.

'I was getting to that,' I said. 'Sixteen cups of water, four teaspoons of kosher salt, a half a cup of sugar, two onions, and two carrots.'

'I put the stock in a pot, roll the fish into balls, and simmer for, what? About an hour?' He bit his lower lip. 'You're leaving something out. This ain't so very special.'

'There was a guy who lived across the hall from us when I was a kid,' I said. 'He was from, like, someplace in India. Anyway, he introduced my aunt to curry. So. In the fish there's fenugreek. In the stock there's cardamom pods.'

He made a face. 'No. That's not right.'

'It's amazing.'

'Naw.' He continued to protest. 'It's not even Jewish!'

'You may be interested to know,' I told him, 'that Yemenite Jews believe fenugreek is the Talmudic spice rubia. You use it the first night of Rosh Hashanah.'

'You're making that up.'

'So now tell me more about Roan.'

He was suspicious of my ethnic history lesson, but he told me about Roan anyway. Seems he and Roan were in the weed trade from Baton Rouge to New Orleans for several years. Completely benign enterprise that got out of hand when larger drug cartels started horning in. Roan wanted out. He backed away, and nobody heard from him for a while. He started a family. He had a kid. Then his wife got sick. Then she died. Then Roan killed the doctor and went to prison, where, as far as Yudda knew, he was still incarcerated. Not really much of a story. When the Canadians came to town, they threatened Yudda with all kinds of bodily harm. He found it especially cruel to threaten him with his ex-wife, and especially weird that Bobby had pretended to be Roan in order to get me involved in the whole mess. He looked down, and then he apologized.

In short, he had no choice but to rat me out, and he didn't know as much about Roan as I had hoped.

Still, something was lurking. I could feel it. Nobody had heard from Roan for a while, he'd said. What did that mean? And what about Roan's trial? If he'd had drug money squirrelled away, he would have gotten a lawyer smart enough to get the charges bumped down at least a little, given the circumstances. Unless the doctor was connected to bigger fish. And what about Roan busting out of jail and then disappearing?

So, while Yudda's story hadn't helped me out as much as I'd thought it would, my brain was lurching forward.

I thought maybe I should find out more about the murder of Dr Bainbridge.

I got off the stool and tapped the bar. 'I'm expecting gefilte fish the next time I come in here.'

'Where am I gonna get fenugreek and cardamom?'

'Long-distance call to Kalustyan's on Lexington Avenue,' I said. 'Put in a rush order. Tell him Shayna sent you. Ought to have it by the end of the week.'

I didn't turn around when I was walking out, but I could hear Yudda dial the phone.

TWENTY

D r Adam Bainbridge made a lot of money selling his cancer cure. That's the first thing I found out. He had nearly two million dollars in the bank when he was killed. No heirs, no will. The second thing I found out was that the cancer cure was a repackaged patent medicine from the nineteenth century, *Dr Goodheart's Brilliant Curative*. It was a mixture of carbonated water, cane sugar, and *Cannabis Indica*, weed with a high level of THC. Which was why patients thought they were getting better. They *felt* better. Right up until the time they died. Dr Bainbridge was, as it turned out, a descendant of Amelia Drake, the inventor of the *Brilliant Curative*. Right after that I found out that his medical degree was as worthless as his medicine. Guttenberg University of Stuttgart didn't exist. Gave me a lot of faith in the medical establishment. Guy could make up a degree, fake a medicine, kill a bunch of people, and make a couple million dollars. God bless America. And the fact that I could find all that out from just a couple hours' worth of phone calls and a little library research only reinforced my disdain for the establishment. Why hadn't anybody else bothered to check on the guy the way I had? I ended up agreeing with Maggie Redhawk that Roan deserved a medal, not jail time, for killing the guy.

My next step was a mystery even to me. No idea why I decided I had to go to Cross City Correctional to see what I could see about Roan's time there. And about his escape from the place. Sometimes you had to follow a hunch. And I had a fairly insistent one about Roan's incarceration.

My assumption had been that he busted out to be with his kid. But that idea had come mostly from Bobby, the fake Roan. And he'd only given that impression because he wanted to find Etta and learn her secret.

What if, no matter what Etta thought, Roan was out for other reasons? Like, for example, revenge on the guys that put him in Cross City in the first place. There was a place in my old neighborhood that only played old movies. I always liked *The Count of Monte Cristo*. There was a guy who earned his revenge. What if *that* was Roan?

And while I was at it, I decided to pay a visit to my new friend Elvin in Lake City. I was curious to know how the Lamberts got their claws on Etta; what their connections were. They'd tried to give me the impression that they were innocents afraid of the bad men, but they certainly did their best to run over Mordecai when they had the chance. Like they knew who he was, and what kind of trouble they were in.

In short, I was going to have to drive to Lake City again.

The T-Bird was parked by the docks. The sun had set, and the moon was up. I realized I had to wait until morning. Elvin's office would be closed, and the correctional facility wouldn't be admitting visitors. So maybe a good night's sleep and an early start were in order.

But when I pulled into the parking lot at my apartment, there were lights on in my place. Never a good sign, because I always turn them off. Light equals heat, and Florida's hot enough all by itself.

I eased out of the car and around the building. Thought I might get a peek in the sliding doors in back. When I did, I was a little surprised. John Horse waved, and Etta started laughing.

I tugged on the sliding door and shook my head.

'You have to stop moving the kid around like this,' I said to John Horse. 'She needs a stable environment.'

'I know,' he agreed.

Etta was still laughing a little. 'He said you'd come around back. Then he heard your car, and he said we should go into the kitchen and wait for you to come to the back door. He knows everything.'

'Yeah,' I told her. 'He's a riot.'

'We were halfway back to the swamp when she said something.' John Horse looked down.

How he could wear a flannel shirt and jeans all the time in Florida was a mystery. But I knew he felt the same about my wearing a suit, so we'd quit talking about it a while back.

'What did she say?' I asked him.

'I told him that the Lamberts know something,' Etta said. 'Something about what I know that I don't remember. The thing. The reason these guys are after me.'

'Where are they?' John Horse asked.

I stared. 'They ran over a guy and then beat it out of town.'

'You should find them,' he told me.

I shook my head. 'You could have delivered Etta to your house, put ten or fifty of your guys around her, and she'd be safe now. Then you could have come here to tell me this. Why did you bring her here? Why did you really come back to town?'

'Someone in my camp is working with the gangsters,' he said softly. 'I realized that a little too late.'

I took in a deep breath. I'd wondered how so many urban criminals had found the Seminole camp way in the middle of the swamp. Although it was hard to believe that any Seminole would even *know* New York gangsters, let alone work with them.

'You think she's safer with me?' I asked.

'I think it's harder to hit a moving target,' he said. 'You should take her with you when you go to Lake City tomorrow.'

'No,' I protested. 'And what makes you think I'm going to Lake City?'

He just smiled. How he knew that I was planning to do that was completely without explanation. He'd pulled off some pretty spectacular tricks before, but this was the biggest in a while.

'Why are we going to Lake City?' Etta wanted to know.

'I have to visit my new friend Elvin,' I began.

'Elvin! I *love* him.' She looked at John Horse. 'He told me all about Foggy. And he knew that the adoption with the Lamberts was hinky.'

'He did,' I agreed. 'And I want to find out more about that.' I looked around.

'Where's the dog?'

'I sent him to the camp,' John Horse said. 'He wanted to be outside.'

I thought there was more to it than that from the way he said it, but I let it go.

'So, look,' I said to Etta. 'After we see Elvin, I'm going over to the prison where your father stayed. Until he broke out to find you. Are you up for that?'

'That'll be weird,' she said. 'I've never seen a prison before.'

'Good,' John Horse concluded. 'It's all settled. I'll wait here in your house, Foggy.'

I studied his face. 'Why would you do that?'

He wouldn't look me in the eye. 'It's for the best.'

I'd learned a long time before to trust John Horse, *especially* when he wouldn't look you in the eye.

'OK.' I yawned a little on purpose. 'I'm going to sleep now. Etta, you take the sofa. John Horse, I have your sleeping bag from the other times . . .'

'Already got it out,' he said, pointing toward the living room. 'And blankets for the sofa. You go on to bed.'

I nodded, heading for the bedroom. 'We'll get a very early start in the morning.'

TWENTY-ONE

Six hours later, I woke up to the smell of coffee. They were trying to be quiet in the kitchen, but sometimes that only made every little noise louder. Like a spoon clinking in a cup, or a cupboard door closing. So, I got up. Shower, shave, and a sporty gaberdine suit later, I was at the table with them.

Etta stared. 'Why do you wear a suit? I mean, if you don't have to.'

I sat and sipped a little coffee before I answered. 'I was partly raised by a guy who told me that a suit equals authority. You wear a cheesy shirt and jeans, that's who people think you are. It's a superficial world. Take, for instance, your T-shirt.'

She was wearing a T-shirt with a peace sign on it. 'What about it?' she asked me. 'It belonged to my mom.'

'But that's not what people see,' I told her. 'They see a kid wearing a shirt that's ten years too late.'

'And what does that make them think?' John Horse butted in. 'These *people*?'

'Makes them dismiss her.' I sipped. 'People are always looking for the stupid visual cue, something that helps them make a decision about you, so they can move on.'

'So, it's working,' Etta said. 'I *want* people to dismiss me.'

'What about you?' I asked John Horse. 'What about your costume?'

He smiled. 'Like you,' he told me, 'I wear clothes that address a cliché.'

'You dress up like an old Seminole man.' I nodded.

'Or,' he said, 'I dress this way because these are the only clothes I have. Most of what I wear has been given to me by someone else.'

'Why are we talking about this?' Etta interrupted.

'You started it,' I said.

'He wants you to change into something else,' John Horse told her.

She sat back and thought about it for a minute. 'We need to make a certain impression on Elvin,' she said. 'Or the people in his office. Also, to the people at the prison, I can't look like an urchin.'

I nodded.

'But I don't have anything else. My bag is still at the Seminole camp.'

I stood and finished my first cup of coffee. 'I keep a stash for just such an emergency. Every so often I'll have to get a kid out of a house, like, really fast. So, I got some clothes in my bottom drawer. From the Goodwill, just in case.'

'Throwaway clothes?' Etta shook her head. 'I don't think so.'

'I got this suit at the same place,' I told her.

'My point exactly,' she said.

'A shirt that makes no impression at all,' I insisted, 'and some mundane pants. That way people don't think they can figure you out right away. They have to work at it. And that's when you give them what you want them to know about you, not what they assume from the cover of your book.'

Again, she thought about it. Then she stood up too. 'Plain white blouse, square collar,' she began, heading for the bedroom. 'Black shorts, if you've got something like that.'

John Horse went into the living room and put Miles Davis on the stereo, *Seven Steps to Heaven*, which meant he was going to take a morning nap. I had no idea why he was staying at my place. Or why he'd *really* brought Etta back to my place. I didn't buy the idea that he wanted to keep her safe by keeping her moving. Didn't seem his style. It seemed more likely that someone in the Seminole camp had, in fact, ratted him out, somehow. But everything was too helter-skelter. And that wasn't John Horse. My guess was that he knew something that he wasn't telling me. But that was always the case.

'You put on your favorite Miles Davis,' I said. 'Are you planning to stay here in my apartment?'

'Just want to get my nap,' he told me, not looking me in

the eye. 'Then I have to go back to the standing stones and talk some more with the dog.'

In other words, he didn't really want to tell me what he was doing. He just turned up the stereo and sank down on to the sofa.

Twenty minutes later, Etta and I were in the car and on our way to Lake City.

She fiddled with the radio, talked about her dog and about some television show she liked. Then she fell asleep for a while. I turned the treble way down low and put the radio on some college classical station. Thought that would help her sleep.

She woke up about the time I was getting hungry. It was early for lunch, but we were close to Lake City and I thought we might visit Madge, have a little pie. Etta was enthusiastic about the idea, so I pushed the accelerator a little harder.

'Look, I've been meaning to ask you,' I said, 'about the stuff you left in your house, or the Lamberts' house, I guess. You left poems and instructions for your dad. And then around Den's neck, you told him to go to Yudda's.'

She stared straight ahead, like the horizon was fascinating.

'Just seems odd,' I nudged.

'My dad's a quiet man,' she began. 'He doesn't talk much, and he's always nice. When my mom got sick, he was even nicer. When she died, he stopped talking altogether. But sometimes I would wake up and there would be notes from him on my pillow. He'd say funny little things, or sometimes he'd draw stupid animals. So, I started leaving him notes too, like in the pocket of his coat or taped to the fridge. After that, one night at the diner, he told me about how to leave him secret messages. Just in case.'

'In case of what?' I asked her.

'He didn't say.' She shrugged. 'But that's why I did it. I guess I'm a little surprised that you found them.'

'I like the poem about blueberries.'

She smiled. 'I wrote that when I was just a little kid.'

'Still,' I said. 'You got a knack.'

She looked down. 'You think?'

'I do.'

By the time we got to Madge's diner, the day was hot, and the sky was white. The air conditioning in the diner was cranked, and it felt like heaven. All the stools at the counter were filled, and the seashell pink and aquamarine blue hurt my eyes. The place still smelled like clams.

Madge, cigarette dangling from her lips, the smoke swirling into her eyes, squinted when she saw us come in.

Etta waved and went for the only empty booth. Madge dropped her cigarette on the floor, crushed it with a delicate toe, and nodded. 'You found her,' she growled.

I nodded.

'Usual, please,' Etta said enthusiastically.

'Same,' I told Madge.

That was all. No emotional reaction. No fuss. Five minutes later, Etta and I were eating our fried chicken sandwiches in silence. Mine was very good and Etta had no complaints. When we were done, Madge came to the table and stared at our empty plates.

Before she could comment, I said, 'Morris told me to get the pecan pie.'

'Morris is a dumbass,' Madge answered. 'That pecan pie is made all the way up there in Georgia. We make the key lime ourselves. Right here.'

'In this diner?' I asked.

'Betty's Bake Barn,' she snapped. 'Two blocks down. Betty brings it in fresh every morning.'

'We'll have two pieces, please,' Etta interrupted.

'That's *right* you will,' Madge said, staring me down.

When Madge left our table, Etta leaned in close to me.

'Madge and Morris used to date,' she told me.

Before I could comment, the door of the diner flew open and two very large guys with two very black guns stormed in.

Now, some people will react to an event like that by making a noise or ducking under a table. Both wrong, but that's what most people in the diner did. I noticed that Madge just stopped moving and stared. Etta folded her hands in front of her on the table top. I turned toward the guys, making sure to show both my hands.

The guys were a sort of stereotype: dark suits, low-brimmed

fedoras, necks too thick for their collars. They saw Etta after a second and moved toward us carefully.

When they got close, I stood up and held my hands out wide.

'Boys, boys,' I began.

'No,' one of the guys said, 'sit back down.'

'The girl comes with us,' the other guy said, 'or this place is a butcher shop.'

'Colorful,' I said, 'but here's the thing. When you say something like that, you have to be prepared to make good on it. And I'm not going to let you take the kid without a whole lot of fuss. So, are you *really* ready to shoot up the joint, or was that just a line?'

They looked at each other like it was the first time anyone had ever asked them a question. About anything. Basically, what I was hoping for.

I batted one of the gun hands, it knocked into the other guy's gun and they both went off, shattering the window next to our booth. Etta was up and around them in a flash, and Madge had produced a sawed-off shotgun from behind the counter. She fired one barrel right away and it took off one guy's hat. I back-elbowed that guy in the jaw and he fell into the other guy. They both tumbled into the booth where I'd been sitting. Etta was already at the door. I pulled out my Colt and shot one of the guys in the foot. He howled. I put the muzzle on the other guy's left ear. They were both still floundering in the booth. I pulled their guns loose and tossed them back behind me. I heard them clatter on the linoleum floor. Madge was beside me by then, the shotgun very close to the hoodlums' faces.

I looked at her. 'I'm kind of in love with you.'

'I get off at six,' she said.

'What about Morris?'

She grinned. 'Yeah, what about him?'

'Foggy, come *on!*' Etta insisted, holding the door open.

'You OK?' I asked Madge.

She laughed. I took that as a yes.

Etta and I were in my car ten seconds later.

TWENTY-TWO

We pulled out of the parking lot, tires screeching. 'You know how to get to Elvin's office?' I asked her.

'We're not going to the police?' Etta replied.

'I think Madge is probably taking care of those boys,' I said, 'and it seems more important than ever for us to figure out a couple of things about you. Besides, I met one of the cops from Lake City, and I'm pretty sure he's bent. Not on your side.'

'Yeah, I guess,' she agreed, 'but how's it going to help you to find out about my phony adoption?'

'What I really want to find out is more about your father. And they're supposed to have that kind of information in Elvin's office.'

That seemed to satisfy her a little, and she sat back.

'Take a left in two blocks,' she said.

Five minutes later we were through the doors of the Lake City Child and Family Services building, a squat 1950s number with no character and lots of florescent. There were three desks, a small waiting area, and a bank of file cabinets. A stern, husky woman in a polyester suit looked up when we came in.

'You're Mrs Bannon,' I guessed.

She glared. I flashed my Child Protective Services badge.

'This is Etta Roan,' I went on. 'You erroneously placed her in a dangerous household and I'm here to investigate that. So, on your feet and fetch the files.'

She blinked.

Then, around the corner from what must have been a break room, holding a mug of coffee, came a young man in a vest and bow tie, crew cut, flappy ears, and ridiculously engaging grin.

'Elvin!' Etta called out.

'Etta!' he shouted, then turned my way. 'And you have *got* to be Foggy Moscowitz.'

'I suppose I've *got* to be,' I agreed. 'Especially if you're Elvin.'

'Which I am.'

Mrs Bannon finally found herself. 'Now see here . . .' she stammered.

'Files!' I snapped.

'I'll get them,' Elvin said patiently.

He set his mug down on the closest desk and went to the file cabinets.

'You can't just barge in here . . .' Mrs Bannon began again.

'I'm *this* close to having you arrested,' I fired back. 'You placed a *child* in the hands of a certain notorious Manhattan *crime* family. Don't you know *anything* about investigating your adoptive couples?'

'What is he talking about, Mr Bradley?' Bannon looked at me. 'It happened before I got here.'

'I don't care,' I told her. 'You're in charge of this office!'

'But Mr Bradley . . .' she said weakly.

'Got it!' Elvin called, holding up two thick files.

'Mr . . . Mr Moscowitz,' Bannon scrambled.

I turned to Etta. 'Are you still intent on pressing charges against this woman?' I improvised.

Etta picked it up right away. 'Or course I am. She endangered me.'

'Well, someone did,' I agreed, 'but she says she's new to this office.'

Etta studied Bannon. 'Yeah, I don't remember seeing her. What happened to the other woman?'

'Mrs Yearly!' Bannon blurted out. 'She's the one. She's the person who was here before me. Right at this desk.'

You had to admire the speed with which Mrs Bannon was willing to finger someone else.

'That's right,' Elvin sang out. 'Poor old Mrs Yearly. She barely knew her own name by the end of her time with us. She suffered from acute, advanced dipsomania.'

Etta looked up at me.

'Mrs Yearly was a drinker,' I explained.

'Of prodigious proportions,' Elvin added. 'Came to the office in nothing but a red slip and a panama boater toward the end, there.'

'Of course, I heard the rumors,' Mrs Bannon mumbled, valiantly trying to remain a part of the conversation.

'You think maybe the Delanys used that to get me penned up with the Lamberts?' Etta asked.

I nodded, looking at Elvin.

'Don't know any Delanys,' he said, 'but Mrs Yearly was certainly coaxed into signing off on Etta's adoption without any of the proper research or safeguards.'

'You told me on the phone that you were suspicious,' I said to Elvin.

'But the higher-ups were so freaked out about Mrs Yearly's condition,' he said, shaking his head, 'that there was a significant degree of CYA. I was told to keep my mouth shut and peddle my papers.'

Etta looked at me again. 'This is why I liked Elvin in the first place. I don't know what he's saying half the time, but I like the way he says it.'

'His bosses were more concerned with covering themselves than they were about checking your phony-baloney adoption, and they told Elvin to mind his own business.'

Her eyes lit up. 'Does CYA mean *cover your ass*?' she whispered.

'Yes,' I said, 'but don't say that word, it's not for kids.'

Etta nodded contritely and looked right at Mrs Bannon. 'I'm sorry for saying *ass*,' she said, staring hard into Bannon's eyes. 'I really try to watch my language.'

I tried not to grin.

'That's better,' I told Etta. 'Now, Elvin. Let's have a look at those files.'

Elvin handed them over and all four of us spent a good half-hour scanning the papers.

Etta sat back in her seat. 'You're sure we don't have to worry about those men in the diner?'

I could see that she'd been trying to stay cool, but her eyes kept glancing toward the door and her feet couldn't seem to stay still.

'You mean you're afraid of what Madge might do to them,' I said, not looking at her.

Elvin looked up from his reading.

'Men at the diner?' He glanced my way. 'Someone had an adventure before they came to see me.'

'Madge fired a shotgun,' Etta said right away.

'Here it is!' I announced, interrupting.

'What?' Etta scooted closer to me.

I read aloud. '"Father, Nelson Roan, incarcerated. *Canada native*," and it gives his passport number. So, that's news.'

'Does it say anything about my mom?' Etta asked, more softly.

'Not much. Says your mother's deceased; she was an American citizen, born New York. Her name was Elizabeth. I don't think I knew that.'

'How does any of this help you?' Etta asked.

'When I first met you,' I said to her, 'you *told* me that the Lamberts were working for the Delany family. I was too surprised by that revelation at the time, but now I can ask you the obvious question: how did you know that?'

Her face changed. It got blank and cold.

'Yeah.' Her voice was barely audible. 'How did I know that?'

'This is your memory thing, your problem thing,' I said to her. 'Sometimes you know stuff, but you don't know how you know it, and you don't want to go poking around memory lane because of what might happen there. Am I right?'

'Exactly,' she managed to say. 'But I am kind of on the edge of it: I remember Mr Lambert talking on the phone a couple of times, saying, like, "Yes, Mr Delany" and "No, Mr Delany." And then, when he'd hung up, he'd tell his wife what he'd been talking about. And then . . . Wait. Wait a minute.'

Etta's face went sheet-white, her eyes rolled back in her head, and she slumped down in her chair, then spilled on to the floor.

Mrs Bannon stared. Elvin and I were out of our seats in a flash. He had Etta's head on his knee and I was checking her pulse.

Before either of us could do anything else, she opened her eyes.

'Uh-oh,' she mumbled. 'I passed out.'

'You did,' I confirmed. 'Happen often?'

'Oh, you know.' She sat up.

'That was a seizure,' Elvin said.

'I guess.' Etta tried to stand up.

I took her elbow. 'You saw something or thought of something.'

'Right.' She got to her feet. 'Mr Lambert hit me.'

I glanced at Elvin.

'When?' I asked.

'Couple of times. He kept asking me about my dad. It was always after he'd talked to these Delany characters.'

'What did he want to know, exactly?' I asked her.

'Can't remember. I need a Coke or something.'

Elvin was up in a flash.

'Do I need to get you to a hospital?' I whispered to Etta. 'Because I'd rather take you back to Fry's Bay. Maggie Redhawk is the best person . . .'

'No.' She squeezed her eyes shut. 'I'm OK. Happens all the time. I'm fine.'

First, I could tell that it didn't happen all the time. Second, I was pretty sure she had remembered something important. I figured she just didn't want to blab in front of Mrs Bannon.

'OK,' I announced. 'We're going to scram.'

Elvin was back with a Coke. In a bottle. Handed it to Etta.

'Are you certain that's best?' he asked me.

'I'm kind of on the trail of her father.' Then I shook my head. 'Funny. At first, I thought I was trying to find Etta for her father. Now it's the other way around.'

Straight-faced and somber, Elvin said, 'That is funny.'

'I don't want you to think I've forgotten our deal,' I told him. 'Drinks are on me. Just not now.'

'Not in the middle of the day,' he agreed.

'What *deal*?' Mrs Bannon managed to ask.

'Best way to get to the Cross City Correctional Facility?' I asked Elvin.

He was wise. 'You're going to find out about Nelson Roan's daring escape from there.'

'It was daring?' Etta asked.

'It's about fifty miles south-east of here,' Elvin said, turning to his desk. 'Let me draw you a map. They've got a new warden over there. Supposed to be a real idiot. That should make it easier for you guys.'

In short order, Etta and I were back in my car, nice little hand-drawn map on the dash, headed for the last known whereabouts of Nelson Roan.

I waited until we were mostly out of Lake City before I said to Etta, 'You remembered something.'

She sighed. 'I did.'

'It wasn't good.'

'No. It wasn't.'

'Are you going to tell me?' I asked.

'Mr Lambert would pop me in the back of the head when I didn't answer his questions fast enough,' she began. 'Didn't hurt so bad, but it rattled my brain, you know?'

All I did was nod.

'So, this one day, a couple of weeks ago, after one of his phone calls from the Delanys, he really laid into me. I guess he hit me one time too many, because Mrs Lambert shot him.'

That slowed the car down.

'What?' I took my eyes off the road long enough to stare for a second.

'OK, shot *at* him, so he'd quit hitting me.' She sniffed.

'What was it that Lambert wanted to know so bad?'

'Something about my dad busting out of prison; something about a murder,' she said, softly. 'And he seemed scared.'

TWENTY-THREE

Given the new information that Etta might pass out at any minute, it seemed extra foolhardy to have her bouncing around the countryside with all the goons on the loose.

'Look,' I told her, 'maybe we should head back to Fry's Bay.'

'No. We have to find out why it was so important to Mr Lambert to find out about Dad's escape. And what Lambert was scared of.'

I slowed the T-Bird a little. 'Yeah, I hate to agree, because I think it's probably the wrong thing for you, but I've been thinking a lot about that.'

'You have?'

'Your dad *wanted* to get put into the joint,' I said.

'Why would he want that?'

'No idea. Tell me a little bit more about your father, can you?'

'He's funny,' she said, 'and he can make up great stories. He's got a—'

'I meant about his work, if you know anything about that,' I interrupted.

'Oh. Right.' She took in a deep breath. 'He didn't think I knew he was a criminal, but I did. He and Yudda used to work together. In New Orleans, before I was born and before my dad met my mom.'

'I hope you don't have any idea what the work was about.'

'Weed,' she said right away, and then shrugged.

'A person your age really shouldn't know about that sort of thing,' I told her.

'It's the 1970s, Grandpa,' she said. 'Who doesn't know about weed?'

'OK, but what I really care about is the connection between the good old-fashioned weed trade and all this hubbub about you. Your father is, of course, a part of that connection. How much do you know about why your father went to prison?'

'He killed the doctor that killed my mother.' She was staring out the window. 'Eye for an eye sort of thing.'

I couldn't tell by looking at the side of her face if the ice water in her veins was inherited or just a function of all the terrible events in her life. I also couldn't decide if I should tell her my suspicions about his incarceration.

'Anyway,' she went on, 'he didn't stay in jail that long, did he?'

'Yeah,' I ventured. 'That's why I say it seems like he wanted to go to prison. Like, what if there was someone on the inside who was also associated with your mother's death?'

I'd been thinking it, but saying it out loud sounded weird, even to me.

But Etta just nodded. 'Right.'

I could tell her brain was working overtime. She had a faraway look and she was as still as stone.

After a while, she closed her eyes. 'Who is Amelia Drake, do you know?'

I tried not to seem surprised. 'How would you know that name?'

She shrugged.

'OK,' I went on. 'The thing is, the doctor who, in essence, killed your mother . . .'

'Dr Bainbridge.' She nodded. 'I know.'

'Anyway, this Amelia Drake was a con artist from way back who sold phony medicine. And Bainbridge is her, like, grand-nephew or something. He jazzed up the old recipe and sold it to cancer patients instead of getting them treated the right way. That's the reason your mother died, or at least that's what your dad thought. She was taking a fake cure. So, I'm asking again: how do you know the name Amelia Drake?'

'Foggy?' Her voice sounded like she had cotton in her mouth.

'What is it?'

'Could you pull the car over to the side of the road?'

I did.

As soon as we stopped moving, Etta opened her door and threw up. I started to make a fuss, but she waved me off.

'I'm OK,' she insisted. 'Here's the story of what Amelia Drake means to me, and it just came to me in one big flash. Happens that way sometimes. My brain shoves a memory out.'

'Can you tell me what it was?' I asked.

She began.

In 1906, Congress passed the first Pure Food and Drug Act. It didn't ban the alcohol or narcotics in patent medicines; it only required them to be labeled. It wasn't until 1936 that the statute was revised to ban narcotics and alcohol from the medications. So, little items like Coca-Cola, Grape-Nuts, and Angostura Bitters couldn't be sold as medicinal any more. That same year, the propaganda film *Reefer Madness* was produced. The next year saw the passage of the Marihuana Tax Act of 1937, which made cannabis possession illegal, with the *exception* of industrial or medical uses. So, Amelia Drake's remedy was kosher again. Then, a couple years ago, weed was officially outlawed for any use, medical included, by the passage of the Controlled Substances Act of 1970.

That history mattered, according to Etta, because of the relationship between Dr Bainbridge and the Delany family. Bainbridge was a large-scale purchaser of choice weed in the 1950s and 60s, for the nefarious purposes of his spurious potion. When weed became completely illegal, he got nervous and wanted to make sure he couldn't be nabbed for possession, so he sought out the special services of someone already tangentially associated with his enterprise. He sought out his local supplier. He sought out my friend Yudda.

Bainbridge threatened to call the cops on Yudda unless they came to a multi-faceted agreement. And since Yudda was already on the run and hiding out in Fry's Bay, he acquiesced. Especially since the terms were still economically beneficial to him. Bainbridge wanted three things. First, he would keep buying weed from Yudda if Yudda would *only* sell to Bainbridge *and* stash the weed at Yudda's restaurant. Bainbridge would come have lunch every once in a while, and he'd pick up a big to-go box filled with the illicit produce. Second, Yudda would hawk the doctor's worthless medicine to members of the criminal establishment whenever possible, thus extending the doctor's sales base into a previously untapped population. Third, Yudda would keep entirely quiet about the whole set-up, on pain of being arrested by the local cops, who would love nothing more than a nice drug bust to make them look good in front of the geezer population of Florida, which, believe me, was mighty.

The unfortunate thing was Nelson Roan heard about the new 'miracle' cure for cancer. Roan was desperate to save his wife. So, unbeknown to Yudda, Roan contacted Bainbridge.

'And the worst part,' Etta concluded, her voice like ice, 'was that my father had basically provided the weed that went into the medicine that resulted in the death of my mother.'

I didn't know what to say.

But she went on. 'All of which you might have known or figured out on your own. But here's a little item not many people know. In the same prison as my father there was a guy called Crawdad Davis. He supplied Yudda with crawfish from Louisiana, under which he hid a truckload of weed, buried in the ice. Because after a while Yudda became more of an administrator than a leg man, and Crawdad was the worker bee. My dad had also moved on to other work, stuff that paid more, so he could keep up with the hospital bills. Wasn't working with Yudda any more. Don't know what my dad was up to. But if you're looking for a reason that my dad might want to get into this Cross City prison place? My guess is that it had something to do with the man who delivered the marijuana to Bainbridge.'

It probably also had to do with why Yudda was *so* nervous. If Roan was willing to go to prison just to get next to someone like this Davis character, what would he do to Yudda?

'Well.' I sat back. 'That's quite a story.'

'It's got a crap ending. My mother died.'

I shook my head and nosed the T-Bird back on to the road.

'We're not anywhere near the ending yet,' I said. 'You just sit back, and we'll have a little talk with the people at the prison. Are you up for a little improvisational theatre?'

'A little what?'

'Let's see if we can pass you off as a poor little girl who just wants to see her incarcerated father,' I told her, 'little knowing that your father has absconded.'

'I just came to see daddy,' she began sweetly, picking up her role immediately. 'What do you mean he's not here?'

She gave a little sniff; even managed a tear in her eye.

'You ought to be in pictures,' I told her.

'Can't this car go any faster?'

TWENTY-FOUR

The Cross City Correctional Facility was, indeed, a military barracks. Flat wooden buildings with a sense of order that substituted for any particular design. The front-gate security was more military than most prisons I'd visited, but the empty mix of authority and boredom was still the prevailing sense of the guard there.

The little gatehouse was about the size of two telephone booths. Paint was peeling. You could see the rest of the compound from where we'd stopped; it was dry and hot and seemed deserted.

The guard stood, hiked up his uniform pants, shook his head, and looked like he'd eaten bad fish. 'Nuh-uh,' he mumbled.

That was it.

I carefully pulled out my credentials.

He stared like he couldn't read. 'So?' he finally said.

'This child,' I began, pointing to Etta, 'who is under my care as an agent of the Florida government, has come to visit her father. If you turn her away, I'll come back with a warrant, and a message from the governor. He's especially fond of Child Protective Services, the Governor of Florida is. We occupy a special place in his heart. So. Call up your warden or whoever you need to, and say that Etta Roan, a juvenile in the custody of the state, has come to visit her father, Nelson Roan.'

The guard stood mute. The shirt of his uniform had mustard on it, and his eyes gave away a certain predilection for off-hours drinking. He was sober at the moment, but his sweat smelled like bourbon. About five-foot-five, maybe two hundred pounds, he didn't appear capable of tying his shoe, let alone formulating a response to my speech.

He managed a single word. 'OK.' He made a show of not caring, and then went back into the booth to make a call.

'I hope Daddy's OK,' Etta said loudly.

I tried not to crack a smile at that. But it was clear that Officer Dumbass was new. If he'd been on the job for any kind of time, he'd have known that Roan wasn't there.

He spent a little longer on the phone than I thought he should have, and when he came back to me, he'd adjusted his attitude.

'If you drive straight down this road, you come to a brick building that says *Warden* on it. Mr Donaldson will be waiting for you.' Then he looked down.

All I did was nod and drive away. When we pulled up to the brick building, Donaldson was waiting outside. It was a hot afternoon, and he was sweating. His dark-blue polyester was darker at the armpits, and his eyes were almost closed against the sunlight. He started talking before we got out of the car.

'I've just come on as warden here,' he was saying. 'You wouldn't believe what a mess this place is.'

Etta slipped around the car and stood beside me, doing her best to look helpless.

'I'm looking for Nelson Roan,' I said firmly, flashing my badge.

'Uh-huh, uh-huh,' he stammered. 'Let's, um, let's just come into my office.'

He turned around and almost ran to the door.

The air inside his office was ice cold. Felt good after the humidity festival outside. Otherwise it was a standard military-style room. American flag in the corner; WWII oak desk.

'The previous warden,' Donaldson began before he sat down, 'was dismissed after the incident involving Nelson Roan. I'm not sure it's the kind of thing you want this little girl to hear about.'

'You came on when?' I asked.

'A week ago,' he said. 'Less.'

He stared down at the top of his desk and licked his lips.

Before he could say anything more, Etta started up with him.

'I know my father's a bad man,' she said, sniffing, 'but I love him, and I want to see him, OK?'

Sounded just like a lost little girl.

'Well.' Donaldson thinned his lips. 'All right.'

But he didn't go any further than that.

'You're reluctant to tell us something,' I prompted. I knew what it was, but I was enjoying his discomfort. Not a good trait of mine, but I got a kick out of messing with men who had that kind of power.

'Your father, uh, Miss Roan,' he mumbled, 'is gone. He's escaped. It was in the news.'

He looked at me for help. 'Escaped?' I stared. 'No one informed my office.'

'My daddy's gone?' Etta squeaked.

'I'm very sorry to tell you that he injured a guard and killed another inmate during his escape.' Donaldson sat back in his chair. 'We're seeking to try it as a capital offense.'

Etta looked at me. 'What does that mean, Mr Moscowitz?'

She knew what it meant, she just wanted me to say it out loud to the warden. Apparently, she enjoyed messing with him as much as I did.

'If they find him and convict him,' I said, 'he'll be executed.'

'No!' She fell forward, face in her hands.

Donaldson didn't know what to do.

'How did it happen?' I asked.

'The escape?' He shook his head. 'As I say, I wasn't here. But the report says he was in the showers. Choked the other inmate to death, and then called the guard to say that the other man had slipped and fallen in the shower. While the guard was examining the dead man, Roan rendered him unconscious and took his uniform. After that, he just walked out.'

Etta wailed. It was getting a little too dramatic, so I thought I should put a stop to it. I stood up.

'This is outrageous,' I said. 'Why wasn't my office informed?'

'We . . . I'll have to look into that, Mr – what was it?' he stammered.

'Moscowitz,' I snapped. 'I'm going to want details. I'm going to want to see the report.'

'Of course.' He practically jumped up.

In seconds I had an incident form in front of me. The guard

who'd been 'injured' in Roan's breakout had mostly suffered a severe blow to his dignity. The guy sat in the showers tied up in his underwear until he was found by inmates. Also said he caught a cold. The second page was the important one. The inmate who had been killed during Roan's escape was Halford 'Crawdad' Davis.

'Well, Etta,' I said, 'he's right. Your father is gone. Look.'

I showed her the second page with my thumb tapping next to Davis's name.

'Oh.' She gulped.

I was having a little trouble with reality. I was struggling to separate the story that Bobby, Etta's *fake* father, had told me from what the real father had done. *Fake* father broke out of jail to look for his daughter. *Real* father killed a guy and split without getting in touch with his daughter. I was confused. In short, I didn't really know what to believe about Roan, or how he felt about Etta.

'And you have no idea where Roan is now?' I asked after a moment.

'All turned over to the proper authorities,' Donaldson assured me. 'I have a facility to straighten out. I'm not really in the business of chasing after something that someone else lost.'

I nodded. 'Can you tell me anything about this Davis guy?'

'Only what's in the report.'

The report said almost nothing.

Etta sniffed loudly, sat forward, and asked, 'Did my daddy leave anything here? Like, in his room?'

'What?' Donaldson squinted.

I saw what she was getting at. What if Roan had left messages in his cell the way Etta had left messages in her house? If that was a thing they'd done together, it was possible that Roan had left us some clue.

'His personal effects,' I said, all business.

'Ah.' Donaldson reached for his phone. 'I'll have them brought. There's not much.'

It only took five minutes for a small box to be delivered to Donaldson's desk, even though it seemed like an hour. He used that time to complain about the heat, his wife, his shoes, his back, and money.

'Then you factor in the cost of air conditioning, which you can't live without around here,' he concluded as a guard set the small box on his desk.

I stood, opened the box, and stared in. Etta came to my side. A hair brush, a toothbrush, a wallet, a set of keys, an old book.

'Where are his clothes?' I asked. 'The street clothes?'

'He came to this place from the courthouse,' Donaldson answered, 'already in his county fatigues. I assume his regular clothing is still somewhere in the Lake City jail.'

But that wasn't true. Otherwise his wallet and keys would still be in Lake City too.

Etta was more interested in the book, *Spelling Studies*, published by Rowe in 1923. Page twenty-nine was marked by a newspaper article folded up like a book mark. The article was about me helping a kid called Lena a while back. The page itself had a sentence underlined. She read it out loud.

'*The orderly arrangement of his time is like a ray of light which darts itself through all his occupations.*'

She showed it to me. The top of the page said *STUDY 42: Words Pertaining to Numbers*.

'Interesting,' I said. 'But I'll just fill out Form 87-b for release of personal effects and be on my way.'

It took Donaldson a second to figure out what I was saying, and then he got up, went to a file cabinet, and got the form I wanted.

'Does she have ID, as the actual relative of the deceased?' he asked, eyeing Etta.

'I don't know,' I said, looking at her. 'Do you?'

She reached into her pocket and produced a crumpled library card with her name on it.

He sighed. 'I'll release the items to *you*, Mr Moscowitz, as an official of the state.'

I was already filling out the form. Etta gathered up the contents of the box. We concluded our visit with a minimum of further interaction, and were back in my car moments later.

'What a dweeb,' she muttered, climbing into the passenger seat of the T-Bird.

Then she began scrutinizing the book she'd been clutching.

'You think he might have left you a message,' I said. 'That occurred to me too.'

'My dad? Yeah.' She bit her lip. 'I mean, you saw the newspaper article. Maybe he knew you'd bring me here.'

'Maybe.'

She held up the book. 'What's the deal with this quote that's underlined?'

I glanced as I drove toward the dinky guardhouse.

'Or maybe there's something in the list of words pertaining to numbers.'

'Huh.' She glared at the page. 'Some of the words have dots next to them. This is just the kind of thing my dad used to leave around the house for me. Like, a puzzle.'

I was about to make another suggestion when a big black Cadillac roared up behind us. It was the one I'd seen close to Yudda's when the Lamberts clipped Mordecai and put him in the hospital. The one that pulled up to the donut shop when I was in there with Tony.

'This may be a problem,' I said quietly.

She looked up from the book. 'What?'

'The car behind us.'

She turned, then nodded. 'Who are they?'

'Fake FBI agents,' I said, eyes glued to the rearview. 'Wonder how they got away from the cops in Fry's Bay.'

I sped up. The Caddy kept pace. I was headed for I-10. It went through the Osceola National Forest. It was familiar to me, or at least more familiar to me than it would be to the guys who were following us. If I was lucky, I thought, I could lose them in the forest, run into some Seminoles, throw John Horse's name around, and everything would end nicely.

But things didn't go that way.

I was about to tell Etta my plan, when the left-rear tire of my beautiful Thunderbird blew out. Because somebody shot it. I still had control of the car, but I wasn't going to outrun a Cadillac.

So, I turned on my lights. Which from behind looked like I'd hit the brakes. The Caddy slowed. I pulled a spectacular U-turn and when the Caddy came up beside me going the opposite direction, I waved to the driver. Sure enough, it was the guys from the donut shop. The driver was slow to figure what had happened. By the time he stopped and tried to manage his own U-turn, there were cars coming, and I got a little distance.

I pulled over.

'What are you doing?' Etta demanded.

'I'm about to attract a lot of attention. You stay put.'

I got out of the car with my Colt in my hand. The Caddy was barreling down. I aimed and fired. The Caddy's windshield blew out. The car swerved. Then I shot out both front tires. Took a couple of tries, but I did it. There was no controlling the big car. It made a mess all over the road, smashing into an old Ford pickup and leaving rubber everywhere.

I didn't want to give them time to think about it. I ran to the car. The guy in the pickup was staggering out of his seat and traffic was already piling up in both directions.

I got to the Cadillac and pulled open the passenger door, my Colt in the guy's face. But it wasn't necessary. He hadn't been wearing his seatbelt, and he'd broken his nose on the dash. Blood all over the place. The driver was worse. Some of the glass had cut his face, and his eyes were half-shut.

I hid the Colt fast and went to the guy in the pickup.

'I never saw a double blowout like that,' I said to him.

'What?' he squinted. 'Is that what happened?'

'You just hang on,' I told him. 'I'll go call the cops.'

I ran back to the T-Bird.

Back in Brooklyn I changed a tire in two minutes and seventeen seconds once. But to be fair, I'd done it because the owner of the car was lumbering out of a bar a block away and I really wanted to boost it: a sky-blue Alfa Romeo.

I managed to get the new tire on to my T-Bird in under five, and we were on the road again. The traffic was backed up something awful around the Caddy, but I had smooth sailing going away from it. We were about half a mile from the wreck before Etta spoke up.

'That was exciting.' All deadpan. 'Now what?'

'Well, I learned what I wanted to know at the prison,' I told her. 'Your dad went in deliberately.'

'So that he could kill this Crawdad Davis guy?'

'Right.' I stepped on the gas. 'So, where's your dad now?'

'I'm telling you, Foggy,' she said. 'He's in Fry's Bay.'

She held up the newspaper article about me that was in the spelling book.

'Why in the world would he go to Fry's Bay just because of that article?'

'Jesus, Foggy,' she said, like I was an idiot. 'He *knows* you.'

TWENTY-FIVE

My problem was that I knew, or had known, plenty of nefarious types in Brooklyn. Lots of them thought they knew me, or said they knew me, because of my association with Red Levine when I was younger. Red was dead, but his influence was still felt. So, it was possible that Roan and I had met, maybe in a group or under other names. But I didn't think it was likely.

What I had to admit was that maybe Roan had heard about me, my hoodlum-saint rep, which has been greatly exaggerated by gangster gossip.

Still, I didn't want to tell Etta that her dad may have over-estimated his association with me. A kid likes to think that their dad is on the square.

'You know how your memory is so great?' I said after a minute. 'Mine is exactly that bad. I'd forget my middle name if it wasn't on my driver's license.'

'You don't remember meeting my dad,' she confirmed.

'What makes you think I ever did?'

'Well, he obviously trusts you, like, with his only daughter. He knows you. He set this all up, my being with you.'

It was clear to me that he had not, in fact, set anything up. That Etta was making connections that weren't really there.

I was of two minds. If Roan really was in Fry's Bay, waiting for us, then of course it would be best to go there. But that's also where Canadians and Manhattanites had converged in order to get their hands on Etta. So, it would be best to avoid going there.

Also, it *was* possible that I'd met Roan in New York in my former life. He could have been at any one of a dozen bars or a hundred gatherings. Maybe I'd bumped into him. Maybe he'd remembered me when my rep got righteous and he thought I was just the saint to help his little kid.

To me that was the weird thing about having a reputation as a good guy. Too many people expected me to be good. Which I wasn't, especially. I was just a guy trying to make up for what he'd done wrong. It was mostly selfish. I just wanted to feel better.

Reputations. Why would anyone want to have one?

But to the present situation: where were we supposed to go?

'Foggy!'

Etta's voice snapped me out of my reverie. I was on the wrong side of the road going ninety miles per hour.

I veered back right and slowed way down.

'What the hell?' Etta continued.

'Sorry,' I told her. 'I was, you know, thinking.'

'OK, well, pull over or something. You're gonna kill us driving like that.'

I straightened the wheel and concentrated on the road. 'Here's the deal,' I confessed. 'I don't know your dad. Never met him, as far as I can remember. So, if he sent you to me, and I'm not convinced he did, it wasn't based on any personal knowledge.'

'Huh.' That was all.

We drove in silence for ten minutes.

Then Etta said, 'I'm a little scared.'

The sound of her voice would have told me that without the admission.

'Yeah.' I wasn't sure what else to say.

'I mean I'm scared of what I might remember. What if I remember something about my dad that I don't like? What if that's the real reason all these guys are after me? Stuff about my dad that's not so good. Stuff that I've repressed.'

I glanced her way. 'Where do you get such a grown-up word as *repressed*?'

'When you have a memory like mine,' she said, 'and you've also got a mom who's really smart, you go to a shrink a lot. A *lot*.'

'But you said that your mom gave you a way to avoid some of the troubles with your memory deal,' I said, 'and it wasn't repression.'

'Yeah, but, Foggy, who knows what my brain's doing?' she said. 'It's pretty messy up in here.'

She rubbed her temples.

'Yeah, me too,' I commiserated, 'but for, like, different reasons. Still, I'm afraid it may be time for some harsh examination of facts. Some hard decisions.'

'You mean I'm going to have to see if I can figure out what it is that everybody wants from me.'

I nodded.

'But do this,' she said. 'Think, for a second, about the donut shop where you met me.'

I nodded again.

'What happened there?' she asked me.

I recounted the events briefly. She shook her head.

'I remember the pattern in the Formica on the bar,' she said. 'Blue swirls on a pinkish background. The lady behind the bar was wearing hospital shoes with one broken shoelace. The man who wanted coffee was wearing a ring that had a black stone in it. My stool squeaked when it turned. Yours didn't. Mixed in with the smell of donuts and coffee, someone was wearing Arpege perfume, the kind my mom used to like. The thing is, I could go on like this until tomorrow this time. I got a million of 'em. See, my problem isn't remembering stuff, it's picking out what stuff is *important* to remember. Out of all the millions. And you can't help me, because we'd sit around for days with me just saying stuff like I said about the donut shop and you'd eventually go nuts.'

I could tell she was getting a little worked up, so I interrupted.

'Got it,' I said. 'I treat you like a Benny Bag.'

She turned my way, twisting in the passenger seat. 'A what?'

'When I was a kid about your age,' I began, 'I did favors for my mentor, Red. Sometimes the favor would be to deliver a bag to a guy named Benny in Queens. The first time Red handed me the bag and told me the address, I asked him what was in it. He told me that it didn't matter, at least not to me. What mattered to me was that the bag *itself* was important. And I was responsible for it. *Benny* was the guy who'd sort it all out. So, from then on, whenever I had what you also might call a pig in a poke, I referred to it as a *Benny Bag*. Doesn't matter what's in that memory of yours. I just have to take care of *you*.'

'Until we find our Benny.' She nodded. 'Good.'

'Not that I know who Benny would be in this particular instance, but yes. That's the general idea.'

'I like it,' she told me. 'Takes the pressure off.'

'It *does*,' I agreed. 'I been worrying about why these goons are chasing you down, but all of a sudden, I don't care. It doesn't matter.'

'You just gotta make sure I don't get kidnapped or killed until we find the elusive Benny, whoever or whatever he may be.'

I smiled big.

'I gotta tell you, kid,' I said, 'I do my best not to get emotionally involved with my clients, but I'm crazy about you.'

She sat back in her seat. 'Ditto, Mr Moscowitz.'

We were back in Fry's Bay an hour later.

TWENTY-SIX

'd already decided that my apartment and Yudda's restaurant were places to avoid; same went for my office, the donut shop, and any open street corner. That's why we were parking in the lot at the hospital. Lots of people, places to hide, and friends in high places.

Head Nurse Maggie Redhawk and I had liked each other since my first few days in Fry's Bay. I'd had to visit the hospital after an encounter with some kid's beefy, abusive father left me with a crack in my forehead and a few regrets about my life. Like, why did I end up in Florida? But the crack healed, the regrets went away, and Maggie and I got close.

Only when she saw me coming down the hall with Etta, she started shaking her head. At first, I didn't understand, but when I saw Officers Haley and Banquer loitering close to the nurses' station, I grabbed Etta's arm and we ducked into the closest room. We were just lucky it was empty.

'Cops,' I whispered.

'Cops?' She stared. 'Why are we hiding?'

'Because I believe these particular cops might be friendly with the Delanys.'

She nodded. 'Maybe we should just lock the door and wait in here until I'm, like, twenty. Think this might all blow over by then?'

I had to admit I was feeling a little bit that way myself. We were hemmed in. Not just at the hospital, but everywhere. I couldn't think of a single place that was safe. Bad guys had even found John Horse's camp. Between the Delany family and the Montreal crew, every single option for safety was blocked.

And just as I was thinking that trouble was everywhere, the door handle began to turn.

I pulled out my Colt and shoved Etta behind me. The door cracked open a little.

'Foggy?'

I lowered the gun. 'Maggie?'

She stepped into the room and closed the door. 'Put that away,' she said, glaring at my gun.

'Sorry,' I said. 'When I see cops hanging around, I think there's going to be trouble.'

She nodded. 'Well, there is trouble. These new cops are trying to question the Canadian who got clipped by the car. The guy you called Mordecai. And I don't like the way they're doing it.'

'Yeah,' I said, 'but here's the thing: I brought this kid here to be safe, not nabbed by the police.'

Maggie stared.

'This is Etta,' I said. 'She's the crux of the biscuit.'

Etta waved.

'It's maybe too much to explain right now,' I said. 'But Etta's in trouble. She's the reason all these hoods and cops have converged here in our little town. It's possible that this Mordecai character was sent here to kill her, even.'

Maggie continued staring. 'Why?'

'There you have the part that's too much to explain.'

She nodded. 'OK. How about this: the kid checks into this room with a head injury. Bandage across her face, registered as older, local, and half-Seminole. Got it?'

'Perfect,' I said.

'Wait,' Etta protested. 'I have to stay in this room?'

'Yes,' Maggie said.

She said it with such authority that the kid shrugged and sat on the hospital bed.

Sure, I was uncomfortable leaving Etta so close to the cops and the notorious assassin Mordecai. But I recalled once again the story about the purloined letter. Etta would be hidden in plain sight. Plus, Maggie was looking out for her. If I had a choice between a band of guardian angels and Maggie, I'd choose Maggie. Besides which, my acquaintance Tony was in the hospital keeping an eye on things too.

'So, about my friend Tony,' I began.

'The other phony check-in you got me involved in,' she interrupted.

'Not phony. He was genuinely shot in the leg.'

'He's genuinely a pain in the ass,' she countered. 'Complains about the food and ogles Nurse Ryan.'

'Well, to be fair,' I said, 'everybody complains about the food, and Nurse Ryan always unbuttons the top two buttons of her uniform. On purpose.'

Maggie shook her head. 'Tony's in room seventeen. I'll take care of Etta.'

And that was that. Maggie was on the job. I'd never really thought about marriage, but a guy could do a lot worse than Maggie Redhawk.

I glanced at Etta. She nodded; I split.

Room seventeen was around a corner, and the door was open. I could hear Tony's voice before I got to the threshold. He was talking softly, but I knew his voice. I peered in. An orderly was nodding, and Tony was handing him a twenty.

'What's going on here?' I snapped.

The orderly turned around. He couldn't have been more than nineteen. Not savvy enough to grab the twenty and scram. He just gulped.

'I'm bribing this gent to nab me some vodka,' Tony told me reasonably. 'They give me orange juice when I ask for it, but what is orange juice without vodka?'

'They call it a *screwdriver*,' the orderly volunteered.

'Yeah, I know what they call it,' I said. 'Beat it.'

The orderly evaporated.

'OK, hello Foggy.' Tony sat up a little. 'I been here in the hospital for, like, a month waiting for you.'

'A couple of days,' I corrected, 'and you're not here to get the staff in trouble.'

'I'm here,' he whispered, 'to keep an eye on you-know-who. But he ain't woke up. And his buddy, the guy who come in with him, he's always there. He don't move.'

'Who's come to visit them?'

'Nobody. Except until just now, when the local cops showed up. That's why I was trying to get the vodka, see? I gotta steady my nerves.'

'No one's been in or out?'

'Not a soul,' he assured me. 'Only these cops just now.'

So, I had two choices: sneak out or dive in. I wasn't feeling great about leaving the kid alone in what was maybe a lion's den, so the choice was made. I turned around.

'What are you doing?' Tony asked the back of my coat.

'Going to see a man about a dog,' I told him, heading for Mordecai's room.

Out in the hallway, Officer Haley saw me first. 'We been looking for you,' he said.

'Not very hard,' I told him. 'I haven't been hiding.'

'We sorted out some of the ruckus,' he went on. 'The guy in a coma and his partner? We believe they're connected to a criminal organization out of Montreal.'

'The same way you're connected to a similar enterprise from New York,' I said right back.

No use mincing words, I thought. I knew Haley was crooked. He knew I knew it. What was the point of dancing?

Haley shook his head. 'In the first place, you underestimate me.' He sighed. 'In the second place, it's a lot more *involved* than that, and you know it.'

He had me there. It was *involved* all right.

'How is it that I underestimate you?' I asked.

'I'm a cop first,' he said simply. 'I had my hand in the cookie jar a couple of times, sure. But when you got a sick wife who needs expensive medicine, you'll do just about anything. I drew a line. There were things I wouldn't do.'

'Yeah, but you know the old joke: guy says to his friend, "Would you kill somebody for a million dollars?" Friend says, "For a million? Yeah." Guy says, "Would you do it for a dollar?" Friend says, "A dollar? What kind of a person do you think I am?" Guy says, "We've already determined that. Now we're just haggling about price."'

Haley nodded. 'I heard it different, but I heard it, yeah.'

I shrugged. All Haley did was look at the floor.

'So, why are you here now, exactly?' I asked him. 'I mean the *real* reason.'

Banquer took a breath to answer, but Haley beat him to it. 'We were ordered to check out the competition,' he said, and his voice sounded like a man down a well.

'By the Delanys.'

Banquer muttered something.

'It's not like he doesn't already know,' Haley said to Banquer.

'What did you find out?' I asked.

'Less than nothing so far,' he told me. 'One guy's still in a coma, and the other guy might as well be. Silent as the grave. Still telling us that his name is Benny Smith. From Illinois. You told us his name was Scarlatti, and that the conked-out guy is Mordecai. Scared Banquer to death with that one. But now I'm not so sure.'

'Oh, he's a Canuck all right,' Banquer sneered.

Haley shook his head. 'Mr Moscowitz would not tell us anything like the truth.'

'I have certain loyalties,' I disagreed. 'A few friends left in New York.'

'Maybe.' Haley let go a sigh.

'Well, I'll give you something for free,' I said. 'This kid everyone is looking for, Etta Roan, is not, as some have said, the *Holy Grail*.'

'Who called her that?' Haley wanted to know.

'Mordecai.' I thought if I repeated the name, it might at least keep Banquer off guard.

'The thing is,' Haley snapped, 'that it doesn't make sense. I've been thinking about this. Why would Montreal send their biggest hitter to a dinky backwater town like this? I think maybe Mr Moscowitz has what they call ulterior motives.'

And that was why I liked a crooked cop: too much thinking about the angle. Too much believing that everybody had one. It's what made a secret weapon out of being completely honest. No one expected it; no one believed it. And you could take advantage of that.

'You think I was trying to scare you guys by mentioning the demon Mordecai,' I said, doing my best to sound sly.

'I do,' Haley confirmed.

'Well, it didn't work,' Banquer piped up. 'That guy ain't Mordecai.'

'Plus which,' Haley went on, 'when you say that Etta Roan is not important, it makes me think that maybe she's the most important thing of all.'

'And by the by,' Banquer sneered, 'just what are you doing here at the hospital?'

Before I could answer, Maggie came to the rescue, from behind me.

'Mr Moscowitz?' she sang out. 'That patient in room twelve is ready to talk to you now. But don't keep him too long. The little guy's had a hard couple of days.'

'Thank you, Nurse Redhawk,' I said without turning around.

'What's up?' Haley wanted to know.

'My job,' I said. 'Kid bashed in the face. Needs a little looking after. *That's* why I'm here.'

It was smart of Maggie to refer to Etta as a guy. Keep the cops off the scent. And with the bandages on her face, Etta could fake being a boy for a while.

I shook my head at Haley, to indicate that he was an idiot, and then beat it back to Etta's room.

Maggie had given her the quick-bandage mask. Reminded me of the Invisible Man movies I'd seen on television.

'I look stupid,' she said as soon as I came into the room.

'You're incognito,' I said. 'Plus, as far as the cops are concerned, you're a boy right at the moment.'

'Oh, great,' she moaned. 'Like I don't have enough issues about my *nature* as it is.'

There was a moment of dead silence. But the sound of her voice had told me that recent events had taken their toll, and Etta was letting off some steam that had been kept under pressure for a while. That's what it sounded like to me, anyway.

'What do you mean, your *nature*?' I finally asked.

'Well, I'm mature for my age, I don't know who to trust, and . . . and I like Jennifer. It's very confusing how much I like Jennifer.'

'OK.' I knew better than to say too much.

'I mean I *like* Jennifer.'

'Got it,' I said. 'But, see, you're eleven. You've got plenty of time to work out—'

'I kissed her,' she interrupted. 'And she kissed me. I don't know what it means.'

'My guess would be that it means you like Jennifer,' I said. 'Tell me about her.'

'She's in my grade,' Etta said right away. 'She's shy so nobody knows that she's very smart. She has long red hair, but she doesn't have freckles. And she loves Robert Frost like I do.'

'Well,' I allowed, 'she sounds great.'

'She is,' Etta went on, 'and I wanted to call her or something. Tell her where I was. But I was afraid that if I did, these guys that are after me might get her.'

'Where is she?' I asked. 'Lake City?'

Etta nodded.

'I could get word to her,' I said. 'What's her last name?'

Another moment of silence.

'Would you do that?' she asked me, voice like a ghost.

'Consider it done.' I glanced at the chart in the nook on the door. 'By the way, your name is Tommy. Tommy Ten Trees.'

'Got it. Jennifer Baker; she lives at 2147 Cascade Road. Are you going there?'

'I've been driving around too much lately,' I told her. 'I think I'd better stick close for a while. But I'll figure something, and I'll tell you when it's done.'

'Foggy?' she whispered.

'Yeah?'

'You're really looking out for me, and I appreciate it. I don't have so much of that kind of luck since my mom died. I just wanted you to know.'

'It's my job.' I shrugged.

'You can say that,' she said. 'But you're not doing it like a job. You're doing it like something else.'

I didn't want to get into a whole rigamarole about how I was guilty, and I needed to feel better about it. I just told her the other truth.

'I'm doing it because I like you,' I said. 'That's all.'

She yawned and nodded. The kid had been through a couple of pretty hard days.

I stood in the doorway until she went to sleep.

I closed the door as quietly as I could and went to the nurses' station. 'What phone can I use that won't get in your way?' I asked Maggie.

She was busy with a patient chart and didn't look up. 'You can use my little office.'

Her little office was the size of a broom closet. Table, not desk; one file cabinet. No pictures, one lamp. I stood over the phone for a second, then picked it up and dialed.

'Number for the Bakers in Lake City.' I waited.

There were three, so I said, 'The ones at 2147 Cascade Road.'

Got it. Dialed. Got lucky: a kid answered.

'I'm calling Jennifer with a message from Etta,' I said.

The kid on the other end gasped. 'Where is she? Is she OK?'

'You're Jennifer?'

'*Yes*,' she snapped. 'Where's Etta?'

'Safe. Thinking about you.'

That calmed her down a little.

We talked for five minutes. It was all I could do to keep Jennifer from jumping through the phone to make me tell her where Etta was, but in the end, she saw the logic of secrecy.

'I have to go,' I said after that.

'Mister, you take care of her,' Jennifer warned me. 'Or you'll have me to deal with.'

'Etta said you were shy,' I said, smiling.

'Not where she's concerned,' the kid said, all business.

We hung up, and I took a second or two to meditate on the way so many people dismissed kids, especially little girls, as not-real-people. As far as I was concerned, Etta and Jennifer were about as real as this world could stand, and the world was better because they were in it.

Or maybe I was just tired. I always got a little sentimental when I was tired.

TWENTY-SEVEN

A lot of things about my little world in Fry's Bay had been moved around. I had always taken Yudda for a friend, but it turned out maybe he was more what you'd call a familiar face. And I'd always considered John Horse's camp to be a fortress. But that wasn't the case either. In fact, Fry's Bay was shaping up to be a little like a slice of Brooklyn. A hot, humid, sandy, fishy Brooklyn. Which, in turn, forced me to consider if maybe *I* was the problem. Was Florida really like my old neighborhood, or had my old neighborhood followed me down?

Either way, I had to ask myself: what would I do in a similar situation in Brooklyn? And the answer was simple: talk to the guy you figured you could trust the least. And why was that the answer? Because if you trusted him the least, then you'd be on guard the most. You'd be wary. But you'd also be cool, because you knew where you stood.

I could trust Yudda about as far as I could throw him, which wasn't so far since he was a large man. But I knew Yudda, at least a little, and I thought I could read him; tell the truth from a good story he might tell.

So, off to Yudda's restaurant I went.

But when I parked my car in the alley two blocks away, I could tell his place was crowded. There was a ring of cars around the front door, and five or six more stretching down to the docks. That meant every booth and all the stools at the bar were filled. I couldn't ever remember his place being that crowded. And it was after the dinner hour.

I was a little worried about who might be packing into the joint, so I approached slowly, making a little too much noise. And let me tell you, it was with great surprise that I opened the door into a room full of Seminole businessmen.

Everything stopped. I stood in the doorway. The business men all turned my way. Everyone was dressed like they were going to a party at the Rockefeller mansion. Silence prevailed.

Then Maggie Redhawk's brother, Mister, stood up from the last booth. He was dressed in a suit that cost more than my car, with cufflinks that might have purchased a small country.

'Hello, Foggy,' he said steadily. 'The restaurant's closed.'

'I can see that,' I told him.

'Gentlemen,' he said to the assembled, 'this is Mr Moscowitz, the man who has Etta.'

Lots of nodding, a few cold eyes, and one smile.

'I never disagree with Mister Redhawk,' I told everyone, 'but I don't *have* Etta. She's her own person. I do, however, wonder why such an illustrious group of well-respected businessmen would know anything about a little girl from Lake City.'

I'd chosen my words carefully, well-schooled by John Horse. I wanted to make certain that everyone in the room knew I had nothing but admiration for them. I wanted them to know that I also held Etta's individuality in the highest esteem. And finally, I actually wanted to know what the hell they knew about Etta.

Redhawk shook his head. 'You remind me of your story about the man named Daniel.'

It took a second before I realized he was talking about a lion's den. Which was a coincidence since I'd just been thinking that about leaving Etta at the hospital.

'Here's the thing,' I began. 'I like Etta. She's a great kid and, at the moment, she's my job. So, unfortunately, I have to ask again: how do you know her?'

'You really mean "what do we want from her?"' Redhawk said.

'That too,' I acknowledged.

And just at that moment Yudda came in the back door with an entire swordfish in his arms.

'Oh,' he said, stopping when he saw me. 'Foggy. Um. We're closed.'

'We've already gone over that,' I told him. 'We're to the part where we're talking about Etta.'

His eyebrows lifted, and he set the fish down on his carving table.

'There's a gambling establishment in Lake City,' Mister Redhawk said.

'John Horse told me about it,' I said.

That got a reaction. I knew that it would. The mention of John Horse's name was a little bit of a hat trick. I wanted everyone in the place to know that I was friends with the guy. But before I could go on about it, Redhawk told the rest of his story.

'What you don't know,' he pressed, 'is that something is happening in that casino this week.'

I stared. 'That's a little vague.'

He sighed and, in a rare moment, let down his guard. I could tell.

'We don't know exactly what it is,' he admitted. 'That's why it's vague. But it's important. Very important.'

'I don't understand,' I said.

He nodded. That's all. He was waiting to see if I could put it together. Which I did, after a second or two.

'This something big that's going to happen,' I ventured, 'is the thing Etta Roan has in her head. The thing everyone wants.'

The room shifted.

'She's told you?' Redhawk asked.

I shook my head. 'She hasn't, because she doesn't know what it is. She has no idea what the fuss is about. She just knows there's a fuss.'

'And where is she now?' one of the other men asked.

I put on my best mask. 'She's under the protection of John Horse. I thought you guys would know that.'

It was *sort* of true.

Several of the men looked at each other. The rest looked to Redhawk.

'That's why he isn't here.' Redhawk bit his upper lip. 'That's why his camp is empty. He's hiding.'

That's what I'd hoped for, that Redhawk had been to John Horse's village, or sent someone there, and found it empty. Not even Mister Redhawk knew about the other place, the one with the standing stones.

One of the men stood up. 'If this girl is under the protection of John Horse,' he told Redhawk, 'then the matter is settled.'

Then the guy turned toward me and started walking. He was in his fifties, long grey braided hair down his back, Brooks Brothers suit that cost as much as my entire wardrobe, and Italian shoes that cost even more.

'Is the girl with John Horse now?' Redhawk called out.

When I didn't answer right away, the old guy heading my way stopped.

I knew better than to lie to Mister Redhawk. But I didn't want to tell him what I didn't want him to know. 'She's under the protection of John Horse,' I repeated.

'Foggy,' Redhawk said, a little softer.

'But she's not *with* him at the moment. Her dog is. Probably. I thought that would count.'

One man nodded. I figured he was a dog owner.

'Will you tell me where Etta Roan is?' Redhawk went on.

'I won't tell anyone where she is,' I said. 'It's not just you.'

'Maybe if you told Mr Moscowitz the nature of our concern,' the dog owner suggested to Redhawk, 'he would be more willing to help.'

Redhawk closed his eyes for a moment. The gent who had decided to leave stood still. I took a second to wonder what Yudda was going to do with that swordfish.

'The men who own the casino in Lake City have disappeared,' Redhawk began. 'They got in touch with me about a month ago to arrange some sort of industrial-strength security at the casino for a very important visitor. They wouldn't say who. But they *would* say that this mysterious visitor was coming to talk to John Horse about a matter of great importance to the Seminole tribes. And now they're gone.'

I could tell by the sound of his voice how much he hated revealing that much about Seminole private business.

'Is that why John Horse was telling me about the casino, and pari-mutuel betting?' I shook my head. 'I was wondering if that had something to do with Etta.'

'Their phone message was clear,' Redhawk told me. 'The men said we should find Etta Roan. They wouldn't come back from wherever they were hiding until the entire affair was over. They were very afraid.'

So, just to keep the score card straight: that was Canadian

mobsters, crazy New York Irishmen, and now the Seminole elite, all looking to find Etta. And I still didn't know why. I knew it didn't have anything to do with legal gambling in Nowhere, Florida. The real criminals made too much money off illegal gambling in the major cities. But maybe it did have to do with this mysterious visitor to the casino in Lake City. Maybe.

'This is something important, Foggy,' Redhawk said.

I don't know how he accomplished making those few words sound so final, and so profound, but the entire place was filled up with the serious consequence of what we would do from that moment on.

So, I did what was absolutely the only thing I could do at that moment. I asked Yudda about the swordfish.

'They say the best part of the swordfish is the liver,' I began. 'Is that true?'

Yudda looked at me. 'Depends on how you cook it. You're speaking to me now?'

'Well, about cooking, yes. The other stuff, you know, might take a while.' I folded my arms. 'So, what about the liver?'

'I was gonna use it to make fish liver dumplings for these guys, to go along with the swordfish steaks,' he said.

'Why did you want to know about swordfish liver?' the man who was thinking about leaving asked me.

'Stalling for time,' I answered honestly. 'I'm trying to think of the best way to help Mister Redhawk *and* Etta Roan at the same time.'

'Oh.' He nodded. 'That's reasonable. I'd like to see how that comes out.'

He went back to his seat.

'Did you ever make swordfish liver dumplings before?' I asked Yudda.

'It's an experiment,' he admitted.

'Foggy,' Redhawk pressed.

'Yeah, OK,' I said to Redhawk. 'I came into this place thinking I was going to ask Yudda about a couple of things. I didn't expect to run into you guys. Etta's here in town. She's with your sister, in fact. But now I'm trying to piece together what three such divergent groups as you guys,

Montreal hoodlums, and the Delany family could possibly have in common. And it's not pari-mutuel betting.'

'John Horse would know,' the dog lover said, mostly to himself.

'John Horse isn't here,' I said. 'I'm asking Yudda.'

I turned his way.

He was a sad combination of dishevelment and exhaustion. The swordfish stared up at him and it was hard to tell which one of them looked more lost.

'OK.' He looked around and pulled up his personal stool, the one he kept behind the bar. When he sat on it, it creaked like a door in an old house. 'Here's what I know. There's some kind of crazy contract out on a guy. This guy is supposed to meet John Horse in Lake City. But ain't nobody know who the guy is, or where or when is the meeting, see?'

'Except we think it might be at this casino in Lake City,' I interrupted.

'OK.' He shrugged. 'That's what everybody's after, that information. It's a big contract. It's a million.'

'And Etta knows,' I said. 'Or at least everyone thinks that Etta knows. But she doesn't.'

'She was in the room, Foggy,' Yudda said softly. 'She was there when it was discussed.'

'What makes you think that?' I asked him.

'Declan Delany.'

The current head of the Delany clan.

'Go on,' I said.

'Declan knows me through Roan. He got in touch. He's the guy who – you know, the main guy who held stuff over my head to make me screw you over. He's also the one who sent that guy Bobby to your apartment, masquerading as Etta's dad. See, Declan Delany's heard of you.'

Which only proved my point about the negative aspects of *reputation*.

'OK,' I said, 'but what I want to know is what makes Declan so sure that Etta was *in the room* and what the phrase *in the room* means.'

'Right.' Yudda sighed. 'So. Roan, Etta's dad, was the guy that was given the one-million contract, for some reason I do not know. But as you might have noticed, Roan ain't that easy to find at the moment. So Declan, who would like to complete the contract and collect the million for himself, is after the next best thing: the kid. This is what I've heard, anyway.'

I shook my head. 'This only brings up about a hundred other questions. Like: why would Roan be given such a big-deal contract? Who put out the hit? What was Etta doing in the room when Roan was contracted? And what's it got to do with a Seminole casino in Lake City? Come on, Yudda. You're trying to sound like you're clearing things up when you're actually just stirring up mud.'

'Am I scared? Yes. Am I stupid? I think you know I am. But swear to God, Foggy, I'm telling you what I know.'

'This is getting us nowhere,' Redhawk interrupted. 'And, frankly, I don't care about the hit or the hitman or even his daughter. I care that people I know are in trouble, and that John Horse might be at a meeting where someone is supposed to be killed, and maybe he's going to be killed too.'

Most of the men in the place nodded their heads. They didn't care if a bunch of white hoodlums shot someone. They cared about their own. I'd heard John Horse say it a dozen times: 'White people are a violent bunch. If we wait long enough, they might just kill each other off and rid us of all our problems.'

And I had to admit that I was thinking something like that myself. All I cared about was Etta. None of my business who put out a hit on who, or what hood was going to pop some other hood. I just wanted to keep Etta safe.

But where was she going to be safe?

I took in a breath. 'We're kind of at a stand-off, I guess. You think Etta knows something, but she doesn't. It may be in her brain somewhere, but it's in there with a million other things and it would take a magician to get it out of her. She *doesn't know* the answer to your question, Mister Redhawk.'

His eyes burned into mine. 'I know that John Horse is your friend. You know that you don't want anything to happen to him. You have to help.'

'I don't think anything *can* happen to John Horse,' I said. 'I think he can't die.'

Some of the men nodded again.

But to be honest, I was just employing the same kind of malarkey that John Horse used on me: his Indian spirit schtick. I was plenty worried about him. He was obviously in trouble. Someone in his own camp had given away its location to the Delanys. He was hiding out in a weird part of the swamp with a little girl's dog.

'Well,' Redhawk said, 'then I suppose I'll go visit my sister.'

He said it like it was a threat. He was going to get Etta. I had to come up with something.

'I do have an idea,' I said, scrambling. 'I have some stuff in my car that Roan left behind when he busted out of prison. There's a book. Etta thought it might be a message from her dad.'

I waited.

'He used to do that all the time,' Yudda volunteered. 'Roan used to leave puzzles and clues and hints all over the house for the kid. Kept her mind occupied. So that she didn't freak out.'

I could tell that Redhawk was skeptical because he hesitated. He did that very rarely.

'Let me go get the book and we'll see if we can't figure something out,' I said, backing out of the doorway.

Redhawk flinched and two men close to me moved like lightning; had me by each arm, one on either side. Redhawk thought I was trying to scram.

'This is an insult,' I said calmly. 'You know me better than this.'

He looked at some other guy and said, 'It's the black Thunderbird parked out in the alley a couple of blocks that way.'

He indicated with his chin, and the guy took off.

'You're going to stay here,' he told me in no uncertain terms, 'and I'm going to take the book with me when I go visit Etta Roan. My sister told me she's in the hospital.'

I smiled. 'You know I can't let it happen like that.'

'You don't have a choice,' he said.

But I did.

All I had to do was lift up my legs. My weight did the rest. The guys on either side dropped me like a sack of spuds. I landed a little hard on my backside, but the pain helped me focus. I grabbed a strange ankle and pulled hard. One of the Seminole men dropped face down. The other one was still trying to figure out what had happened. I rolled backward, fetched my Colt, got to my feet, and put the barrel of the pistol next to his left eye.

'No,' was all Redhawk said.

'I just want to go with you when you take the book to Etta,' I told him. 'I'll overlook this little bit of rude behavior.'

It was a bold thing for me to say, calling Mister Redhawk rude. The man with the gun to his head was very still. Everyone else stared.

Then the dog lover spoke up. 'Mister Redhawk is under a lot of pressure, Mr Moscowitz,' he said.

'Why's that?' I asked.

'We're the Seminole Tribe of Florida, *Inc*.' The man blinked. 'That's what this group of men you see here in this questionable establishment is. Mister Redhawk is the CEO of that organization. Do you understand?'

I shook my head. 'You guys are a corporation?'

'The company was founded in 1957,' he said amiably. 'It's based in Hollywood, Florida. Lots of money in gambling. And in oil. We were thinking of buying Cuba.'

'That's enough, Ralph,' Redhawk snapped.

'Ralph?' I smiled. 'This is a Seminole name?'

Ralph smiled back. 'It's from the Viking name Radulf. It means *strong*. My mother thought that the Seminoles were a lost Viking tribe. But she also thought that if you touched the color yellow, your liver would disappear. So.'

I spoke to the guy who had my gun in his ear. 'I like Ralph, so I'm going to back away from you now, and I really don't want to shoot you. But I will if you do anything I don't like.'

He looked at Redhawk. Redhawk gave out another one of his heavy sighs and nodded. The man stepped away from me and went back to his seat in a nearby booth.

'Now,' I continued to Redhawk, 'there was really no need to send your guy to my car for the book. Let's go, you and me, to the hospital. I'd kind of like to see what's going to happen there.'

Redhawk started my way. 'I suppose I have felt a little pressure. My thoughts are . . . divided.'

It was as close as I was going to get to an apology.

'I'm gonna cut up this swordfish now,' Yudda piped up.

Redhawk said, 'Everyone else can stay and finish the meeting. And the swordfish. Mr Moscowitz and I are going to the hospital to see if we can't find out something about this alleged assassination at one of our casinos. Don't kill anyone until I get back. Unless you have to.'

No one said a word.

TWENTY-EIGHT

I guess I shouldn't have been surprised to see John Horse standing at the nurses' station when we got to the hospital. Redhawk wasn't.

John Horse was talking to Maggie and she was laughing. She stopped when she saw me.

John Horse turned my way. 'The dog is in your apartment, before you ask.'

He was dressed in his usual: flannel shirt, dirty jeans, construction boots. His long grey hair was in a braid down his back. His face was remarkably smooth for someone who was supposed to be two hundred years old.

'That's not close to the first thing I was going to ask.' I looked around. The cops were gone. 'Like: "What are you doing here?" springs to mind.'

'I came to see the little Seminole boy in room twelve,' he said. 'Tommy Ten Trees.'

It took me a second to remember that was Etta's hospital name.

'Where are the cops?' I asked Maggie.

'Asleep.' She smiled at her brother and said, 'Hello.'

'Sister.' He nodded cordially. 'We are here to speak with . . .'

'Tommy Ten Trees,' she affirmed. 'Room twelve.'

John Horse nodded.

'You know that the entire corporation is in town talking about you,' Mister Redhawk said to John Horse.

'I do.' He ambled toward room twelve.

'They're afraid for your safety,' Redhawk went on.

'I think Foggy probably told them I couldn't die, right?' he said.

His back was to us, so I couldn't be certain he was grinning, but I was pretty sure he was. He knew me well enough at that point. He knew I'd probably said something to his Seminole brothers.

Redhawk shook his head and we followed John Horse into Etta's room.

She woke up with a start when we came in. Her face all bandaged up, she looked like a mummy.

'It's OK,' I said.

She glared at John Horse. 'Where's my dog?'

'At Foggy's place,' he answered. 'I knew *someone* was going to ask me that.'

'Did you leave him a bowl of water?' she demanded.

'Yes.'

'OK, then.' She sat back.

'I called Jennifer,' I told her, sidling up to the bed. 'She's not quite as shy as you said she was. Not where you're concerned.'

Even in the bandages I could tell she was smiling.

'This is Mister Redhawk,' John Horse said to Etta. 'He has something for you.'

Once again, I had no idea how John Horse knew that Mister Redhawk had the spelling book in his suit coat pocket. But Redhawk produced it and handed it over to Etta.

'There's something in there, on page twenty-nine, that may be the key to helping you remember something that's very important.'

That was it. No introduction, no explanation.

Etta looked at me.

'There's a theory,' I told her, 'that your father left you a clue, like the puzzles that he used to leave for you around the house, that would help you remember whatever it is that's got your world in an uproar. Mister Redhawk believes that has something to do with friends of his that own a gambling casino in Lake City.'

'Why would my father do that?' she asked.

I looked at Redhawk. 'Good question.'

Redhawk's eyes told me how tired he was. 'Everyone believes that you have something in your head that will help them. Your father thought that too. He was aware of your apparent difficulties with memory, as I have discovered. So, he gave you a key.'

'No,' Etta said, 'I mean why would he need to make me remember something that he already knows?'

I smiled. The kid made me smile.

'It's very important,' Redhawk repeated.

Etta didn't move. 'What people don't realize,' she said, almost to herself, 'is that I can't afford to fool around with this kind of thing. I could get messed up. Really messed up.'

'There are men who would like to kidnap or kill you,' Redhawk said harshly. 'Wouldn't that be worse?'

She turned his way. 'Not really. It only takes a second to be dead. It could take a lifetime to recover from wandering around in my memories.'

If I hadn't already been nuts about the kid, that sentence would have done the trick.

But John Horse beat me to a response: 'That's the smartest thing I've ever heard a white person say; a white person of any kind.'

'And if we had time to indulge in philosophical dialog,' Redhawk snapped, 'I'd offer my own thoughts on the subject of things worse than death.'

He tossed the spelling book down on Etta's bed. She looked at me.

'He thinks there might be a clue in the book,' I explained, 'on that page that was marked.'

'A clue to what, exactly?' she asked. 'Does he know?'

'We think someone is going to be killed,' John Horse said. 'Someone important. Some people think it's me.'

'We think you know who. And where.' Redhawk stared. 'And when.'

'Is it possible,' I ventured, 'that the clues in this book – if, in fact, they *are* clues – might be designed to help you come up with something specific so that you don't have to wander around in the forest, like you said?'

She didn't blink. 'Can I please take these stupid bandages off my head?'

'No,' John Horse told her softly. 'You need to stay hidden.'

She shrugged, then picked up the spelling book. She stared for a while; don't know how long, really. And then she said, 'Huh.'

'What is it?' I asked.

'Here's the sentence: "The orderly arrangement of his time

is like a ray of light which darts itself through all his occupations." And here are the numbers: nineteen, fourteen, two and
then two, two-three, three-four, four-five. All of these are
marked in some way. I ran it forward and backward, and I
don't know if it makes any sense. But here's what I come up
with. The nineteenth word's second letter, the fourteenth
word's second, third and fourth, and the second word's fourth
and fifth letters. That's the pattern that makes the most sense
to me. Don't know why.'

'What does it spell?' Mister Redhawk asked.

Etta pointed to the letters one by one.

John Horse sat down in the only chair in the room.

'What is it?' I asked him.

'Do you know that name?' he asked Etta. 'Do you have any
recollection of a conversation about a man with that name?'

'No.' She closed the book. 'That's why I don't think I got
the clue. Usually when I get a memory clue, I can't keep the
avalanche from falling, the memories from drowning me.
With this? Nothing. So, I'm wrong.'

'No,' John Horse said. 'You're right. I was afraid it might
be this. I just wasn't sure.'

'What *is* it?' I insisted.

But before he could answer, there was a commotion down
the hall. Maggie had left the door open. Someone was shouting
in a way that a person wouldn't ordinarily do in a hospital.

I got out my gun again. John Horse froze. Mister Redhawk
slipped over to Etta's bed, snapped up the book, and put it
in his pocket. The yelling continued. It was incoherent for a
while.

But after a stream of unrecognizable words, we all heard
the man say *Etta*.

I got to the door and closed it, but Etta was already up and
out of bed, ripping the bandages off her face.

'That's my dad!' she screamed.

She shoved past me and ran into the hall. I chased after
her. The big noise was coming from another hospital room.
Etta raced toward it. Then, all of a sudden, there was Tony,
out in the hall in his hospital gown with a nasty-looking
Luger in his hand.

Before I could get to her, Etta was in the room. By the time I made it to the doorway, she was already up on the bed and in the arms of the guy who'd told me he was Mordecai. Officers Haley and Banquer looked about as stupid as they could because Scarlatti was guarding Mordecai and Etta with a pistol of his own.

I stood there for a second, trying to sort it out. Tony appeared a little behind me. Maggie was nowhere to be seen.

But one thing was clear: that guy was Etta's dad. They were holding on to each other like a life raft after the *Titanic* sank. Etta was crying her eyes out.

That scene went on for a while, a weird tableau of guys and guns, and then Mordecai – or was he Roan? – caught my eye.

'You're Moscowitz,' he said. 'I recognize you from a newspaper picture.'

'It's my dad,' Etta sobbed.

She sobbed so hard, in fact, that I finally got an idea just how much she'd been holding herself together.

'I only have about a million questions for you,' I said, lowering my gun.

Tony poked me in the back. 'It's OK?'

I turned. 'I'm impressed with you, running out in the hall like that.'

He shrugged. 'I used to be better than I am now. Every once in a while, it comes back to me. But if this is OK, I'm going back to my room. I got chocolate pudding.'

'Go,' I said.

He did. I turned back to the family portrait.

'You told me your name was Mordecai,' I said to Roan.

'It is,' he told me. 'Professional name.'

'And you chose that name because . . .?' I asked.

'Last verse of the book of Esther,' he said. 'It says, "Mordecai the Jew was second in rank to King Xerxes, and held in high esteem by his fellow Jews, because he worked for the good of his people."'

'You think you're held in high esteem by the Jews?' I glared.

He let go a sigh. 'I was your father's last apprentice. I worked with your old man in The Combination. I was just a kid.'

'Like hell,' I said.

'I was his second.'

'So, he's supposed to be King Xerxes in this story?' I snapped, ire growing.

I knew what he was trying to do. He was trying to knock me off guard by mentioning my father. What he didn't realize was that I never knew my father. I heard stories. He was good at what he did. He died guarding Red Levine, which was why Red was always so nice to me. But all that was well-known hoodlum lore in Brooklyn. Anybody could make a claim like he did.

'It was his idea that I go to Canada,' the guy went on. 'His idea that I infiltrate the Montreal organization. Only he got popped before we could work out the solids with our bunch. Somehow Declan found out I was, like, a double agent. Gossip, probably. But he started taking advantage of my position with Montreal. Which wasn't your father's intention. Exactly.'

'You understand that I don't believe a word you're saying, right?'

'Why do you think I sent Etta to you?' he said. 'Family connection.'

'No,' I began.

'This was. I met a girl in Montreal,' he interrupted. 'She got pregnant; I wanted out of the business. I got out, in fact. For a short while. We beat it down to Podunk Florida, the family and me. But then the wife got sick.'

'Stop,' I said, mostly for Etta's sake. 'I know the rest of the story.'

He sat up a little. 'You don't begin to know the story,' he said. 'I needed money, so I accepted work from the Delanys. Which was a wrong move on my part. I admit that. But I gotta do it, see? Now, one of the few things that Declan told me directly about my current job was that I had to find some joker named John Horse.'

I glanced at Haley. He shrugged.

Then, from behind me, a voice said, 'This ought to be very interesting.'

John Horse pushed past me into the room. He went to sit

on the edge of the bed and stared into Roan's eyes. After a
minute he said, 'Oh.'

Then he turned my way. It was very unsettling. I'd never
seen panic on his face before. John Horse stood up and said
to Roan, 'You don't know.'

Roan just nodded.

'He doesn't know *what*?' I asked.

'That antique spelling book,' Roan said. 'Declan sent it to
me. It was my instructions. He was always doing that kind
of crap. He liked to think he was in the CIA or something.
But I couldn't figure it out. I even took it with me to the joint.
I went in to pop a guy there who—'

'I know this part,' I interrupted. 'Skip on down.'

'I had to leave the book there when I busted out. I was
gonna go back and get it.'

'But we got it instead,' I concluded.

'You didn't leave it for me?' Etta asked, her voice very
small. 'As a clue?'

'What?' he snapped. 'No. Why would I do that?'

'You used to leave little puzzles all over the house for me,'
she said.

'To keep you occupied,' he told her. 'To keep you quiet.'

Etta didn't understand, I could tell from her face. But I
did. And I didn't like it. It was about that time that I noticed
the distinct absence of Maggie and her brother. I thought
maybe that was a good clue for me to beat it.

'Let's leave your dad with John Horse, Etta,' I suggested,
'and you and me go back to my place and see your dog.'

'You don't know who you're supposed to assassinate,'
John Horse said, ignoring everything else. 'You weren't able
to figure out the puzzle.'

Roan nodded. 'I have no idea who I'm supposed to
pop. And if I don't do it, I'm screwed. I already took half the
money.'

'Well,' Etta began, 'I tried to figure it out, but all I got was—'

'Doesn't matter,' John Horse said a little too loudly. 'Let's
go get Etta and her dog back together. The dog is very eager
to see her.'

'Exactly.' I headed for the door and motioned to Etta.

But she wasn't having any of it. 'I want to stay with my dad,' she protested.

She jumped on the bed and hugged him as best she could with all the hospital paraphernalia attached to him.

'What?' Roan began.

John Horse intervened. 'Your father needs rest. He got hit by a car.'

'The Lamberts,' I added.

'The Lamberts hit my dad with a car?' she railed.

'So, let him recuperate,' I went on, 'and let's go take care of Den, right?'

Etta looked up at her dad, but he didn't look back at her.

'In fact, everybody should clear out,' Officer Haley piped up.

He'd finally woken up enough to say a coherent sentence. Banquer was still rubbing his eyes. They had both been standing there like mannequins. But I could tell that Haley was anxious to grill Roan, now that Roan was out of his coma and admitted to being Mordecai.

I could also tell something else, something that made my entire chest cavity hurt. Roan didn't care about his daughter. Certainly not the way she cared about him.

'Let's go see about your dog,' I said again to Etta.

'He's worried about you,' John Horse added.

Etta thought about it. 'But we can come back to the hospital, to my dad, right?'

'Of course,' I told her. 'I mean, now that we know where your dad is, we can relax, don't you think?'

She was reluctant, but she came along. She followed me; John Horse followed her.

Out in the parking lot, Etta climbed into the cramped space behind the seats of the T-Bird, and John Horse settled into the passenger side. As we were pulling out of the parking place, Etta poked me in the back.

'My dad must have really gotten hurt by the car that hit him,' she said. 'He was acting weird.'

'He was unconscious for a pretty good while,' I agreed.

'Otherwise he'd remember that those guys, the ones from Canada, they sent me puzzles all the time.'

I stopped the car. 'What are you talking about?'

'Remember I told you how Mr Lambert would get so mad after he talked to those Delanys on the phone?'

I nodded.

'One of the things he wanted to know about was all the puzzles the Canadians sent me. Or, sent to my dad, I guess, *for* me. For me to solve.'

'You think that the spelling book was meant for you,' I concluded.

'I do.' She sat back. 'What I don't get is why my dad doesn't know that. Is he pretending not to know because the police are in his room?'

Once again, I had to give it to the kid. Sharp as a tack.

'I won't try to guess what your dad is thinking,' I told her. 'But are you telling me that these Canadian guys would send you, like, coded instructions? And that those instructions were things they wanted your father to do?'

'For years,' she told me. 'Dad said it was a way to protect everybody. He said that I was his "key to the kingdom".'

I glanced over at John Horse. He nodded.

'So,' I said. 'It's entirely possible that you could remember *all* those puzzles. All the instructions over the years. Everything.'

'Oh, definitely,' she said. 'It's all in here somewhere.'

That was it. Etta Roan was the secret file cabinet of the entire Montreal mob.

TWENTY-NINE

It was genius, really. What cop or FBI agent in the world was going to suspect that a little kid would know everything about an entire mob operation? I wasn't even sure I believed it. But it also betrayed a lack of understanding about Etta, I thought. She may have had all that stuff in her brain, but getting it back out would be tougher than breaking Fort Knox.

We made it back to my apartment in no time; girl and dog reunited.

While they wrestled in the living room, John Horse waved me into the kitchen. 'How about some coffee?' he said.

But I could tell by the way he said it that caffeine wasn't foremost in his mind.

Standing over the sink, he whispered, 'I'm not sure what to do.'

Another John Horse first. Panic on his face in the hospital, uncertainty at the kitchen sink.

'About what, exactly?' I whispered back.

'I think my vision is clouded by white politics.' He stared out the window over the sink. You could see the ocean, but he was looking at whatever was in his mind.

'What are you talking about?'

He turned around. 'I've gotten myself mixed up in something that I should have stayed out of. It's my own fault.'

'What is it?' I insisted.

'It's the American Indian Religious Freedom Act.' He sighed. 'I've told you that many of our religions are illegal in the United States. I was hoping to change that. I've been talking with someone who's willing to change that.'

I shook my head. 'I still don't understand.'

'I have to sit down,' he told me. 'Have to think.'

He went to the kitchen table. It was a junk store purchase,

1950s style bent chrome and Formica with a nice kind of Jetsons pattern. John Horse dropped into a chair and leaned forward on his elbows.

'White people are strange, aren't they?' he said, mostly to himself.

I realized I would just have to wait until he was ready to talk with me. He was working out something in his mind, and when he was ready, he'd tell me about it.

Meanwhile Den and Etta's horsing around had subsided, and they wandered into the kitchen.

'I'm hungry,' Etta said.

Den went to John Horse and sat beside him. John Horse patted the dog's head without looking.

'Eggs?' I suggested to Etta.

'I would like a dozen, please,' she told me, and then went to sit at the table.

John Horse looked up at her. 'What are you hiding?'

She stared. I was about to come to her defense when she spoke up.

'OK,' she confessed, 'I have a secret.'

'You know more than you've ever told anyone,' John Horse said.

Etta shook her head. 'Wrong. I told my mother.'

'And she told you to keep it from your father,' he surmised.

'Yes. And everyone else.'

'What the hell are we talking about?' I interrupted. 'What are you keeping from everyone else?'

'If I want to,' she began, 'I can remember anything. Without much trouble. The whole "it's like a forest I get lost in" was something Mom came up with.'

'Why?' I asked her.

'All of my dad's friends are criminals,' she said.

Her voice had grown colder. I wasn't sure if it was because she'd lied before, or she was lying now.

'After all that stuff about how you can't remember anything,' I said slowly. 'Now you want me to believe that you've got a bucketful of secrets in your head? Secrets that you can pour out any time you want to?'

She turned to John Horse. *'Bucketful of secrets?'*

He nodded. 'I told you that he had a colorful way of talking sometimes.'

'The thing is, Foggy,' she said to me, 'I didn't lie. Both things are true. Sort of. I *do* have a forest in my head. But my mom gave me a way of dealing with it.'

'You told me,' I interrupted. '"Quicksilver Girl".'

'Right, but that was only part of it.'

Without warning, John Horse stood straight up. His chair scraped across my kitchen floor.

'You haven't said everything that you found in the spelling book,' he said, not looking at Etta.

She avoided him too. 'Right.'

'You found a date and time,' he went on.

'And place,' she said.

'I know the place.' He closed his eyes. 'Why didn't I go to the corporate meeting? What's the matter with me? I think I'm getting old.'

I had to interrupt. 'Would somebody please tell me what's going on?'

'I didn't want my dad to kill anybody else,' Etta told John Horse. Her voice was very small. 'At five thirty tomorrow morning.'

'Oh.' That was all John Horse said.

But I wanted more, and I thought I was figuring it out. Roan, as Mordecai, was supposed to ice some joker, but Etta was trying to prevent it. Only if he didn't do it, he'd be in trouble with the Delany clan – the kind of trouble you don't recover from. How John Horse was involved was beyond me at that point.

He seemed to realize that I was thinking about him and turned my way.

'Can you take me to Lake City?' he asked me.

'What?' I blinked. 'When?'

'Now.'

'You're not going without me,' Etta snapped.

'We're not going at all,' I said.

John Horse took two steps my way. 'Foggy,' he said softly, 'this is very important. We have to get there before five thirty.'

His eyes pierced mine and I knew he was dead serious.

That was the moment the phone rang. It was Maggie. Chaos had visited the hospital. Detective Banquer was dead; Haley was wounded; Roan and his buddy were gone. No word on my acquaintance Tony.

'Roan figured it out,' John Horse told me as I was relating the basics. 'He's headed for Lake City. We have to go *now*.'

Without waiting for me to respond, he headed for the front door. Etta took one look at me and followed him. The dog glanced up.

'You stay here and guard my apartment, OK?' I said to him.

He must have agreed; he went into the living room and curled up on the sofa.

John Horse and Etta were already out the door.

THIRTY

I drove in silence for the first twenty miles or so, Etta crunched into the space behind the seats and John Horse clutching the passenger door handle. But out on the open road, I couldn't stand it.

'If somebody doesn't tell me why I'm driving to Lake City in the dark of the night,' I said to no one in particular, 'I'm going to pull this car over and pretend I'm out of gas.'

'I think John Horse is going to save the man my father is supposed to kill,' Etta ventured. 'Right?'

John Horse nodded. 'This is what I get for mixing in white politics.'

'You've said that a couple of times,' I told him, 'about white politics. What's that all about?'

'Carter.' He sighed. 'That's the name Etta got out of the spelling book.'

'Right,' she confirmed. 'But . . .'

'*Jimmy Carter?*' I shook my head. '*That's* who Roan is supposed to ice?'

'Yes,' he said.

'Why?'

'Why do these white hoodlums want him dead? Who can say?' He shrugged. 'Why am I involved? Because Carter seems to be serious about the American Indian Religious Freedom Act. I want that to happen. I was supposed to meet him at this casino in Lake City to talk about it. Very secret. But something has happened to the men who own the place.'

'That's what Mister Redhawk said,' I added.

'So now we have to go there and – do something.'

I looked at the side of his face. 'Do something.'

'I think we're going to stop my dad,' Etta volunteered. 'Like I said.'

'How are we supposed to do that?' I asked, because I certainly wasn't going to shoot Roan. Not with Etta around.

'We clip the roots,' John Horse said.

The fact that I knew what he meant wasn't the scary part. The scary part was that he meant taking on the Delany clan.

I slowed the car.

'A car thief, a little girl, and an old Seminole man with outstanding warrants – you think we have a chance in hell against the Delanys?'

He turned to Etta. 'Sounds like one of those jokes.'

She nodded. 'A Jew, an Indian, and a hitman's daughter walk into a bar.'

He laughed a little. 'I'd like to hear the punchline to that one.'

'The punchline,' I snapped, 'has something to do with three different caskets! And by the way, Etta, when did you get such a grown-up attitude about your father's occupation?'

'He always thought we didn't know, me and Mom. But we did.'

There was a deep sadness in that sentence. Maybe it was about the death of her mother. Maybe it was about knowing something so adult at such a tender age. Whatever it was, it made me a little sad too.

'OK,' I said at length, 'but you didn't seem to know when your meeting with Carter was. Why are we zooming to Lake City *now*?'

'The men who run the casino are missing,' he answered. 'I think they got wind of what was going to happen. I have to find them, warn Carter, stop Roan, protect Etta, and scare off these Delany miscreants.'

That did it. I pulled the car over to the side of the road and stopped altogether.

'No.' I thought that said it all.

'Listen,' Etta said to John Horse, 'Foggy knows more about the Delanys than we do. He's the one who can figure out how to stop them from killing Carter and get them to lay off my dad.'

I turned to face her. 'You're a very scary person. You *look* like a kid, but you talk like a career criminal.'

She held up one hand. 'Apple.' She held up the other close to it. 'Tree.'

'And I don't have any idea how to deal with the Delanys. Nobody does. Because they are who they are: the lunatic fringe of the minor league mobs in Manhattan. Besides, no power on earth could stop them from doing something by five thirty this coming morning!'

John Horse sat forward. 'If she thinks you can do it, Foggy, I do too.'

I gripped the steering wheel and tried to keep from blowing up.

'Listen to me, both of you,' I managed to say steadily. 'I'm going to drive back to Fry's Bay, drink a little Scotch, and forget that I know either one of you. Because one of the easiest ways I know of to get dead is to mess with Declan Delany. He's the one in charge of this caper. And he is entirely without moral compass or spiritual content. Maybe we could stop this particular hit from happening, but then you'd have Declan to deal with. He's an insane parody of an insane crook. You said you want to scare him off, but you're wrong. There's nothing on earth he's afraid of!'

Etta smiled. 'He's afraid of me.'

And there it was. The final piece of her puzzle. She didn't just have all kinds of information *stored* in her head, she knew how to use it. And she knew something about Declan Delany.

'Declan Delany,' she began, like she was reading a book report in a schoolroom, 'April third, 1974, snuck into his parents' house and smothered his older brother, Sean, who was asleep in his bed. Everyone thinks it was a heart attack. Sean was the favorite son. Nobody liked Declan. But with Sean gone, Declan took over as the head of the Delany *business*. And the thing is, the mother is a super-Catholic. Believes that Sean's spirit is still in the house because he died in his sleep. The father is long dead. And the mother runs the *family*. See?'

I didn't want to see, but I did. First, it was the main reason Declan wanted Etta, because she knew that secret. Second, it was also the thing that Declan was *really* afraid of: his mother. Third, it was probably what was going to get us all killed.

'I guess this is probably the information that Benny found in the bag,' she went on.

'Yeah.' I kept my eyes on the road, steamed that the kid had kept that information from me. 'And how would you know this?'

'I was in the room, Foggy,' she said. 'I was in the room when they were talking about Carter. My dad said it was crazy to kill a man running for president, and Declan said he didn't care; he was crazy enough to kill his own brother. Strangled him in his bed. He was trying to scare my dad. And it worked.'

The wheels in my brain started spinning. 'Yeah, this is . . . this is . . .'

They were both looking at me. And my misfortune was that I already had a plan hatching in my fevered brain. I should have just ignored it and turned the car around, followed my first plan of Scotch and memory loss. But I didn't do that. I started up the car again and headed for Lake City.

'You've got something,' Etta said cautiously.

I just nodded.

'Are you going to tell us?' John Horse asked me.

I shook my head. I didn't want to tell them because I was afraid that if I heard it out loud, I would realize that I was insane. Because I was.

The plan to nip the roots of the Delany family involved, unfortunately, my Aunt Shayna. She and my mother lived together in a fairly large brownstone in Brooklyn. Shayna had been with us since my father died; she was his sister. She came to take care of my mother in her grief, and me in my relative infancy. She was a short, round bundle of loving kindness, and a world-class cook, in my opinion.

She also kept the books for The Combination, which was the real name for what the press called Murder, Inc., an enclave of the most professional hitmen on the planet. The rumor was that Shayna had dated Allie 'Tick-Tock' Tannenbaum when he lived in Brooklyn, but that was unsubstantiated. Allie and my dad *did* work on hits together once or twice. I know that for a fact. Even though I never knew my father, his legend was huge in our neighborhood.

The point was that Shayna knew guys who knew guys. I

mean, they were all a little up in years at that point, but they would be of the same generation as Declan Delany's mother. Same age and same inclination. And the only thing Shayna liked better than a good kosher meal was the exercise of her influence on the community. Primarily in the form of gossip. And if I could get her to stir up something about the death of Declan's older brother that would get into the ears of the widow Delany, then Declan's goose would be cooked, eaten, bones tossed into the Gowanus Canal.

Anyway, it was a working theory. And gossip of that sort had been the death of more minor criminals than anyone might imagine. Shayna was going to love it.

How that was going to help the immediate situation was a little unclear. Gossip was an uncertain sword. Like Damocles, you never knew when it was going to get the job done.

I pressed the accelerator. 'First things first,' I mumbled. 'See if we can't meet up with your dad, Etta, and talk him out of making a million dollars.'

She sat back. 'That shouldn't be hard. What does he need with that kind of money?'

John Horse laughed, and we drove farther into the night.

THIRTY-ONE

Lake City, Florida, was dead at four in the morning. Not a soul on the streets, not a light in any house.

'Where am I going?' I asked John Horse.

'The casino is on the east edge,' he said, 'off Baya Drive. Let's start there.'

I steered the car through town. After a while on Baya we came to what I thought they called a Butler Building. Said *Casino* across the big double doors.

'This is where you were supposed to meet a man who's running for president of the United States?' I asked softly.

'We both thought it would be unexpected,' he told me. 'And private.'

'You said, and Mister Redhawk too, that the guys who run the place, your friends, have vanished.'

'They were scared away.'

I nodded. 'The Delanys are scary.'

'So why did we come here,' Etta asked, 'if we know they're not around, the men who run this place?'

'Trying to think like your father,' I began. 'He thinks the hit is still on. He doesn't know that it's all mixed up now. He's gonna show up early, case the place, figure out the best vantage point, the best approach. That kind of thing.'

'How do you know?' she pressed.

'Because that's what I'd do,' I said, getting out of the car.

The night was quiet, the moon was high, and the air seemed clearer than usual.

'The thing is, Foggy,' John Horse said softly, coming to stand beside me, 'I haven't called off the meeting. I just found out there was a problem, you understand. Carter still thinks it's on.'

'Right,' I realized. 'How would he know the whole thing's weird?'

There was a sudden scraping sound from inside the

building. Like someone was dragging something heavy across a wooden floor.

I reached for my Colt. 'I feel obligated to tell you both to stay here. I don't suppose that'll do any good.'

'It's nothing,' John Horse said dismissively.

'I've never seen the inside of a casino before,' Etta added, bounding ahead.

So, all sane considerations to the contrary, the three of us headed for the front door.

Etta got there first, but when I saw her put her hand on the door knob, I sped up and pulled her away.

'You stand to the side when you're about go into a strange place,' I instructed. 'That way you won't get hit if they shoot through the door.'

'Oh.' She nodded, like she was learning a new math trick or a history lesson.

John Horse had stopped a few feet short of the door, but without warning he began to sing.

It was in Hitchiti, one of the Seminole dialects – one that I didn't know. I'd learned a few phrases in the various Seminole languages, but what he was singing was all a mystery.

After a second Etta tugged my suit coat. 'What's he doing?'

I tried to answer, but I had nothing. I'd seen John Horse do some pretty strange things in the time I'd known him, but this was inexplicable.

I grabbed the kid and got her behind me. Then I eased the safety off my gun. I was sure there was about to be a whole lot of shooting.

John Horse's voice rose higher. His eyes were closed, and the song seemed to grow more intense, although I still had no idea what he was saying.

Then, in a kind of explosion, the door I was standing beside burst open and two guys sizzled out, guns in front of them with both hands. It was the two guys we'd met in Madge's diner.

John Horse didn't bat an eye or take a breath. He just kept singing.

It was such a strange scene that Etta started laughing, which only added to the surreal nature of the tableau.

I stared at the guys with the guns. Backed by the florescent light from the casino, they didn't look like big-time hoodlums. They were in cheap suits and I realized they both had tans. Local hires, that was my guess. And as the seconds ticked away, it was increasingly difficult to understand why they weren't shooting.

Then I saw it.

Etta quit laughing. John Horse stopped singing. I lowered my gun.

Because there were maybe a dozen Seminole men and women all around us. Every one of them had a rifle or a shotgun. It was like they'd just appeared out of the darkness. Silent as the grave.

John Horse addressed the two men who had come out of the building.

'You're trespassing on Seminole land,' he said calmly. 'These people are going to shoot you now.'

Without hesitation several of the Seminole rifles went off.

The two local hoods dropped their guns and dived to the ground. I kicked both guns away into the darkness and stood over the men. Neither one had been hit. They were just scared.

'Man, did you guys make a mistake,' I told them. 'First you mess with Madge, now you're in trouble with *these* guys. What the hell do you think you're doing trespassing on Seminole property?'

One guy turned his eyes my way. 'We was only supposed to wait here for Mordecai.'

'To help him or to pop him?' I asked.

'Help him get the job done,' the other guy said, sitting up very slowly.

'Hey,' the first guy said, looking around. 'Where did all them Indians go?'

I cast an eye about. He was right. They were almost all gone. There was one old woman standing by a tree, her face hidden in shadows from the moon.

John Horse stepped up. 'What Indians?' he asked innocently.

'You guys are from the Delanys?' Etta asked, poking her head out from behind me.

The first guy stared in awe. 'Are you Etta Roan?'

'Who?' she asked.

'This is my second cousin, Ida,' I said instantly. 'She's visiting. She's never seen Florida before.'

'I don't care for it.' She shrugged. 'Always smells like dead fish.'

'You guys were waiting here for Mordecai?' I went on. 'He's on his way. Busted out of a hospital to get here.'

'Hospital?' the second guy asked.

'The Lamberts clipped him with their car,' I said. 'He was with Scarlatti.'

I thought a little dose of truth would get their guard down.

The first guy said, 'That ain't no second cousin from Brooklyn. That's Etta Roan.'

Brooklyn. Why had he said that? He knew who I was. OK. I could make use of that.

'The first thing that Red Levine told me about the Delanys was that nobody in the entire family was very smart. You guys seem to be proof of that.'

The guy flinched a little, so it worked.

I glanced to Etta, then back at the two men. 'What should we do with them, cousin?'

'I think we should just kill them now and quit playing around,' Etta said.

I turned to her, careful to keep my gun pointed at the guys on the ground.

'Don't say *kill*,' I told her. 'It's impolite. Say *ice* or *pop* or *zotz*; it's nicer. OK?'

She lowered her eyes in mock contrition. 'Sorry.'

I turned to the guys. 'She has a point, though.'

'Let's just get these two inside,' John Horse suggested. 'I want to talk with them.'

'You're gonna have to tell me about the singing and the sudden appearance of your Minute Men,' I said, 'but for now I agree: we should get these goons inside and wait for Roan to show up.'

He nodded.

'By the way,' I went on, 'who's the old woman?'

He turned around. He stared. He stopped breathing.

'Huh.' He shook his head. 'What's she doing here?'

'Who is it?' I asked again.

'Well,' he drawled. 'That's Philip's grandmother. I think you met her once before.'

'Wait,' I said. 'The one he said was dead?'

John Horse nodded. 'This could be a problem.'

I looked again.

She was gone.

THIRTY-TWO

We herded the two locals back into the darkened casino. Even in shadow you could tell it wasn't an especially well-ordered room. Cavernous, poorly built, drafty, smelly, and mean. Just right for cheap gamblers and locals under the erroneous impression that they might hit a jackpot or double the Friday-night paycheck.

I cast my eye about. 'What the hell was it you were moving around in here that was making such a racket? Sounded like you were shoving a tank over a parking lot.'

Neither one said anything, but when I flipped on the lights, it was obvious. They had turned over a couple of heavy tables and arranged them like a barricade right at the front door. They'd be shielded and have a good chance at getting off a couple of rounds against anyone who came in the front door.

'You were expecting company,' I said.

Which made me think. They were waiting for someone to show up that night. Their job wasn't to make sure Roan did his. Their job was to take care of Roan. Someone had tipped them off that he'd busted out of the hospital. And Roan's idea was to go to the casino and set it up for the hit. Only somebody had decided that Roan wasn't working out. Or that his alter-ego Mordecai was too much of a wild card. The more I thought about it, the more my imagination ran wild.

I sat the two nameless hoods down. 'Off with your belts,' I said, and motioned with my Colt.

They hesitated, but they did it.

Without my asking, John Horse retrieved the belts and used them to tie each guy's hands behind his back and to the chair he was sitting in. They could get up, but they'd look pretty silly doing it. Especially after I shot somebody's leg or somebody else's foot.

Etta had found the bar and poured herself a Coke. She was

standing behind the bar, only her head and shoulders visible. Good place to hide if things got weird.

I decided to play a kind of guessing game I'd learned from the cops in Brooklyn. You pretended to know what was going on, and you said it out loud like it was a fact, even though it was a guess. Half the time you'd be right, and your guess was confirmed. If you were wrong and the person you were questioning was not particularly bright, you could get them to correct you. It was really all in the way you said it.

'You got a call from Scarlatti,' I began, completely confident in my guess. 'He told you that Mordecai wasn't himself, and that you'd have to pop him the second you saw him. That much I know. What I don't get is why Scarlatti would do it.'

They both stared at me. One said, 'We know you're Foggy Moscowitz.'

I smiled. 'What makes you think that?'

'You kiddin'?' the second guy asked. 'You look like a hood, and you got a kid and an Indian with you. Who else would you be?'

'John Horse is a *Seminole*,' I corrected, 'and the kid is my cousin, I told you. And PS: you two look like hoods. Cheap suits, bad shoes, and monkey hands. Locals. Out of your depth. This thing here involves *Mordecai*, man. *And* the Delanys.'

'This suit costed a hundred dollars,' one guy said.

'Why do you think we dragged those tables in front of the door?' the other one asked me. 'We knew we had to get the drop on Mordecai.'

'You were supposed to pop him,' I said. 'You had no intention of helping him get the job done.'

He shrugged. But so far it looked like I was right about the rest. What was the deal with Scarlatti? Why did he rat out his partner? Was he with the Delanys too? And why order a hit on Mordecai? And these birds, the two locals – why get them involved? Declan Delany already had his guys down in Florida. Too many questions, not enough answers.

Like she'd read my mind, Etta started up.

'So, boys,' she asked the two men tied to chairs, 'how did you get mixed up in this? Canada and Manhattan, I understand. But wouldn't you two rather be fishing or something?'

Thing One turned to Thing Two and whispered, 'That's *got* to be Etta Roan.'

Thing Two nodded, his eyes all lit up, and a lightbulb went on in my head. These guys were after the big prize: Declan Delany's file cabinet, the one in Etta Roan's brain. They thought it was their brass ring. Give it to Delany himself and go up in rank, or maybe even sell it to the highest bidder, make a pile and retire somewhere far away from the New York mobs. They figured that if they got rid of Mordecai, they'd eliminate the worst part of the competition. They didn't realize that Mordecai was, in fact, Etta's dad.

Etta must have seen something like that, because she stopped talking. The hungry look in their eyes was enough to shut me up too.

Without warning, and apropos of nothing I could figure, John Horse started up, sauntering toward the two guys.

'The thing a lot of whites don't quite understand,' he began, 'is that the Seminole tribe is the only one that never signed a peace treaty with the United States government. We're still at war with you. That makes you enemy combatants. Isn't that what they're called, Foggy?'

'Yes.' I really wanted to see where he was going. 'Yes, it is.'

He reached into his construction boot and produced a very long hunting knife.

'Tommy Ten Trees gave me this knife to hide after he killed three FBI men with it,' he said.

I glanced at Etta, who stifled a laugh. Tommy Ten Trees was the name that Maggie Redhawk had made up for Etta when she was hiding in the hospital. John Horse was screwing with these guys and he wanted us to know so that we'd play along.

'It's already had a taste of white blood,' John Horse went on. 'It's hungry for more. Can you hear it singing?'

He held it close to Thing One's face. The guy lost some of his tan, and he swallowed hard.

'Oh, all right,' John Horse said to his knife. 'Just a little blood, then.'

Thing Two started to speak but I interrupted.

'Your problem,' I said calmly, 'is that John Horse has spent time in a Federal prison. He's also over two hundred years old. There really isn't anything you can say to make him stop this. Except to tell him the truth about what you guys are doing here.'

'True,' John Horse said. 'And also: I enjoy it.'

He twirled the knife in his hand, like it was dancing, eager to taste blood.

'Oh,' Etta sighed in mock distress, 'I can't watch.'

'Christ!' Thing One exploded. 'We heard about the kid. We came to kill Mordecai. Scarlatti tipped us off. It's them two you want to cut up, not us. We don't mean a thing. It's that damned Mordecai you gotta worry about. He's a maniac! He peeled a guy's skin off while he was still alive! In front of the guy's mother! It took three days! Do you understand that?'

John Horse hesitated. 'Interesting,' he said, and turned my way. 'The first time I heard that, about peeling a man's skin off in front of his mother, was from an Apache I met in Oklahoma. He told me he was going to do that to some government agent, as soon as we all got out. I asked him where he got such a terrible idea. He said he'd heard something like it in a John Wayne movie. About Apaches, as a matter of fact. I thought that was ironic.'

'No.' I shook my head. 'It's something the Inquisition used to do to Jews who wouldn't convert to Christianity. Like, in the middle ages or something.'

'Actually,' Etta chimed in, 'it's something that the ancient Sumerians did to their enemies. Or so they claimed. But it's been discovered that they only circulated that as a story to scare their enemies. My dad and I read about it in this book he got me. It was called *The Sumerians: Their History, Culture, and Character*. We read it together. It was fun.'

Thing One turned to Thing Two and said, 'I don't know what's going on.'

'Why would Scarlatti tip you off?' I asked, another non sequitur.

'He's a Delany plant in the Montreal mob,' Thing Two said, keeping an eye on John Horse's knife.

I took a second to reflect on the fact that Roan had told me he was a plant in the Canadian mob too, something he claimed my father had told him to do.

'They know, the Delanys, that Mordecai is trying to retire,' Thing Two went on. 'And he ain't been seen in almost a year. They think he's going after this Etta Roan kid so that he'll have something on Declan Delany. See, because the kid knows things about Declan. Nobody knows what it is she's got on him, but it has to be something big. Because he's worried.'

'Worried and crazy,' Thing One agreed. 'It's a bad combination.'

'So,' Thing Two concluded, 'we thought we'd get rid of Mordecai, grab the kid, and end up in the catbird seat, like they say.'

John Horse looked at me. 'I think your cousin was right, we should just kill these two. They're too stupid to live.'

'I agree,' I said, staring at them. 'Man, you guys have no idea what you're in the middle of. See, Mordecai is coming here to set things up for a big-time hit *for* Declan Delany. If you take Mordecai out before he does that, it won't matter what else you do, he'll keep sending guys after you until you're deader than disco.'

'Disco's not dead,' Etta objected.

'What you guys have to do,' I continued to the two thugs, 'is back off. This is not your day. Not your win. Your best move is to try and stay alive for the rest of the week.'

'Well, that's the other part of the story,' Thing Two volunteered. 'We knew Mordecai was coming here for a hit. Later this morning. So, we thought, you know: if we could pop him *and* ice the mark, that could put us in a good place with Delany.'

'We're working a lot of angles here,' Thing One added.

Thing Two eyed Etta. That was clearly another one of their angles: get the girl.

'Only Carter would never come here without a confirmation from me,' John Horse assured me.

'*Mordecai* is coming here for a hit that isn't going to happen,' I concluded.

'Well . . .' Etta piped up.

I turned her way. 'What is it?'

'I was thinking he might be coming here to get me.' She looked down. 'I slipped him a note in the hospital. When I jumped up on his bed to hug him. Because I knew this is where he was supposed to go, the message from the Delanys. I'm sorry. I knew it was what he wanted and, I mean, I didn't know it was something . . . I didn't realize exactly . . .'

And she was done. She was a tough kid, but she was dealing with stuff way beyond her years. I should have realized it before that moment. I should have known she was on overload. The full weight of what her father was coming here to do finally hit her.

I glared at the goons. 'You two birds just stay put, all right? I really don't want to shoot you, but I also am very capable of doing it.' I put my gun away and went to Etta.

She started crying a little. 'My dad was acting so weird in the hospital. I was, you know, expecting him to be really glad to see me. And it didn't look like he was. Did it?'

I just shrugged, because I didn't really want to tell her what I thought. Because what I thought was that Roan was a little more like the fantastic monster Mordecai than maybe he wanted to be. How many times had I heard it said: *be careful what you pretend to be.*

None of that would do Etta any good. She was just an eleven-year-old kid who'd lost her mom and needed a parent of some kind in her weird world. The complexities of invented persona, contract murder, and a distant father were too much to take in.

Or was that just me? Like a dope, I only just that moment realized how similar Etta's childhood was to mine.

She must have seen something on my face, because her expression changed, and she stopped crying. 'Geez, Foggy,' she said. 'You look worse than I feel.'

I thought about telling her my story. About how I never knew my father. That he was a legend, not a person. That he killed people for a living. That I hadn't really had much choice but a life of criminal activity. That a horrible accident ran me out of New York, scared, all the way to Florida. That I was spending my life trying to make amends. And, finally, that she was one of my amends.

But before I could get my thoughts arranged, the door flew open and there was Roan, backed by the faintest light of the rising sun, with a submachine gun in his hand.

THIRTY-THREE

Everyone froze for a moment.

Etta broke the silence. 'That was a very dramatic entrance.'

Roan hesitated, then he cracked up. 'Yeah, I guess it was. I saw cars, I thought maybe . . . I mean, I didn't really know who was in here.'

He stepped inside and closed the doors behind him. 'Took me a while to get myself together after you gave me that note in the hospital,' he went on. 'And then I had to remember where this stupid casino was. That took a minute. Anyway, gang's all here, I see.'

Etta pointed at the two guys tied to chairs. 'They were gonna kill you. Foggy tied them up.'

'John Horse helped,' I said.

John Horse still hadn't moved.

Roan glanced at the overturned tables and nodded. 'One of you guys named Carter?' he asked.

They didn't answer.

'Look,' I said firmly, 'the guy you're supposed to pop today, he isn't coming. He was supposed to meet John Horse, but John Horse never contacted him. These geniuses in the chairs here, they thought they could get you, get the contract, *and* get Etta.'

He stared at them and nodded. 'Climbing the ladder.'

'I think I might start singing again,' John Horse ventured.

'Hold off on that for a second, OK,' I suggested. 'I think I can sort all of this out.'

But Etta had other ideas. 'Look,' she said to her father. 'Are you happy to see me or not?'

'What?' Roan asked, a little too distractedly for my taste.

'See,' I intervened, 'we've been looking for you. *Hard* looking.'

'Foggy knew I was in the hospital,' Roan told Etta. 'He saw me get clipped by the Lamberts.'

'I didn't know you were Etta's father,' I objected. 'Your name was *Mordecai.*'

'Oh.' He looked around for a second like he'd lost something. 'Right.'

'*That's* Mordecai?' Thing One asked Thing Two.

'What you don't understand,' Roan went on, 'is that if I don't get this particular job done, Delany will send other guys after me. Guys a lot smarter than these two. Declan's out of his mind, and he's already mad that I went missing for a little while, to take care of the business in the prison. That guy.'

'Declan was mad that you went on a personal vendetta instead of attending to his agenda?' I confirmed.

'He didn't know where I was. That made him nuttier than usual. Because he was afraid maybe I'd switched loyalties or maybe even gone to the cops.'

'You know he arranged for the Lamberts to get custody of Etta,' I said.

'I *didn't* know that,' he told me. 'But the Lamberts were weasels.'

'Can we get back to my question?' Etta interrupted.

'What question?' Roan asked.

Etta glanced my way, and the look on her face made me up the ante.

'Declan Delany wants to get a hold of Etta because she has all his secrets locked up in her brain,' I snapped. 'What I want to know, on Etta's behalf, is what the hell you're going to do about *that.*'

'I told you that was Etta Roan,' Thing One whispered to Thing Two.

'Jesus, man,' Roan complained to me, 'what *can* I do? Declan's got a battalion of toads as nutty as he is. I don't stand a chance. I can't kill *everybody.*'

'Don't say *kill,*' Etta interjected. 'It's impolite.'

'The thing is,' I said louder, 'with Etta's help, I've come up with the perfect way to get rid of Declan for good *and* screw up his organization for a long time. And it doesn't even involve a gun. It involves a phone call.'

Everyone stared.

Thing Two broke the silence. 'This I *gotta* hear about,' he said softly.

I declined to tell the local idiots anything about my plan. And after only another second's thought, I determined to keep it to myself altogether. Why jinx it by saying it out loud?

Instead I said, 'OK, Roan. Keep an eye on things here while I go find a phone, OK? Also, you should be aware that John Horse has a battalion of his own. Seminole warriors have this place surrounded.'

Roan blinked.

'It's true,' Etta said. 'I saw them.'

He still didn't know what to say, but I didn't feel like waiting for him. I cast an eye about for something like an office. Didn't take long. In the back of the large hall there was a suite of rooms with windows that looked out on the action. There had to be a phone somewhere in there.

The doors were all locked, but it took me about seven seconds to jimmy one of the doors. A desk, a chair, and a phone. I made sure to face the congregation, because I didn't trust Roan, and I dialed.

The conversation with my mother started, as it always did when I called home, with a complaint that I hadn't been calling as regularly as I should have. Then it moved on to my health, the weather in Florida, the weather in Brooklyn, and who had died since the last time I called. I knew I just had to let it all play out, because there was no rearranging my mother's telephone etiquette.

But as soon as there was the merest lull, I asked to speak to my Aunt Shayna. My mother thought it was nice that I would include Shayna in a long-distance call, even though I always did.

Shayna got to the phone by complaining all the way from her room to the telephone. I could hear it: why did I call so early in the morning; how was she supposed to talk on the phone before she had coffee; why did her knees hurt so bad?

'Did you hear who died?' was her opening gambit.

'I did,' I assured her. 'But I got bigger fish to fry. To wit: how would you like to take down a criminal empire today?'

'Depends,' she said. 'Whose empire?'

'Declan Delany.'

'You mean Moira Delany,' she corrected me. 'Declan runs the business, but the mother runs the family.'

'This is only one of a hundred reasons I love you, Shayna.' I laughed. 'You know everything.'

'Only a hundred reasons?' she complained.

'I've got Declan's number, Shayna. Something that I hope will take him out permanently.'

'Good,' she said firmly. 'He's crazy.'

'More than you know,' I told her. 'He killed his older brother, Sean. Smothered him in his bed. Nobody knows.'

'Then how do you know?' she asked me.

'I got a hold of his file cabinet.'

'I don't know what that means, exactly,' she said, 'but if it's true, and the mother finds out? Well – Declan's dead. Worse than dead. And the whole Delany . . . oh, I get it. You want me to crank up the gossip machine. God in heaven. What did Declan ever do to you?'

'Me? Nothing. But there's this kid . . .'

I let her figure the rest out, which she did in short order.

'Well, Declan is an equal-opportunity rat: he'd just as soon pop a kid as anybody, I guess. Especially now I know he killed his own brother. And now that I think about it, there was always a question about Sean's death. This might not be so hard at all. His mother *already* doesn't like him so much. Man-oh-man. I would not want to be in Declan's shoes when Moira finds out that Declan killed the favorite son.'

'So, you think you can make this happen?' I pressed.

'By about three this afternoon, if you'll get off the phone and let me do my work.'

Maybe there *were* more than a hundred reasons I loved her. One of them was this eagerness to get the job done. But I could also tell how much she relished being back in the game, like the old days, if only for a day.

'You gotta do this very carefully, Shayna,' I began. I was worried about somebody finding out that she was the source of the rumor.

'Who do you think you're talking to, Mr Big Shot? I been doing this stuff since before you were born.'

'You know I love you, right?'

'What's not to love?' she asked. 'You want me to call you when it's done?'

'I'm not sure when I'll be home. Better let me call you.'

'I'm hanging up now,' she said, 'before your mother gets back on the phone and keeps you all morning. She's got the sciatica again, and she won't shut up about it.'

And that was that. Shayna hung up the phone.

Across the room, out of nowhere, John Horse announced, 'I feel funny.'

But he wasn't laughing. I'd come to trust his feelings in general, because they were more reliable than most people's facts. So, I wasn't laughing either.

I headed back across the huge room. But before I got to John Horse, the front door flew open wide. Again.

No one appeared this time. I understood after a second and motioned to John Horse to move away from the door. Etta was still behind the bar. I crouched down a little and pulled out my Colt. Because whoever shoved the door open had done exactly what I might have: open the door and step back to see what might be flying out at me. I put my finger to my lips, hoping everyone would see.

Seconds ticked by. No one came in.

John Horse was a statue. 'I think my friends just want to see what's happening in here.'

Etta had ducked down behind the bar, nowhere to be seen.

The two guys tied to chairs were trying to look small and unimportant.

Roan had ducked down behind the tables.

'Where's Etta?' he mumbled without a hint of emotion.

'Not sure,' I answered before Etta could speak up.

'Well,' Roan went on, turning my way, 'I really didn't expect to see you here.'

He seemed more than a little vague. Stoned, maybe. Or maybe he'd just let himself out of the hospital too soon. Maybe the morphine hadn't worn off. Whatever it was, something wasn't right.

He turned to the guys in the chairs. 'Who are they, again?' he asked me.

'Good.' I straightened up slowly. 'I'm going to put my gun away now, and introduce you to these gentlemen, OK?'

He nodded.

I moved, again, very slowly. 'They came here to kill you,' I went on. 'Gentlemen,' I said to the backs of the boys, 'as you have already surmised, this is Mordecai.'

They both twitched around and tried to see. Roan moved fast. He was standing in front of them before I could blink.

Roan shook his head. 'I don't know them.'

'They're local,' I explained. 'Declan Delany sent them to polish you off, and they thought they might be able to get their mitts on Etta.'

Without even taking a breath, Roan fired his Tommy gun into the floor of the casino. The floor responded by splintering up pretty good. The guys in the chairs responded by freaking out like nobody's business. Yelling, crying, begging, bargaining, praying.

Then it was very quiet.

'I tied them up,' I concluded, like nothing had happened. 'So they couldn't do that.'

I'd always thought that the best response to mayhem was to ignore it. Like it didn't matter. In this particular instance, it seemed to work. Roan sighed, then nodded.

'Declan Delany,' he muttered.

Without a whisper of warning, John Horse spoke up.

'You think you've come here to kill a man,' he said clearly. 'But you've really come here to find something.'

Roan turned toward John Horse and stared at him for a long time before he said, 'What are you talking about?'

'I'm talking about your shadow demon,' John Horse went on. 'I saw it when you were talking in the hospital. You wear it like it's a shield, but it's only a shroud.'

Roan turned my way. 'What is he *talking* about?'

I shook my head.

John Horse went on. 'You should put that loud gun on the floor now. Just in case.'

'Just in case?' Roan repeated.

'In case my friends think you might want to do something with it,' John Horse said.

I didn't see the Seminole guards *come* to the open doorway. They were just suddenly *there*. Rifles all aimed at Roan.

'I don't want you to be dead,' John Horse continued, 'before I learn more about your demon. It's very interesting.'

'These Seminole men and women,' I explained to Roan, 'don't bluff. They're pointing their guns at you because they intend to use them. Your best bet is to lay down the Tommy and try not to sneeze.'

Roan seemed to really give it a lot of thought before he dropped his gun. I knew he probably had a couple more smaller weapons on his person somewhere, but at least the military-grade armament was gone.

Only then did John Horse move toward Roan. The rest of the Seminoles stayed put. I edged my way toward the bar, trying to be as inconspicuous as I could possibly be. I wanted to get closer to Etta, just in case.

John Horse got right up next to Roan and started sniffing.

Roan tilted his head. 'What are you doing?'

'I'm trying to smell the demon,' he answered. 'But it doesn't have any scent.'

'Maybe it's not made out of anything real.' That was Etta's voice. She stayed crouched behind the bar. 'Maybe it's made out of lies.'

John Horse nodded slowly. 'A demon made out of lies. There are probably lots of those.'

'That's why you can't smell it,' Etta whispered. 'I guess.'

'I guess.' John Horse stared at Roan's face like it was a really hard riddle.

Roan looked my way. 'What the hell are they talking about?'

'Not sure,' I told him, 'but I think they're talking about Mordecai. He was a lie you invented to make your job easier. Only, as I was just thinking a little while ago: you've got to be awfully careful what you pretend to be. He's your shadow demon. And that's what John Horse thinks you've come here for, today. He thinks you want to get rid of what you've pretended to be.'

'Because that's what you've become,' John Horse concluded.

'Look,' Roan began, 'you don't have any idea what I'm up against.'

But I could tell he was eyeing his Tommy gun, and the distance between him and the Seminoles.

Before he could make a move, I felt I ought to intervene.

'The thing is,' I told Roan, 'your troubles are about to be over in a certain regard. Declan Delany is about to be out of the picture for good.'

'You think you can get him knocked off?' Roan snapped. 'You can't. I've tried.'

Was that another reason Declan had sent the two local goons after Roan? Retaliation for some botched hit Roan had tried on Declan? Then it occurred to me why Roan had been given the million-dollar contract to kill someone who was running for President: because Declan not only wanted to get rid of Carter, for whatever reason. Declan wanted a fall guy. Roan was supposed to get caught by the cops or the Feds. Declan would make sure of that. Which altered, once again, my thinking about the two guys tied up in chairs.

I took a few careful steps in their direction.

'You two guys haven't been entirely forthcoming with me,' I said.

Thing One piped up. 'What?'

'Declan hired you to get here, to this casino, stake it out, wait for Mordecai. You were supposed to see that he got his job done, and then shoot him, wound him if you could, so that the Feds would catch him, and the assassination would be solved right away.'

They were both silent; avoided eye contact. Which told me I was more or less right.

'Declan set me up,' Roan said, nodding. 'He told me if I did this job, I'd be out of trouble with him. Why did I believe him?'

'But that's what I'm trying to tell you,' I said. 'Declan's not going to be a problem for very much longer.'

'Unless you've got maybe a small atom bomb,' Roan said, 'you don't stand a chance.'

'I've got something *much* better than an atomic bomb,' I assured him. 'I've got two women.'

THIRTY-FOUR

Before Roan could blink, let alone respond, Etta laughed. 'Gotta say,' she announced, 'I love being referred to as a *woman.*'

'Right,' I said. 'You're one and my Aunt Shayna is the other.' Roan stared. Thing One and Thing Two gave me the horse laugh. John Horse squinted.

But we couldn't get any farther into my revelation, because Mister Redhawk appeared in the doorway then. He was dressed in an Ermenegildo Zegna tailored suit, best rags ever. Cost him close to ten thousand dollars. I knew what it was because my Uncle Red went to Italy to get one once. That's when I realized that Mister Redhawk kind of reminded me of Red, flanked by bodyguards with weapons drawn, and all.

Redhawk surveyed the scene serenely. He nodded once. All the rest of the Seminoles vanished. He stepped across the threshold into the casino.

'First,' he announced, as if we'd all been waiting to ask him a question, 'the meeting with our friend from Georgia has been . . . rescheduled.'

John Horse smiled.

'Second,' Redhawk went on, 'despite what my sister might have told Mr Moscowitz, no one was killed when Mr Roan escaped the hospital.'

Good news.

'Third, I would like to speak with John Horse and Mr Moscowitz in private. Outside.'

Without waiting for any response, he turned and left the doorway.

I looked at John Horse. He lifted his eyebrows and headed out the door. What could I do? I followed.

The night air was turning into morning light very nicely. The horizon was the color of a flamingo, the kind of sunrise you could only get in Florida. I couldn't see the Seminole warriors, but I knew they were there somewhere, behind trees or in the shadows.

Mister Redhawk stood, hands behind his back, biting his lip impatiently. As soon as we were close enough to him so that he could speak to us in a lowered voice, he flared up.

'Would one of you mind telling me what Philip's dead grandmother is doing following you around?'

He was mad, I could see that. But I wasn't sure why. So, I did what I always did when I thought someone was accusing me of something I didn't do. I played dumb.

'How could anybody's dead grandmother be following me around?' I looked at John Horse. 'What's he talking about?'

'It's probably my fault,' John Horse said to Redhawk, ignoring me. 'She just showed up, that day that my little village was raided. I think she came to help Philip. You know, watch out for him.'

Redhawk leveled a look at John Horse that would have killed a lesser man.

'Philip told me that Mr Moscowitz saw her,' he whispered harshly.

'Oh.' John Horse glanced my way. 'Really.'

'That day your camp got all shot up?' I asked him innocently. 'Gee. There was so much going on that day. It was chaos.'

'It was,' John Horse agreed.

'And so much has gone on since then,' I continued.

But Redhawk stopped me. 'You don't have any idea what you've stepped into,' he growled.

I smiled politely. 'Pretty good idea, actually. I've foiled a political assassination, rid the world of one crazy New York mobster, and brought a daughter back to her missing father. And all for the crappy little salary I get paid by the State of Florida. I mean, some people think of me as a kind of saint.'

'While others think of you as a kind of smart-ass.' John Horse laughed.

'Right,' I agreed, eyes still on Redhawk.

'I don't understand white humor,' he said coldly. 'Are you trying to be humorous?'

'No. I'm trying to be light-hearted. Because of the afore-mentioned trilogy of good deeds which I've just pulled off.

Look. I'm tired, I'm hungry, and I want about a half a bottle of Scotch. But I'm also happy because I think I've just concluded a job well done.'

'Almost,' John Horse said.

'What do you mean?' I asked him.

'Not sure you're done with the whole father/daughter part of the story.'

That gave me pause. Because I was afraid that he might be right. I had so many bad feelings about Roan, it was like he'd given me some kind of weird flu. And the thing was, it seemed to me that Etta had her doubts too. In that regard, I wasn't sure what my next move was going to be.

John Horse intervened. 'You should take those two men away from here,' he said to Redhawk. 'The ones Foggy tied up. They were going to kill Roan or kill Carter if Roan wouldn't do it. Any way you look at it, they're bad. Local operatives for Declan Delany.'

Redhawk's face told me he knew who Declan was. Not surprising. Redhawk's business dealings associated him with plenty of unsavory characters; plus, Redhawk had a very careful mind. He would know anybody who might be a problem for him. He just would.

'*That's* the crazy New York mobster you referred to,' Redhawk said to me. 'Declan Delany.'

I nodded.

'You had him killed?'

'Not exactly,' I admitted, 'but that's how it's going to end up. Don't know when, but I'm pretty sure about it.'

Redhawk took in a breath, doubtless to ask me one of the hundred questions he had in his mind about what I'd just said. But after a second, he just exhaled.

'All right,' he said, a little wearily, 'I'll handle the two locals you've got in there. You should tell Mr Roan that the police are on their way. I told them they would find Roan here.'

It didn't surprise me that Redhawk had figured a lot of things out. Because it wasn't really guessing with him. He was like some kind of weird Sherlock Holmes. He could make an entire book out of the scraps of information. I'd seen him do it before.

In short order, the two local hoods were bundled off by armed Seminoles, protesting mightily. Redhawk didn't say goodbye, he just left. John Horse and I went back inside the casino, but I left the door open.

'The cops are on their way here,' I said to Roan. 'You should think about taking a powder.'

'You're letting me go?' His voice was thin.

'How am I supposed to stop you?' I asked him. 'You've got a Tommy gun, and all I've got is an old man.'

Roan glanced at his gun, and then up at John Horse. 'For some reason,' he said slowly, 'I'd make that about even.'

At last Etta stepped out from behind the bar. I was surprised when she came to stand beside me in the doorway instead of going to her father.

'Foggy's right,' she said firmly. 'If the cops are on their way, you'd better get out of here.'

Nobody knew what to say.

I finally said to her, 'You wanted me to find your father all this time. What are you doing?'

She looked down. 'That's not my father, Foggy,' she said, and her voice was very adult-sounding. 'That's not the man who played catch with me in the back yard when I was little. Who left me notes all over the house. Who gave me puzzles for fun. Who stayed with me when Mom got sick. That man standing over there is someone who kills people for a living. Someone who went to prison just to get revenge. I don't know what made him into this *Mordecai*, exactly. But that's who he is now. I figured that out.'

It was a cold and lonely speech. And I didn't feel like pointing out that maybe losing his wife had changed Roan for the worse.

Roan seemed unmoved by the situation. 'What was I supposed to do?' he asked everyone. 'My wife died. I had work to do. I was just trying to provide for my family. Christ.'

Etta looked up at me. 'See? That doesn't sound like my father at all.'

'Sounds more like mine,' I admitted. 'Or so I've been told.'

Roan looked around like he suddenly didn't know where he was. After a second, he looked our way.

'I don't know what to do,' he said.

His voice was very small.

Then, like it was an answer, we all heard sirens in the distance.

'I think maybe Etta's going to stay with me for a little while,' I said. 'Right?'

She looked at her dad. 'Right.'

'While you get your head straight,' I went on. 'And I think we'd all rather not see you in jail. You really ought to scram. I'll figure out something to tell the cops.'

'This isn't really the happy ending I was hoping for,' John Horse said, mostly to himself.

'Not yet,' I told him. 'Sometimes you have to wait a little longer than you want to for the happy ending.'

The sirens were getting closer.

'Etta,' Roan said, like she was an unfathomable mystery.

She said, 'September third, 1970. It was a Thursday. It was the day Blind Owl Wilson died. I was six. We sat in the living room and played that Canned Heat record over and over again.'

'You remember that?' he asked.

'I remember, like, everything, Dad.'

'Yeah. Yeah, I know that.' He sniffed. 'Why did you bring that up now?'

'Now it's your turn,' she told him. 'You have to remember who you are. And when you do . . .'

'OK. OK. That's when I'll come back, when I remember who I am. Right.' He nodded and turned around, heading for the back door. 'I'll be sending regular checks.'

'You forgot your Tommy gun,' I called after him.

He didn't answer. He was just gone.

Officer Haley and his cohorts showed up about five minutes later. John Horse and I were still trying to wrestle the over-turned tables back into place. Etta was sitting at the bar sipping another coke. The sun was up.

Haley asked me a lot of questions, and when he couldn't get anywhere with me, he started pestering Etta. She held up like a trouper, pretending to be a child of eleven when, in fact, she was a soul as old as the air. In the end Haley gave up. He didn't know what had happened, and he decided that he didn't *want* to know. Because it involved Declan Delany, some crazy mobsters from Canada, and incorporated tribes of the State of Florida. In other words, it was too much.

'Screw it,' he finally said, sitting down at the bar with Etta. 'I'm supposed to be retired.'

'You want a martini?' Etta asked. 'I'm pretty good at it. My secret is extra bitters.'

'I wouldn't say no to a Scotch and soda,' he confessed.

She slid off her stool and went behind the bar. 'One Scotch and soda coming up.'

John Horse laughed. 'She's a better bar tender than the old guy they usually have in here.'

'Foggy?' Haley sang out.

'Yes?'

'I don't know how you're going to handle this.' He accepted his Scotch and soda from Etta. 'Where's the kid's gonna live, go to school, maybe work? Plus, I wouldn't want to be anywhere near you when Declan Delany finds out about all this and comes crashing down. That ain't safe for a kid.'

'It's all taken care of,' I said. 'I told you, I'm good at my job. And this is my job.'

It was the voice of confidence. But it was a show for Etta's sake. Honestly, I wasn't at all sure what was going to happen next.

THIRTY-FIVE

It took me a few days, and a little help from John Horse, but I was able to convince Mister Redhawk to give Etta and Den one of the swanky condos in his building, downtown Fry's Bay. A fairly large one-bedroom with a distant ocean view. And since it was Redhawk's castle, it came with a contingent of Seminole watchers. Not bodyguards, exactly. Just people who would look out for Etta when she was there in the building. But she was over at my place every evening at supper time. I had her enrolled in the local school, but she quit going after a week. She said they didn't have anything to teach her. After all, she could read a book on any subject and remember all about it. Every single word. It was hard to argue with.

So, I managed to fudge some paperwork a little. Got my bosses in Miami to hire Etta as 'Admin-1, temp'. They didn't have to know she was only eleven. That way she was not only at my apartment in the evening, she was with me all day long. It was nice. The idea was to get her a salary for hanging out at my office. The reality was that she was great at organizing my particular brand of chaos. My office never had it so good.

A few days later, Officer Haley wandered into my office to tell me his news. The phony FBI guys were freelancers without a clue. Their idea had been to kidnap Etta and ransom her to the highest bidder. They were off to the Feds in Miami for impersonating FBI officers. The two locals we'd nabbed at the casino were being held on trespassing charges. The Seminole owners were prosecuting to the full extent of the law. And finally: strange news. It seemed that Declan Delany had been found dead in his bedroom in Manhattan. Smothered, they said. And since no one knew who'd done it, the Delanys were in turmoil. The kind of turmoil that's hard to recover from.

The word from Montreal was that a local Sicilian bunch had done it in order to get control of a certain part of Manhattan.

But the Sicilians said it was a Montreal job. So, everybody was in a muddle.

Meanwhile, John Horse had moved his entire village deeper into the swamp. Somewhere that would be a lot harder to find. Every cinder block, every chicken shed, every stick and stone. It turned out that one of the Seminole businessmen I'd seen at Yudda's that night had tipped off the mugs who invaded John Horse's camp, Tony and his Delany bunch. Apparently, it was an old grudge. Had nothing to do with Roan or any of that. The businessman resented John Horse's influence on the corporation. That's what came of making a tribe a corporation, I thought: corporate competition. But it was a moot point. That particular businessman had disappeared, and no one was asking where or why.

A couple of weeks later, everything finally settled down. Etta was in the office making little piles out of big ones at her table in the corner one day, when all of a sudden, she looked up.

'You know, if you were married, you could adopt me,' she said out of nowhere.

I did my best to stay cool.

'You've already *got* a father,' I said.

'Do I?' Then she blinked and there was a hint of a smile. 'You're messing with me.'

'A little,' she said. 'But what's the deal with the chicks, man?'

'Don't say *chicks*,' I told her, 'and *what* deal?'

'Exactly! *What* deal? You've got no deal. I mean, I'm eleven and I have a girlfriend. Why don't you?'

'Ah. The complexities of the human heart.'

'What's complex? You just start talking, and she talks back, and you see if it's any good or not.'

'That's how you got next to Jennifer?'

'Oh, no,' she said. 'Me and Jennifer, that's, like, a mystical thing. Beyond words. Beyond space and time, man.'

'Right.' I returned to the paperwork on my desk. 'And how am I supposed to meet someone like that in Fry's Bay?'

'Funny you should ask,' she said, motoring over to my desk. 'You know Bibi at the donut shop?'

I looked up. 'Absolutely not.'

'She's a Taoist.'

'Shut up.'

'I can't because it's true,' she said, delighted with herself.

'And what do you know about Taoism?' I asked.

She took in a breath. 'Nothing. But when I wanted to know if she might be Jewish, she told me she was a Taoist. It's spelled with a T, but the T is pronounced as a D.'

'I'm aware.'

'And she's never been married, she likes Den, and she thinks you're cute.' At this point, Etta was beaming.

'Why are you doing this to me?' I asked her. 'Haven't I always been nice to you?'

'I want to see you happy.'

'And you think that being married is the road to happiness. Have you been talking to my mother?'

Thank God John Horse came into the office at that moment. I stood up. 'I'm very glad to see you.'

'He just doesn't want to talk about his girlfriend,' Etta sneered.

'He doesn't have a girlfriend,' John Horse said.

'That's why he doesn't want to talk about it,' she said.

Before the whole line of conversation could get entirely out of hand, I said to John Horse, 'Look, I've got questions for you.'

'That's why I'm here.' He smiled. 'I knew you had questions.'

'How am I supposed to visit you now,' I began, 'when nobody knows where your village is any more?'

'No, you want to know about Philip's grandmother,' he said.

I started to speak, but he went right on,

'It was probably Philip's *mother*, actually, pretending to be the grandmother in order to invoke the spirit of the grandmother who would watch over you and protect you.'

I shook my head. 'Why would she want to do that?'

'She likes you,' he told me.

'Yeah, but . . .' I began.

'And she also wanted to make sure Etta was taken care of. She knows that Etta is a rare thing. She could tell that right away, from just one meeting. It's important for everyone that Etta is taken care of.'

'No,' I protested. 'I usually let you get away with all your phony shaman baloney, but this is too much. Why would Philip's mother dress up like *her* mother, snap a deer antler in my direction, thinking that it would help Etta? And since when do Seminole matriarchs care about little Caucasian girls?'

Etta butted in, but not the way I thought she might. 'You used the word *probably*,' she said to John Horse. 'It was *probably* Philip's mother.'

John Horse smiled. 'I said that for Foggy's benefit. He has a hard time believing that the spirits of the dead can appear to the living.'

'You think it was really the dead grandmother that Foggy saw?' she asked, her voice hushed.

'Oh, it was.' He turned to me. 'And it wasn't.'

'See,' I told Etta, 'this is what you usually get from this guy: *mishegas*.'

'What's that?' she asked.

'Insanity.'

'It's Yiddish,' John Horse told Etta. 'He likes to throw around the language of his people in moments of distress.'

'I'm not distressed,' I objected.

'You should be,' Etta said. 'You don't have a girlfriend. I was trying to set him up with Bibi.'

'The girl at the donut shop?' John Horse grinned like I'd never seen before. 'That's a great idea.'

'That's a terrible idea,' I said firmly, 'and you should both shut up now.'

'You haven't heard the rest of my news,' he said.

I shook my head. 'I don't want to.'

'It's about Jimmy Carter,' he went on.

'Why did those guys, like Delany I mean, want to kill him?' Etta wanted to know.

'Well, Carter is a very honest man,' John Horse said. 'Unusual for a white politician. Very kind. A genuinely good man.'

'That's why they wanted him killed?' she pressed.

'No. It's because of Carter's promised amnesty to all the protesters of the war in Vietnam, the ones who went to Canada. If he's elected, he's going to bring them home. More than forty thousand.'

'Why do these gangsters in New York care about that?' Etta asked.

'Hold on a minute,' I said slowly. 'Let me figure this one out. The Delanys had some of their guys pretend to be draft dodgers and abscond to Canada in the sixties. So they could keep an eye on the Montreal mob. They were, like, spies for New York. Like Roan.'

'And the guys in Canada would get suspicious about people who didn't want to go home when they got the chance,' Etta chimed in.

'*And* Foggy's right,' John Horse said, 'one of the spies was none other than the man who called himself Mordecai.'

That stopped me and Etta both for a minute. Because it was very complex.

But after a minute, I was able to remember this quote: 'Now there was in the citadel of Susa a Jew of the tribe of Benjamin, named Mordecai, who had been carried into exile from Jerusalem by Nebuchadnezzar, king of Babylon.'

'Declan Delany wanted to prevent Carter from giving out this amnesty,' John Horse said softly, 'to keep Mordecai in Canada. Keep him away from New York.'

'Declan Delany was just nuts,' I said. 'None of that was remotely necessary. None of that makes any sense.'

'Yes,' John Horse said. 'Declan Delany was insane.'

The phone rang then, and I picked it up right away because I was pretty sure I knew who it was. I was right, and it was a short conversation.

'Let's all go get a donut,' I announced after I hung up. 'It's on me.'

They both stared.

'You want me to chat up Bibi, don't you?' I pressed.

They relented, and we all headed out the door, but they were obviously suspicious. Only two minutes before, I'd rejected the whole Bibi thing.

When we got to the donut shop the sign for 'hot donuts now' wasn't on, so the place was relatively calm. We walked in, and Bibi beamed.

'You're here,' she said, and her eyes shifted left, in the direction of the corner booth.

And there, in that corner booth, in a yellow dress with white birds on it, was the happiest kid I'd ever seen. Or, second happiest once Etta saw who it was.

'Jennifer!' she screamed.

She ran. Jennifer was up, and they were holding on to each other like there was no tomorrow. They were both crying and laughing at the same time.

I sat down at the bar and John Horse sat beside me.

'Nice,' he said.

I shrugged. 'School's on a break; I pulled in a favor.'

That's when Elvin sat down next to me.

'You had an OK trip?' I asked him.

'Great.' He leaned over and offered his hand to John Horse. 'I'm Elvin Bradley. Lake City. I was promised a cocktail but I'm sitting in a donut shop.'

'I'm John Horse,' he said amiably, shaking Elvin's hand. 'I was promised a fair deal by the American government but I'm hiding in a swamp. You can't always get what you want, like Mick Jagger says.'

'Bibi,' I interrupted. 'I promised Mr Bradley here a cocktail. We would all like a Manhattan, please.'

'Right away,' she said.

Bibi disappeared into the kitchen laughing, and when she came back, she brought the newest taste sensation from the shop: a cake donut with a little whiskey in the dough, a dash of bitters sprinkled on top, and a maraschino cherry. For select customers only.

We had a good laugh about it, and I'd have to say the donut was pretty good.

But best of all was the sight of the two kids in the corner booth, both talking at the same time, laughing at each other's jokes, whispering secrets. It was one of the happiest things I'd ever seen in my life.

It got me to thinking, just a little, and I watched Bibi's profile while she was working. She was completely out of her element there in the donut shop, but she was doing her best to make it work. Kind of like I was doing in my own job.

But after a moment I turned my attention back to the booth, because it was a miraculous, wonderful thing to behold.

AUTHOR'S NOTE

1. The spelling book referred to in this novel is *Spelling Studies* by Harriet Ewens Beck and Marie J. Henninger, edited by Charles Reigner, published by H.M. Rowe Company, copyright 1923.

2. Jimmy Carter served as President of the United States from 1977 until 1981. His first act as President was to provide amnesty for all Americans who had gone to Canada to avoid serving in the war in Vietnam. His American Indian Religious Freedom Act, Public Law No. 95-341, 92 Stat. 469 was enacted in August of 1978.

3. Samuel 'Red' Levine has often been described as the director of Lucky Luciano's hit squad of Jewish gangsters. He was an observant Jew and would not accept a Sabbath contract.

4. Albert (Allie Tick-Tock) Tannenbaum was a professional hitman for Murder, Inc. during the 1930s.

5. To the date of this writing, the Seminole Tribe of Florida has not signed a peace treaty with the United States. The two nations are technically still at war.

6. Fenugreek is a little seed that the Talmud calls *rubia*. You can still get it from Kalustyan's on Lexington Avenue.

7. John Horse (1812–1882) claimed African and Seminole heritage and fought in the second Seminole War in Florida. He often served as Osceola's translator. He was once captured and held for ransom. His people collected gold and sent it to the kidnappers. When the kidnappers opened the bag, the gold was covered in blood. They

wouldn't touch it, and John Horse had vanished. He disappeared for the last time in his seventies, riding a horse to Mexico City.

8. In the early nineteenth century, the playwright and politician Mordecai Manuel Noah believed, as many people did, that Native American tribes were the fabled lost tribes of Israel. His *Discourse on the Evidences of the American Indians Being the Descendants of the Lost Tribes of Israel* (1837) purported to provide documentation of significant parallels between Jews and Native American tribes. In 1860 stones inscribed in Hebrew were found near Newark, Ohio. *The Occident and American Jewish Advocate*, the first Jewish periodical in America, concluded, 'The sons of Jacob were walking on the soil of Ohio many centuries before the birth of Columbus.'